STANDALONE BOOKS

The Haunting of Willow House

Crow Song

West Street Publishing

This is a work of fiction. Characters, names, places, and events are products of the author's imagination. Any similarity to events or places, or real persons, living or dead, is purely coincidental.

Cover art and interior design by Bad Dog Media, LLC.

ISBN: 978-1-942207-20-7

# CRYPTID QUEST

ANTHONY M. STRONG

# ALSO BY ANTHONY M. STRONG

*For Sonya and the doggies. Next year we'll go to New England.*

CRYPTID QUEST

Opening monologue for the reality TV show Cryptid Quest:


Hi, I'm Darren Yates. Adventurer, explorer, archaeologist. I've traveled the globe from the Nazca desert in southern Peru to the Siberian tundra looking for the mysterious, the unexplained, and the downright weird. And boy, have I found it. Now I want to bring you along on a special expedition into the heart of the Amazon to locate the jungle fortress of a lost civilization and the unknown beasts that guard it. So, what are you waiting for? Pack your adventure gear, put on your explorer's hat, and join my team and I as we push deeper into the unknown, on our very own… *Cryptid Quest.*

# PROLOGUE

---

CHRISTMAS EVE.

SOMEWHERE IN THE AMAZON RAINFOREST.

They huddled in the darkness as the rain lashed down, protected only by the dense undergrowth at the water's edge. In front of them, in a clearing carved out on each side of the riverbank, stood a mighty stone building that straddled the raging waters, which flowed through a tunnel and emerged unhindered on the other side. Almost completely overgrown with vegetation, the ancient structure would be all but invisible from the air. Which was bad. Because even if someone came looking for them, it would be impossible to pinpoint their exact location. Hell, even if a would-be rescuer could find them, there was nowhere to land a helicopter, and any search party hoofing it in on foot would take two days to reach them. Minimum. They wouldn't last anywhere near that long. They probably wouldn't even make it until dawn.

This thought made Darren Yates's gut tighten with dread.

He'd traveled all over the world and faced all sorts of danger, from whitewater rapids to a hungry Bengal tiger, but nothing compared to the horrors lurking in this jungle.

Next to him, Dan Weatherby was mumbling something that sounded like a prayer. Yates jabbed an elbow into the other man's ribs and whispered a terse command. "Stop it. That's not helping."

"It's helping me," Weatherby said. His voice was barely audible over a rumble of thunder that vibrated through the forest.

"Then do it quietly or they'll find us."

"At least I'm doing something," Weatherby whispered. He glanced toward his companion, rainwater streaming down his face, and nodded toward a bulky satellite phone in the other man's hand. "For the love of God, would you either make a call on that thing and get help, or give it to me."

"Too dangerous. The phone is too loud. A lot of static. Whatever is out there will hear us."

"Then we should make a run for it back to the cliff. If we can climb up, we'll be safe. Then you can call."

"We'd never make it," Yates said, "you saw what happened to Evan."

"Saw it? I don't think I'll ever get that image out of my head." Weatherby shuddered, and not just because his clothes were sodden. "I still think we should try."

"You want to make a run for it, be my guest. I'm staying here and riding it out until daylight."

"And what good is that going to do?"

"I don't know. At least we'll be able to see where we're going."

"Yeah, and whatever's out there will see us, too." Weatherby gripped his machete—one of a pair they'd been using to hack their way through the jungle—and looked around. "I don't want to die."

"Neither do I," Yates said.

The sky exploded brilliant white as lightning streaked overhead. Seconds later, another clap of thunder barreled across the landscape. The torrential rain drummed on the tree canopy above them.

The two men strained their ears, listening for any aberrant sound above the storm's cacophony that would indicate the creatures had found their hiding place. What they heard instead turned their blood to ice.

A scream.

It rose from somewhere off to their right, close to the ancient building they had discovered only hours earlier. Then, just as it reached a terrifying crescendo, the scream was abruptly cut short. Another one of their group was gone.

"That sounded like Carlos." Weatherby shifted position and lifted his head, risking an exploratory glance toward the ancient building. "You think it came from inside the pyramid?"

"How would I know?" Yates said.

"If it did, maybe the creatures aren't out here anymore. Maybe the rain drove them off."

"You want to take that chance?"

"I don't want to sit here waiting to die."

"And you think I do?" Yates reached out and placed a hand on his companion's arm. "Just take it easy. Whatever is out there hasn't found us yet. If we stay hidden, we stand a chance. If we move, they might hear us."

"This is insane." Weatherby's eyes were wild with fright. "How could creatures like that even exist?"

"I don't know."

"Did you see the claws on that thing when it took Granger? And the teeth..."

"For Pete's sake, would you pipe down? This isn't helping." Yates rubbed rain from his eyes. "Man, I wish we still had the camera."

6 | ANTHONY M. STRONG

"You're unbelievable."

"What?" Yates shrugged. "If we ever get back to civilization, I want those creatures on film. Think of the ratings."

"Yeah. Your friends getting torn apart by monsters is great TV. Maybe they'll give you an Emmy."

"Really?" Yates whispered, then saw the look on the other man's face. "Oh. You were being sarcastic."

Weatherby stared at him in disbelief but didn't respond.

"Look, I'm sorry," Yates said. "When I'm scared, I don't think straight. Right now, I'm terrified."

"As am I. But I don't deal with it by fantasizing about our TV ratings."

"It's that or dwell on what just happened to Carlos."

"You think there's anyone else left?"

"Beats me. We know they got Granger, and we just heard Carlos. There was at least one other scream, but with the thunder, there might have been more. It's hard to tell."

"This is so messed up," Weatherby said. "We should never have come here. The old man warned us."

"What, that drunkard in Manaus?" Yates snorted, referring to the small city that sat near the spot where the Rio Negro and Solimões rivers combined at a place the locals called the *meeting of the waters* to form the mighty Amazon River. The town was also a staging point for expeditions entering the rainforest, including theirs. "If we listened to every lush with a tall tale who told us not to go somewhere because it'll make the spirits angry, we wouldn't have a show."

"Well, maybe we should have listened to this one."

"Great advice. I'll just hop in my time machine and go back to warn us. You got any other messages for our past selves?"

Weatherby glared at Yates. He was about to reply, but before he could speak, a sound echoed through the forest. A guttural, throaty roar. And it was close. Too close.

"That's it, I've had enough. I'm out of here. Give me the phone."

"No." Yates clutched the satellite phone tight to his rain-soaked body. "You want to leave, go ahead. But I'm keeping the phone."

"Suit yourself." Weatherby pushed at the foliage.

"What are you doing?" There was panic in Yates' voice. "Get back here."

"Not a chance. I'm not hanging around waiting for one of those creatures to find me. I'm going back to the cliff. When I make it to base camp, I'll send help."

Weatherby pulled the branches aside and stepped out onto the riverbank. He glanced all around, then started off, following the river upstream back toward the waterfall they had seen on their way in. He'd barely gotten ten feet when something large came crashing through the understory. A bipedal creature that stepped out onto the bank in front of him, blocking his path. It towered above the petrified man—a good four feet taller than its prey—and watched him with a single enormous eye set into its wide forehead.

From his hiding place among the foliage, Darren Yates turned his head away and closed his eyes. He didn't want to see what was about to happen. But he still heard it...

# 1

SIX HOURS EARLIER.

ONE DAY'S HIKE FROM BASE CAMP.

The jungle pressed thick and humid all around them. The small group of adventurers, along with their producer and film crew, seven of them in all, had spent the previous day hacking through vines and thick vegetation that choked the forest floor. They moved slowly, alert for snakes, spiders, and larger predators such as the jaguar. Even the smallest of insects was formidable in this tropical cauldron of runaway evolution. Get bitten by a bullet ant and you could look forward to hours of unyielding agony akin to being shot, hence the name.

Which was why they hadn't tried to make it all the way to the fortress in a single day. Instead, they moved slowly, careful of step, and when the sun began to slide below the treetops, they found a suitable area and made camp instead of risking a dangerous and possibly deadly night hike.

As dawn tinged the eastern horizon, the group rose early

and ate a quick breakfast, then set off again. The going was tough, the terrain getting more impassable with each hour. Now, after another full day of walking, they were approaching their destination, a large and possibly manmade structure discovered by a lidar equipped helicopter the production company hired to run sweeps high above the rainforest. Lidar, or light detection and ranging, was an advanced technology that allowed them to see through the trees and produce a topographical map of the jungle floor, revealing what was hidden there. Like a foliage-covered building invisible to the naked eye.

"You really think there will be anything worth filming at the end of this nightmare trek?" grumbled Dan Weatherby, the stocky audio technician who was trudging along weighed down by fifty pounds of equipment, plus his tent and personal items, in a knapsack on his back. At forty-three, he was one of the older members of the team, but could keep up with the best of them, thanks to his vigorous fitness regime and adversity to junk food.

"We always do," said Evan Granger, the show's producer, from further along the line.

"No, we don't," Weatherby shot back. "Tell me one genuine discovery we've made in six seasons?"

"There's the yeti footage. That was classic," tech manager Carlos Pardo said. "And what about the Orang Pendek hair we brought back from Indonesia?"

"The yeti footage was probably just a Sherpa higher up the mountain. And as for the Orang Pendek, not being able to identify that hair didn't prove it belonged to an unknown dwarf primate. You'll be telling me we actually found mermaids off the shores of Fiji next."

"There was *something* swimming around in those waters."

"Yeah. Sharks," Weatherby said. "Look, I get it. We shoot vaguely tantalizing out-of-focus footage in the middle of the night and then pretend we captured the Beast of Bray Road or Nessie on camera. It's a bit of harmless fun to entertain the masses. But do we really need to go trekking for days on end through a dangerous mosquito infested jungle just to spend a few hours poking around what will probably turn out to be some weird rock formation?"

"It's not a rock formation," said Darren Yates, the show's archaeologist host and one of its three co-presenters, along with Cassie Locke and Elijah Silverman, both of whom were currently bringing up the rear. "You heard the stories from that old guy we interviewed in the bar back in Manaus. There's an ancient city out here, just waiting to be discovered. A citadel built by the earliest inhabitants of this rainforest and protected by prehistoric creatures that survived the mass extinction."

"Yeah, I'm calling bull on that one," Weatherby said. "The old guy was so drunk he could hardly stand up during the on-camera interview, which means we're going to have a hell of a time using the footage, and we couldn't find anyone else who ever even heard about any of this."

"The old guy went there when he was young. He saw it for himself. Barely got out alive after the creatures guarding the site attacked him."

"So he says." Weatherby chuckled. "Come on, guys, he was playing us. He just wanted another bottle of tequila."

"He had the scars to back his story up." Team biologist Cassie Locke flicked an errant strand of hair away from her face. Still in her early thirties, with thick brown hair and hazel eyes, she possessed a rugged girl-next-door beauty that played well with the Cryptid Quest viewers. And she knew it, even though she hated working on Darren Yates' schlocky show. It was a means to an end. Nothing more. A precursor to her own more serious adventure series, which was already in the works. A few more weeks and the contracts would be signed. Then she could tell Darren Yates goodbye forever. But first she had a part to play. "The guy was covered in them. Looked nasty too. Painful."

"He had scars. I'll give you that. But I wouldn't exactly call it convincing evidence." Weatherby leaned against a tree, but only after checking for snakes. "He could have gotten them anywhere. And what's with the sudden conviction. I happen to know you don't believe any of this crap, and the cameras aren't even rolling."

"Not true. I've been filming the entire exchange," cameraman Michael Vance said, with the smaller of their two digital cameras on his shoulder. "We've got to turn this jungle jaunt into a six-part series, so we need all the footage we can get."

"Especially since we're not going to find anything, as usual," Weatherby said. "Which reminds me, it's Christmas Day tomorrow. I was hoping to be back in the States in time to watch my kids unwrap their presents. That clearly isn't going to happen. Can we at least get home for New Year's Eve?"

"All right, we're going to settle this right now. I heard the grumblings around the campfire last night." Evan Granger brought the group to a halt and turned to face them. "I'm sorry we had to work over Christmas. Filming took longer than expected, but you all knew it was a possibility when you signed your contracts. Having said that, I'll do my best to have everyone back in time for New Year's. We'll spend a day filming at the site, two more days hoofing it out, and then we'll have the helicopter pick us up from base camp and go straight to the airport. Eight hours later we'll be landing at JFK with our expedition in the bag and Auld Lang Syne on our lips. How's that?"

"Perfect." Weatherby felt his spirits lift for the first time since they'd set out that morning. "What are we waiting for, then?"

Granger didn't reply. He turned back to the trail and motioned for the others to fall in and follow him. Then he set

CRYPTID QUEST | 13

off again through the jungle with Darren Yates at his side, machetes hacking and chopping as they went.

They continued for another hour. There was little conversation now. After such an arduous journey, they were all tired and thirsty. Later, as night fell, the temperature would drop by twenty degrees, but right now the tropical heat was taking its toll. At one point, they stopped to allow a snake to cross their path. A five-hundred-pound green anaconda longer than a bus. Which meant they weren't too far from water, probably a tributary of the jungle's namesake river. On land the snake was ponderous, but still deadly enough that the entire group held their breath as it slithered on its way. The bulging lump near the snake's head was the only reason it ignored them. It wasn't hungry.

When the danger passed, they moved again. They continued for another hour, everyone more on edge after their brief encounter with the gargantuan snake. Then, as they drew close to the fortress identified during their lidar sweeps, the ground abruptly fell away as if a giant hand had reached out and scooped a chunk out of the earth.

The group came to a stumbling halt.

The forest floor ended ahead of them in a jagged, rocky drop. A precipice that ran for miles in each direction and fell a hundred feet straight down before disappearing into the canopy of trees populating the tropical basin spread out below them. To their left, a waterfall crashed over the edge and tumbled out of sight.

"A cliff," Weatherby said in awe. "A freaking cliff face in the middle of the Amazon."

"It doesn't look like there's a way around. We'll have to go over and down if we want to continue," Granger said, studying the terrain.

"And how are we going to do that?" Weatherby stayed a safe

distance from the edge. "I don't see a trail leading down there, do you?"

"Doesn't matter. We came prepared." Vance was already filming again, capturing the wide sweep of the forest below, and the impressive scale of the cliff to use for filler shots, known as B roll, later. "This is why we brought rope."

"Hell, no." Weatherby looked green. "Not in a million years. You know I'm afraid of heights."

"Some adventurer, you are," Vance snickered.

"I'm an audio technician, not a mountaineer. I make sure the mics are working and we get lots of nice animal noises for the B roll. Did you forget that?"

"You ever wonder if you chose the wrong production to work on," Vance asked.

"That's enough, both of you," Granger said. "Everyone's going down. No excuses. We need our audio technician at the bottom of that cliff with the rest of us, not trembling with fear up here."

"Don't worry. It'll be fun. I promise." Yates glanced toward the nervous audio technician.

"Fun for you, maybe." Weatherby didn't look convinced.

"Come on, suck it up, you're with the big boys now," Yates shot back, eyes alight with excitement. He clapped his hands. "What are we waiting for, people? Let's break out that climbing gear. And keep the camera rolling too. I want close-ups as I go over. This is gold. Pure gold."

2

It took over an hour to get the entire team and all their gear down the cliff and onto the forest floor below. With the climb behind them, the group wasted no time moving on. Once darkness fell, they wouldn't be able to continue. No one wanted to camp a second night before reaching the fortress. Evan Granger and Darren Yates took the lead once again, their machetes whipping back and forth to clear a path. After a few miles of torturous going, they stopped to rest and passed water bottles around.

"The forest feels different down here," Yates said, taking a deep swig from his canteen. "Did you notice that?"

"I feel it, too," Elijah Silverman, the team's cryptozoologist, agreed.

"And me." Cassie nodded. "It's quieter."

"No birdsong," Weatherby said. "And I don't hear any monkeys in the trees."

"No insects either," said Yates.

"Creepy." Cassie looked up toward the dense canopy of branches above them. "I've never been in a forest this silent."

"Almost like the jungle's holding its breath." Weatherby

glanced around nervously, as if expecting something with big teeth to emerge from the surrounding foliage. "It's not right."

Granger held a calming hand up. "All right, people. Let's not give ourselves the heebie-jeebies. Keep all that good stuff for the camera."

"You want to have the conversation over again, boss?" Michael Vance asked, reaching for his camera. "It'll be great footage, especially for the trailers."

"Shame you didn't get it the first time." Granger looked miffed. "All right, everyone. Let's wind it back a minute and say it all a second time for the viewers at home. Brownie points for whoever hams it up the most."

"Do brownie points equate to real-world dollars in our paychecks?" asked Weatherby.

"You wish." Granger looked at his watch, a Bell & Ross military style chronograph gifted him by the network at the end of season five. "I won't fire you though, how about that?"

"You're all heart." Weatherby fell in with the others, and they repeated their earlier exchange, this time with a little more panache. The cameraman gave a thumbs up once the rehashed conversation was done, and the group continued upon their way.

As they walked, the forest remained eerily quiet. The fortress was less than a mile away now, but they still could not see it. The dense jungle vegetation covered everything in a thick carpet of green leaves and twisting vines that reduced visibility to only a few feet ahead. Which was why they didn't notice the obelisk until they were right upon it.

"What is that?" Cassie asked, spotting the strange and out-of-place object first.

"I don't believe this," Yates said. He rushed forward and pulled foliage from the twenty-foot-tall stone monolith to expose the carved surface beneath. "There's writing here."

"Is this what the lidar picked up?" Weatherby asked.

"No. It's much too small." Cassie joined Yates and together they uncovered more of the towering needlelike four-sided column. "This is something else."

Weatherby stepped forward. It reminded him of a monument he'd seen on a trip overseas, many thousands of miles from this location. Cleopatra's Needle, standing on Victoria Embankment in London. That obelisk was three times the height of the one they were currently looking at, but otherwise they might as well be twins, even down to the strange writing that covered all four tapered faces. He looked at Yates, his eyes wide with astonishment. "Are those Egyptian hieroglyphics?"

"I don't see how they can be." Cassie was still tugging vines away from the face of the obelisk. "We're six and a half thousand miles and an ocean away from Egypt."

"Except they are," Yates said, running a hand along the stone surface, his fingers tracing the carved symbols.

"It gets weirder, guys." Elijah Silverman, the third of the three presenters, was on the other side of the monument. He peered back at the rest of the group. "I have linear B on this side."

"What?" Yates sounded incredulous. He moved to the other side of the column. "Let me see."

"What's linear B?" Weatherby asked.

"It's an ancient syllabic script used by the Greeks starting around 1500 BC." Yates answered without looking up. "And I can't believe I'm saying this, but Elijah is right. This is definitely linear B."

"Are we filming this?" Granger motioned toward Michael Vance. "For the love of God, please tell me you were rolling."

"Damned right." Vance moved closer to get a better shot of the towering object.

"There's another one over here," Cassie shouted, pushing her way through the greenery toward a second vine-covered shaft fifteen feet from the first. She inspected it with growing excitement. "This one has hieroglyphics too."

"No way." Yates stepped back and surveyed their surroundings. "Ladies and gentlemen, do you know what we found here?"

"Not a clue." Weatherby's eyes were still fixed on the strange, picture-like writing that adorned the obelisk's closest face.

"Gates." A grin broke out on Yates' face. "This is an entrance to something much bigger."

"But what?" Cassie asked.

"The fortress, of course. The building we picked up on lidar."

"I still don't get how there's Greek and Egyptian writing here," Cassie said. "It's completely impossible. Neither culture traveled to South America, and certainly not together."

"Maybe someone brought these here afterward?" Weatherby shrugged. "Didn't the conquistadors explore up and down the coast?"

"Sure." Yates noted. "Francisco de Orellana navigated the Amazon River in the 1500s. In fact, he died here in 1546. But I'm pretty sure he didn't bring along any ancient Egyptian or Greek relics."

"Well, somebody put them here, and it sure wasn't the Greeks or the Egyptians," Cassie said. "Unless our history of the ancient world is completely wrong."

"Then maybe it is. Because those obelisks look like they've been here for a long time."

"But what about the writing?" Weatherby asked. "How could there be Greek and Egyptian on the same stone?"

"It's not unheard of." Cassie was still examining the second obelisk. "The Rosetta Stone was inscribed in hieroglyphics, Demotic script, and ancient Greek. It was instrumental in deciphering hieroglyphics, because scholars could read the Greek and all three languages said the same thing."

"And that isn't the only one," Yates said. "Other bilingual stele are known to exist."

"But nothing in the Amazon jungle," Cassie said.

"Until now," Granger said. "And if we've already made such an unbelievable discovery, doesn't it make you wonder what's waiting for us at the fortress?"

"To quote Howard Carter," Yates said with a flourish, "wonderful things. Which is why we should waste no more time here. I have a feeling there are bigger discoveries yet to be made." And with that, he turned and strode off into the jungle, machete swinging.

## 3

Darren Yates was right. There were bigger discoveries waiting for them at the fortress, which turned out to be a towering, stepped pyramid structure with an exterior staircase on each face leading to its flat top. Overgrown with vines and foliage, just like the obelisks they had discovered earlier, the pyramid was reminiscent of Mesoamerican structures such as the Mayan Temple of Kukulkán at Chichen Itza. But what made this even more remarkable was the location. It sat straddling the banks of a fast-moving river. A tributary of the Amazon itself. The rushing water penetrated through the middle of the ancient building and emerged on the other side uninterrupted. If they followed the water back upstream, they would surely arrive at the waterfall they'd witnessed before descending the cliff.

The purpose of this strange and architecturally difficult design was a mystery, but not so much as the hieroglyphics and Greek text that adorned the walls of the fortress, as they had on the twin monuments. It was impossible, but the evidence spoke for itself. Both the Greeks and ancient Egyptians had traveled here in the long distant past.

"This building could be the missing link," Darren Yates said as he studied the script carved into one of the building's lower blocks. "Archaeologists have long wondered how ancient civilizations from both sides of the Atlantic Ocean developed pyramids. The Olmec, Aztecs, Inca, and the Maya, all built them. Some of the earliest date to one thousand BC."

"That's still later than the Egyptians," Cassie said. "They constructed the majority of their pyramids fifteen hundred years earlier."

"Which would make sense if the Egyptians came here and constructed a pyramid in the Amazon, which was later copied by other cultures."

"I don't know." Cassie didn't look convinced. "It's a leap. We don't even know how old this pyramid is."

"The Greek writing would date it somewhere between fifteen and three hundred BCE, and probably closer to the former than the latter." Yates moved on to another stone and continued his examination. "That's toward the end of the Egyptian pyramid building boom. They only built two major pyramids after that date. Piye and Taharqua. But it doesn't prevent the Egyptians having a hand in this construction."

"The hieroglyphics would appear to confirm they did," said Granger. "Besides, the Greeks didn't have the architectural knowledge or enthusiasm to erect a pyramid like this."

"Which means this was built approximately five-hundred years before the rise of pyramids like Chichen Itza. That adds credence to the theory of copycat construction by the indigenous peoples of the Americas."

"Is that actually a theory?" Elijah Silverman shot Yates a quizzical look. "I thought it was just crackpots trying to make a link between cultures using ridiculous ancient alien theories."

"Except we're standing here looking at the proof with our very own eyes."

"No. This building proves only that ancient Egyptians and

Greeks had contact with the Americas. It does not prove that aliens had a hand in any of this."

"People." Granger raised his voice to get everyone's attention. "Let's focus on what's important. This is a huge archaeological discovery. It could be even bigger than Tutankhamen's tomb, or the Dead Sea Scrolls. The first evidence that early European and African civilizations crossed the Atlantic."

"What about the Vikings?" Weatherby asked. "There's plenty of proof they visited America."

"North America. And that came much later. They made it to Greenland around the tenth century. There's no evidence of Norse settlements on the mainland. Even the Vinland map is now considered fake," Silverman said.

"None of that matters." Granger was pacing at the base of the pyramid. He squinted upward toward the top of the structure, which was hard to see among the trees that pressed around it on all sides. "Think of the kudos. The first show like ours to make a genuine discovery."

"Except we're supposed to be finding monsters, not pyramids."

"Who cares?" Yates turned toward the group. "This is the real deal. Now maybe those snooty academics will actually take me seriously."

"Yeah, they'll probably give you tenure at Yale," Weatherby said with a chuckle.

"All right, let's all settle down." Granger raised his eyes to the sky, where leaden clouds had closed in, blotting out the early evening sun. "It'll be dark soon and there's a storm approaching. I don't want to be caught unprepared when the rain starts. Let's set up the tents and call base camp to report what we've found." He turned to Silverman. "You have the satellite phone?"

"Right here, boss." Silverman slipped his pack off and

reached inside. He brought out a chunky handset. "I'll make the call as soon as we make camp."

"Not likely." Yates walked over to his co-host and relieved him of the phone. "If anyone's going to make the call, it'll be me. This is my show."

"Figures." Silverman turned away, looking annoyed.

"What does that mean?"

"What do you think it means?" Silverman turned back to Yates and stared him down.

"Stop it." Granger stepped between the two men. "I don't care who makes the call. Just get it done. There's plenty of limelight to go around."

"Whatever." Silverman folded his arms and stared off into the distance. At six-four, he was the tallest member of the team, yet right now he looked small. The pouty expression on his boyishly good-looking face—which had been a big factor in the casting director picking him for this job—didn't help.

"We all good here?"

"Sure." Silverman shrugged.

"Peachy." Yates lifted the phone and grinned.

"Good." Granger turned his attention back to the rest of the group. "I want those tents erected and a fire going within thirty minutes. That's our priority. Then we eat. Tomorrow we'll see if there's a way into this building. I don't know about the rest of you, but I'm burning with curiosity to see what's inside."

"If it's Egyptian, probably a mummy." Weatherby shucked his pack from his shoulders and dropped it to the ground with a sigh of relief.

"Or maybe a buttload of gold and precious stones." Silverman's eyes sparkled with excitement, his run-in with Yates all but forgotten. "What are the rules in this country about finding stuff like that? Do we get to keep it?"

"What do you think?" Granger stepped away from the building and threw his own pack on the ground. He kneeled and pulled out a lightweight military combat shelter tent, hurrying as a peal of distant thunder rumbled across the forest. "If we find anything of value, we catalog and leave it in place. Those are the rules."

"Your rules."

"The network's rules. Not to mention those of our host government."

"Well, that sucks." Silverman pulled a face.

"I thought you were a professional," Cassie said.

"I am. I hold an advanced degree in Cryptozoology from the Vermont Institute of Metaphysics."

"Ah. The other Ivy League college." Cassie tried to suppress a grin but failed. "I guess you're hoping to add looter of antiquities to your heady resume."

"Whatever. Like your education is so much—"

Silverman never finished the sentence, thanks to the guttural roar that echoed out of the gloom between the trees.

"What was that?" Weatherby took an instinctual step backwards.

"Thunder?" Cassie peered skyward. "There is a storm on the way. Pretty soon it'll be raining so hard we'll drown if we don't get these tents up."

"That didn't sound like thunder."

"No, it didn't," Silverman said. "It was an animal."

"Easy, people. We are in the rainforest. There are all sorts of critters out here." Granger stood up and looked around. "The sooner we build a fire, the better."

"I've been in the rainforest before," Silverman said. "I've never heard a roar like that."

"And you're the expert, what with your advanced degree and all," Cassie quipped, but the tremble in her voice betrayed her fear.

"Quiet," Granger said, waving a hand toward his companions. "I hear something moving through the trees."

"I don't hear anything," Silverman said.

"I hear it. Listen." Weatherby's eyes drifted toward the canopy above them. "It's in the branches. Getting closer."

Now they all heard it. A rustling that grew steadily louder, closing in on their location.

"What is that?" Cassie asked. "Do you think it's monkeys?"

"It sounds too big." Granger shook his head. "Besides, we haven't heard any monkeys since we came down here."

"We've heard no animals at all," Weatherby said.

"Except whatever made that roar." Cassie swallowed hard. Her eyes were wide with fear. "And it's coming right toward us."

"I don't like this." Silverman took a step backwards. "Does anyone have a gun?"

"I do." Granger bent and rummaged in his pack. He came up a moment later with a pistol.

"That's it?" Silverman looked disappointed.

"What did you expect me to have in there, a rocket launcher?"

"I don't know. Something bigger than that."

"Just stay here." Granger took a deep breath and moved away from the group, holding the gun with trembling hands. He lifted his eyes skyward, examining the tree branches above, even as the rustling grew closer.

It sounded like it was right above them.

Then it stopped.

Granger stood a while, the gun pointed skyward, then he relaxed. "Whatever it is has gone now."

He took a step back toward the group. Before he could take a second, something dropped out of the canopy. A creature with dark, leathery wings, and an elongated head sporting a mouth full of sharp white teeth. It gripped Granger's shoulders with curved claws and flew back upward.

The terrified man let out a shriek as his feet lost contact with the ground. And then he was dragged swiftly up, disappearing into the leafy canopy above even as he struggled against his attacker. A moment later, his frantic screams abruptly cut off.

For a few seconds no one moved, too stunned to react. Then, as more roars filled the surrounding jungle, and impossible beasts crashed through the trees, the group finally found the will to run.

---

## 4

CHRISTMAS EVE.

PORTLAND, MAINE.

John Decker parked up in the driveway of the three-bedroom home CUSP had provided for him and Nancy while they got settled and found a place of their own. He went to the trunk and removed the items he purchased on the way home after spending the day at his employer's island facility, completing yet more rigorous training. Sometimes he wondered if it would ever end. He'd been back from Las Vegas for over a month, and they had offered him no new assignment.

This was fine, up to a point.

Some of that time had been used for the move from Mississippi, and Decker was still getting used to his new environment. He'd forgotten just how cold northern winters could be. And the worst of it wasn't even here yet. It hadn't yet snowed.

He was well aware of the misery the fluffy white stuff would bring. He'd worked in New York for many years as a homicide detective and seen his fair share of snowstorms. Nancy, on the other hand, had not. He wondered how well she would fare once winter unleashed its full fury.

But it had been her idea to move, and she'd reassured him that the cold weather would be met with the same stoic perseverance with which she greeted all the obstacles in her life. So here they were.

He slammed the trunk and headed toward the house, climbing the front steps and doing his best to open the door quietly. The bags were full of presents for Nancy, even though she'd said there was nothing she wanted except a quiet Christmas snuggled up with him in front of the fire. His efforts of stealth failed.

Nancy called out from the kitchen. "John, is that you?"

"Yes. I'll be with you in a moment." He made his way upstairs to the third bedroom. This was his domain, kitted out as an office complete with a secure link to the island. A place where he could work without interruption should CUSP require it. So far all he'd used it for was staying out of Nancy's way when she was on a tear unpacking the stacks of moving boxes piled in the garage. Decker had reminded her that this accommodation would probably be temporary, but she was having none of it. Given the likelihood that Decker would end up on a new assignment sooner rather than later, she figured they were going to be here for a while. She wanted to be comfortable.

She also wanted to make the place feel as homey as possible for Taylor, Nancy's daughter, who was attending college in Boston, and had made the trip up to Maine for the holidays. Currently, Taylor was occupying the other spare bedroom, from which Decker could hear loud music playing.

Decker stashed the bags in the closet and went back downstairs, closing and locking the office door behind him. He would wrap them later. When he entered the kitchen, Nancy was busy preparing their meal for the next day. A freshly made apple pie sat on the counter, steam still rising from its crust. The scent of baked goods filled the kitchen.

"Do we have to wait till tomorrow to dig into that pie, or is it available right now?" Decker asked, eyeing it hungrily as he pulled out a stool and sat at the island.

"You know the answer to that. It's for dessert tomorrow."

"Shame," Decker said, disappointed.

"I have this, though." Nancy removed another pie from the oven and placed it on the island in front of him. "Maple pecan. It's a recipe I'm trying out for the bakery."

"Looks delicious." Decker picked up a knife and cut a large slice, then slid it onto a plate. The bakery had been Nancy's idea. Ever since they sold the diner in Wolf Haven, she had been at a loose end. She wanted to make her mark now that they were finally settled in a new town. They had already found a location but wouldn't be able to sign the lease until after the holidays. Once that happened, she would get straight to work, turning the currently empty storefront located in the Old Port district into a bakery and coffee shop. She also planned to bring her native Louisiana cuisine to the area with Bananas Foster, Beignets, and bread pudding on the menu.

"What do you think?" Nancy hovered over Decker as he dug into the pie.

"Delicious," Decker said, between mouthfuls. "You're going to be the most popular bakery in Portland. Maybe even Maine."

"Stop it." Nancy was still holding the tea towel she'd used to remove the pie from the oven. She flicked it toward Decker playfully. "You might be setting the bar a little high."

"Just telling it as I see it."

"Well, that's very nice of you, but we'll let the customers be the judge." She turned back to the oven. "Honestly, I'll just be happy to get through Christmas."

"You love Christmas," Decker said. "Always did. Even when

we were first dating back before I left Wolf Haven you thought it was the best holiday of the year."

"It is. Because it doesn't just last one day. We can look forward to it for weeks, listening to festive songs and watching cheesy movies about people falling in love and running inns in Vermont. There are presents to wrap and a tree to decorate. It's happy. I like happy."

"What's happy?" Taylor appeared in the kitchen doorway.

Decker turned to look at her. "Your mother was telling me how much she loves Christmas."

"That again? It's so sappy." Taylor approached the pie like a predator zeroing in on prey. "I'll take a slice of that."

"I thought you liked the holidays." Nancy cut her a piece and handed it over.

"I do. It's just harder to get into it these days. There's so much awful stuff in the world."

"Doesn't mean we shouldn't try." Nancy glanced toward Decker. "Besides, John's out there making sure the world's a safer place for us all."

"Oh, yeah. The supersecret job on the creepy island chasing monsters."

"I never said my job was chasing monsters."

"You didn't need to. It's obvious. First you got fired as sheriff because no one would believe a werewolf tried to kill us all. Then you went to some middle of nowhere place in Alaska because the locals were convinced there was a monster stalking them. And as if that weren't enough, you almost got my mother eaten by a giant alligator."

"I didn't almost get Nancy eaten by an alligator," Decker said. "She insisted on accompanying me and almost got herself eaten. It's different."

"And how long after that was it before the shadowy government organization showed up recruiting you?"

"John doesn't chase monsters for a living," Nancy said with a grin. "He catches them."

Decker glared at her. "You're not helping."

"See. I knew I was right." Taylor skewered a piece of pie with her fork and popped it in her mouth. She grinned at Decker. "I hope I'm safe showing up here for the holidays. I mean, with your track record, we are likely to have Krampus kicking the door in tomorrow morning."

"Krampus?" Nancy looked confused.

"He's kind of like a bad Santa Claus."

"I don't think Krampus is real," Decker said. "At least, if he is, Adam Hunt hasn't asked me to go catch him yet."

"Give it time." Nancy laughed. "Speaking of which, you did tell him not to disturb you over the Christmas holiday, right?"

"Really can't do that. If they need me, I need to be ready. It's not like I have a regular nine-to-five job."

"Dammit, John."

"Don't worry about it. They haven't had an assignment for me in more than a month." Decker helped himself to a second serving of pie. "Nothing will happen over the next few days."

"Not so fast, mister." Nancy picked up his plate and put the slice of pie back in the dish.

"Hey." Decker protested, even though the look on her face told him it was pointless.

"Nope. If you eat a second slice, you'll spoil your appetite." Nancy glowered at him.

"Even I know not to go for a second piece." Taylor ate the last mouthful of her own pie and put her empty plate in the sink. As she turned to go back upstairs, she looked back over her shoulder at Decker. "Boy, I'd hate to be you when Hunt calls and drags you away from Mom's Christmas dinner."

"He won't call."

"You sure about that?" Taylor said over her shoulder. Then, before Decker could reply, she mounted the stairs and disappeared back to her bedroom.

# 5

Early on Christmas morning, Decker rose and left Nancy sleeping. He slipped out of the house and strode through town. Walking had become a morning routine he enjoyed. The air was crisp and cold, and his breath came out as a fine mist that was snatched away by the gentle breeze. He walked down to the waterfront, where boats of all shapes and sizes bobbed against the piers. On any other morning, the docks would be a hive of activity, with lobster boats preparing to put out. Most people assumed there was a strict lobster season, but in reality boats harvested the tasty crustaceans all year. But not today. Because of the holiday, the waterfront was quiet and empty.

Decker found a bench on a wharf jutting into Casco Bay. He sat down and enjoyed a moment of peaceful solitude. New England was nothing like his native Louisiana. The weather was more extreme. The landscape was more rugged. Local attitudes were different. Superstition permeated the South, much of it revolving around religion and the supernatural. He'd seen real estate listings in New Orleans that touted a lack of hauntings in the same way that one might say a building was free of termites.

Not here. New Englanders were a different breed. They

were practical and down to earth. Hardy. He liked their more prosaic outlook. But New England was not free of superstition and tall tales. Like Champ, Vermont's answer to the Loch Ness monster, that was rumored to live in Lake Champlain. They just handled it differently. He wondered what a born and bred Mainer would think of CUSP's island prison known as the Zoo, within which lurked supernatural monsters beyond their wildest imagination.

Decker watched a lone seagull fly in lazy circles above the wharf, no doubt disappointed that the lobstermen were not there to provide an easy meal. He glanced at his watch and decided it was time to head back. He stood and left the waterfront, walking at a leisurely pace. Nancy was in the kitchen making coffee when he arrived home. Taylor wouldn't surface for another hour.

Later that day, they opened gifts around the tree. Decker had wrapped Nancy's presents the previous night. Now he watched her open them with a smile on his face. He'd bought her a bunch of items, including a pair of thermal socks, because her feet got cold when she was in bed, and a flannel bathrobe. But the big present was an envelope containing the sales receipt for a floor-standing commercial spiral dough mixer for the new bakery and coffee shop. Decker knew it wasn't the most romantic present, but it was the same model she used at the Wolf Haven diner. To most people the gift would be uninspiring, but to Nancy it could not have been any more perfect. For Taylor there was an iPhone, and an upgraded laptop because she'd spent the last six months complaining the one she already had was too slow.

Later, during dinner, Taylor eyed the engagement ring on

Nancy's finger. "When are the pair of you thinking of getting married?"

"Soon. We were thinking the spring," Nancy said. To Decker, she said, "Have you spoken to Adam Hunt about taking time off for the wedding yet?"

"I've mentioned it," Decker said.

"And what did he say?"

"He wants an invitation."

"You know, that's not a bad idea. We should invite him," Nancy said. "If he's at the wedding, he can't interrupt it to order you off to the end of nowhere to catch Bigfoot."

"There are plenty of Bigfoot sightings in New England. Don't need to go very far to find that."

"Except Bigfoot isn't real," Taylor said, then she faltered. "Or is it?"

"Not as far as I know." Decker grinned. "But then again, even if it was, I wouldn't be at liberty to tell you. I work for a shadowy government organization, remember?"

"Hilarious." Taylor rolled her eyes.

Not long after, when the meal was over, Nancy started clearing the plates away. She was on her way back into the dining room from the kitchen carrying the apple pie she'd baked the day before when Decker's phone rang.

She put the pie down, her eyes flicking to his cell, which was sitting on the table. "That had better not be who I think it is."

"It's Adam Hunt." Decker picked the phone up.

Nancy put her hands on her hips. "I thought you said he wouldn't call today."

"Guess I was wrong." Decker stood up. He went onto the porch and pulled the front door closed behind him before answering.

"Decker?" Hunt said.

"Your timing is lousy, you know that?" Decker glanced back through the window. He could see Nancy in the dining room, still standing with an irritated look on her face. "I'll end up divorced before I even get married at this rate."

"Yeah. Sorry. If it's any consolation, I'm not calling to ruin your Christmas. But I will need you on the island first thing tomorrow. Something has come up."

"What?"

"An assignment that needs your brand of expertise. I won't go into the details right now. It can wait until the morning."

"Should I prepare a travel bag?"

"That would be a good idea," Hunt said, "and pack for a tropical climate."

"Guess I'm leaving the country."

"I'll brief you tomorrow. Go enjoy the holiday."

"Sure. I'll be on the island first thing." Decker hung up and stood looking out toward the waterfront a mile away. He could hear the faint lapping of waves out in the bay and the remote clang of a bell buoy. Then, pocketing his phone, he turned and retreated inside, grateful for the warmth that greeted him within, and returned to the dinner table.

Nancy was waiting, but instead of looking angry, there was a resigned expression on her face. "Hunt gave you an assignment."

"Yes." Decker took his seat. "I'll be leaving in the morning."

"Well, at least we have today, then." Nancy sat down and looked at Decker, forcing a smile. "How about some pie?"

## 6

Decker arrived at CUSP's island headquarters bright and early the next morning. He caught the 6 AM ferry from the mainland along with a couple dozen other employees, most of whom he didn't recognize. When he entered the cavernous lobby, with his travel bag in hand, Adam Hunt was waiting.

"John," he said, making his way across the marble floor as if he were greeting an old friend rather than a subordinate he was about to send on a dangerous mission. And maybe he and Decker were friends, to a point. They had stood side-by-side in Clareconnell, Ireland, and faced down the legendary Grendel, and his near immortal mother, Astrid. They had almost died, too.

"Adam." Decker's stomach rumbled. He hadn't eaten before leaving the house, figuring the canteen would be open. He looked hopefully toward it.

"Not yet," Adam said, as if reading Decker's mind. "Briefing first, then food."

"Guess I should've grabbed something before heading down to the ferry." Decker felt a flicker of annoyance.

"Which would've been the smart thing to do. Plan ahead and cover all eventualities. A good lesson."

Decker gritted his teeth and fought back the urge to remind Hunt how he'd ended up in a jail cell in Ireland not too long ago by not covering all the eventualities. It was Decker who sprung him. But it was not smart to remind your boss of their failings, especially when they were about to send you somewhere that could get you killed. He swallowed his annoyance and decided breakfast could wait. "Let's get on with it, then."

"First things first," Hunt said, leading Decker to a security station across the lobby. "You will need to leave your phone here. You can collect it after I've briefed you."

"Why is that?" Decker asked. He'd never had to give up his phone before. It was a handset provided by CUSP, and as such, was impervious to hackers and operated on a private, secure network.

"New security protocols." Hunt waited for Decker to hand over the phone, then spun on his heel and set off toward the elevators. "Follow me."

They rose two floors and in less than a minute were inside Hunt's spacious yet strangely impersonal office.

Decker waited for Hunt to sit down, then settled on the other side of a double pedestal desk finished in dark cherry.

Hunt picked up a remote control from the desk and pointed it toward a flatscreen TV mounted on the wall. The opening credits of a show were already waiting on pause. He pressed play and let the episode run until the opening monologue was over, then paused it again. "Recognize this?"

"Sure," Decker said. "It's that ridiculous monster hunter reality series on the Travel Network. Although I use the word reality loosely."

"Cryptid Quest." Hunt leaned back in his chair, one eye on the TV. "The main presenter is an archaeologist turned wannabee PT Barnum called Darren Yates. He teamed up with a cryptozoologist and a biologist. Together the three of them have been trekking all around the world looking for everything from the yeti to the Jersey Devil. This episode is from the fourth season. It should be right up your alley. The Loup Garou."

"I must have skipped that one."

"Doesn't matter. You didn't miss much. They spent most of the episode running around the swamps outside of New Orleans in the middle of the night scaring each other."

"I guess they didn't find anything, then?"

"They found an alligator that almost bit their producer's foot off. That made for about ten seconds of interesting TV, but no werewolves."

"I'm guessing that happens a lot."

"Which is why they're making bad reality TV instead of working for CUSP," Hunt said.

"They should've looked me up," Decker said. "I could've pointed them in the right direction."

"Maybe you still can, if you can find any of them alive."

"So that's my mission? Rescuing a reality TV crew."

"Ridiculous as it sounds, yes. They've been shooting a six-part special down in the Amazon. Some obscure story told by the locals about an ancient lost jungle fortress defended by monsters. Everyone but the nuttiest of pseudo-scientists have already written the story off as nothing but a myth. Even the production company that makes the series thought it was a load of bull, but that isn't the point of the show. People lap this stuff up."

"Except you don't think it is bull."

"No. I believe they stumbled into a genuine discovery."

"Why?"

"The production company chartered an old Brazilian military helicopter and equipped it with lidar. They spent a couple of weeks making passes over the jungle, looking for anything they could use as the basis for a show, even if it turned out to be nothing out of the ordinary."

"And they found it."

"They got a hit on something big. A structure buried deep in the jungle. It was invisible to the naked eye, completely covered in vegetation. It was also in an unexplored region and hard to reach."

"But they went there, anyway."

"A group set off from base camp three days ago. Seven people including three presenters, a producer, and three production crew. It was a two-day hike in. They were going to spend one day at the structure, then hike back out. They never returned."

"Maybe it just took longer than they expected to get in and out," Decker said. "Or they ran into some sort of trouble. Either way, I'm not sure this has anything to do with us. Sounds like a job for a search and rescue team. Maybe even the military."

"They did run into trouble, but not before they reached the structure."

"Let me guess, they found something you're interested in."

"They found a bunch of stuff. Like a pair of obelisks covered in Egyptian hieroglyphics and ancient Greek writing. And that's not all. There really is a fortress of sorts there. A large pyramid of ancient origin. And it's covered in more of the same."

"Hieroglyphics." Decker wasn't convinced. "In the Amazon jungle?"

"That's what they reported when they contacted base camp via their satellite phone, although the transmission was a bit garbled."

"Poor reception?"

"Not quite." Hunt sat back in his chair and observed Decker. "You remember when I said the myth mentioned monsters guarding the fortress?"

"Sure." Decker had a nasty feeling about where this was going.

"It's not a myth. Darren Yates, the show's presenter, made the call. He was practically hysterical."

"And?" Decker leaned forward.

"He claimed monsters attacked them. Told the rest of the team back at base camp a Cyclops killed his audio technician."

"Come again?" For a moment Decker thought he'd heard wrong. "Did you say a Cyclops?"

Hunt nodded slowly. "That's exactly what I said."

## 7

Decker was momentarily speechless as Adam Hunt's words sank in. Then he rubbed his chin thoughtfully. "How did this information come to us?"

"An asset at the United States Embassy in Brazil used back channels to alert us of the situation. The production company contacted the embassy yesterday to report the team missing. They wanted a contingent of US Marines sent down there to go in and rescue their production crew and presenters." Hunt snorted. "As if that was going to happen."

"Do you believe the sat phone call was genuine?"

"Why wouldn't it be?" Hunt asked.

"Because we're talking about a reality TV show. The whole thing could be a setup. The production crew head off into the jungle, then one of them makes a call claiming monsters attacked them. Which is what their show is about, after all. There's huge press coverage and they get all sorts of free publicity. After they get rescued, they can claim they didn't get the Cyclops on tape. No one will be able to prove anything either way, and they get a ratings hike."

"That's a cynical way to look at it."

Decker shrugged. "Just because someone cries wolf, or in this case Cyclops, that doesn't mean there really is one."

"You're forgetting one thing."

"What's that?"

"Darren Yates went as far as saying the creature killed his audio technician. Difficult to fake that." Hunt raised an eyebrow. "Unless you're suggesting the production company decided murder was worth the ratings boost."

"I think we can rule that out," Decker said. "But come on, a Cyclops?"

"Is it any stranger than Grendel being real?"

"That's a fair point. But even if such a creature exists, what would it be doing in the Amazon? Those things are straight out of Greek mythology."

"And they discovered Greek inscriptions at the site alongside the Egyptian hieroglyphics."

"I guess that makes sense then, in a completely nonsensical way."

"Doesn't have to make sense," Hunt said. "Surely you've seen enough weird stuff to realize that by now."

Decker shrugged again. "I suppose you're sending me down there to deal with this thing."

"And whatever other monsters might be lurking around."

"You think there's more than one?"

"Don't know. But Darren Yates said monsters attacked his team. Plural. Granted, one word in a frantic call from a distressed individual is not much to pin a theory on, but I wouldn't count it out. If Darren Yates is to be believed, both the Greeks and the Egyptians were at that site, apparently together. There must be a reason they would risk crossing a hostile ocean and constructing a building so deep in the jungle."

"You think they took this Cyclops there and imprisoned it in the same way the Vikings put Grendel in that labyrinth under Clareconnell?"

"It had crossed my mind. Then I got to thinking, why do all that just for one creature?"

"Good point," Decker said. "But something still doesn't make sense. If the ancient Greeks took the Cyclops there, or even a bunch of them, they should be long dead by now."

"Do you know how long a Cyclops lives?"

"No, but I'll bet it's not several thousand years."

"Which would explain Darren Yates' use of the word monsters," Hunt replied. "Think about it. A whole population of these creatures."

"They're breeding."

"Bingo." Hunt glanced back toward the TV, and the episode of Cryptid Quest still on pause there. When he looked back at Decker, his expression was grave. "I don't know how many of that production crew are still alive, but I need you to locate and extricate the survivors."

"I'll do my best."

"I also want you to figure out what the Egyptians and Greeks were doing in the Amazon, so far from home."

"That really isn't in my wheelhouse. I'm not an archaeologist," Decker said.

"Which is why you won't be going alone. We've assembled a small team of specialists to help you. An archaeologist with expertise in ancient civilizations and their mythology, an Egyptologist, and a representative from the production company who will be there in an advisory capacity. We've also sent a complement of Ghost Team operatives. Ex-Navy SEALs and Marines with big guns to keep you all safe."

"Ghost Team?" Decker had thought the Ghost Team were primarily concerned with transferring dangerous subjects and mopping up after regular operatives like him. Now he realized they did much more. They really were CUSP's version of a private special force. "This is a military operation, then."

"To a degree."

"That really isn't my style," Decker said.

"But it is a necessity given the hostile terrain. There are many dangers in the Amazon, beyond the snakes and jaguars. You might run across animal or drug traffickers that operate with impunity and won't take kindly to strangers on their turf. Not to mention gold smugglers. The soldiers are a precaution. I don't want to lose anyone down there."

"Who's in charge?" Decker asked.

"You are."

Decker nodded. "One question. Why didn't the production company have protection? Maybe then they wouldn't have lost their crew."

"They did. A couple of ex-Brazilian Army types. There was a dispute over money, and they quit the evening before the expedition was due to set off into the jungle from base camp. Disappeared in the middle of the night. The show's producer decided to continue without an armed escort."

"They hired mercenaries who tried to jack up their fee then left them to fend for themselves when it didn't work."

"They should have stayed away from the locals. A mistake on their part."

"And it might have gotten them killed."

"Or they might have ended up with nine people missing instead of seven."

"Fair point," Decker said. "When do I meet this team that you've put together?"

"Most of them are already in Brazil. They went there direct from other assignments. The Ghost Team have set up a temporary base camp in the Amazon. You'll rendezvous with them before proceeding to the pyramid."

"Sure." Decker had a feeling this was going to be a more complicated assignment than those Hunt had previously sent him on. He wasn't looking forward to tromping through the Amazon. "You said most of the team were meeting me there."

"Right. You won't be traveling down alone. One of the team was already working another job for us, close at hand. He arrived here last night. You know each other, actually. I'm sure he'll be pleased to see you."

"Is it Colum?" Decker asked.

"Not this time, although I admit he would be useful. But alas, we have him on an undercover assignment and we can't spare him."

"Who, then?" Decker asked.

"See for yourself." Hunt reached toward the phone on his desk.

He picked up the receiver and spoke three words. *Send him in.* No sooner had Hunt replaced the receiver than the office door opened, and a figure stepped through.

Decker turned in his chair, recognizing the diminutive man who stood in the doorway right away. Rory McCormick.

---

## 8

Hunt motioned for Rory to enter the room and told him to sit down. The archaeologist took a seat next to Decker and glanced over at him, nodding a quick greeting.

Decker returned the gesture.

Hunt waited until Rory settled down, and then spoke. "Now that I have you both here, there are a few more things we need to discuss." He leaned forward with his elbows on the desk and looked between the two men. "Everything that I'm going to tell you from this point on is compartmentalized information. The key members of your team have already been briefed, including the Ghost Team commander. You are the last to be read in on this. No one else within CUSP knows the details of what I'm about to tell you, and it must remain that way."

"What about the rest of the Ghost Team unit?" Decker asked.

"Like I said, only the commander has been read in. His men will do their jobs, but they are not privy to the more sensitive aspects of your assignment."

"Understood."

"Good. The information I'm about to give you is not to be

CRYPTID QUEST | 47

discussed or shared with anyone outside of your team unless the situation on the ground absolutely warrants it. Do you both understand?"

Decker nodded. "Loud and clear."

"Sure," Rory said. "What's with the extra secrecy?"

"New protocols," Hunt replied without explaining further, just as he had when Decker asked the same question down in the lobby. He pressed a concealed button under his desk and Decker heard his office door lock engage. Perhaps noting the look of surprise on Decker and Rory's faces, Hunt waved dismissively toward the door. "My office doubles as a secure briefing room. All very high-tech stuff. Had it put in last month. Once I activate the system, no one can enter or leave, and eavesdroppers cannot overhear us."

"Is that why the security guard downstairs took my phone before I was allowed up here?" Rory asked.

"It is." Hunt looked at the two men. "Now let's get down to business. There is much more to your current assignment than just rescuing a lost film crew."

"You want us to find what the Greeks and Egyptians were doing in the Amazon," Decker said. "And if there really is a Cyclops running around."

"I want you to do both those things. But your principal objective is finding out what lies within that structure the TV crew found," Hunt said. "Because it isn't just an old jungle temple to some long forgotten ancient deity. There's a power source within the pyramid. Something is running and we don't know what."

"Come again," Decker said. "The pyramid has power?"

"Yes. A considerable amount of power." Hunt leaned back in his chair. "Several hours ago, while the pair of you were tucked up in your beds sleeping, we co-opted a black ops NSA satellite to scan the region. I won't bore you with the specifics of what instrumentation is aboard the satellite. I couldn't even if I wanted to. It's way above your pay grade. Suffice to say, we got back some very unusual readings. We picked up an energy signature within the structure. We made three passes over the area to confirm our data. The energy signature was not the same on all three flyovers. It fluctuated. But there is no doubt. Something is turned on inside that pyramid, and it's using a lot of energy."

"Can you tell us anything else about it?" Decker asked. "Is it dangerous?"

"There's no way to know. But here's the kicker. The energy signature is similar to the one given off by the transit device you recovered from the sunken U-boat a few months ago."

"You're kidding me." Decker was stunned. "Are you trying to tell me there's alien technology running inside an ancient pyramid in Brazil?"

"I'm telling you no such thing." Hunt shook his head. "I said the power signature was similar. Not the same. That doesn't mean it came from an advanced technology, or that its origin is alien. It just makes it unusual. We don't see those sorts of readings every day."

"Understood."

"But we do know it shouldn't be there."

"We'll do our best to figure out what it is," Decker said.

"I know you will," Hunt answered. He cleared his throat. "I'm going to send the coordinates of both base camp and the pyramidal structure to your phones. The data will be encrypted. Only the two of you will have access to it."

"More cloak and dagger," Decker said.

"It's necessary. I can assure you of that." Hunt rubbed his forehead. As if he had a headache. "There's a jet on standby to fly you to Brazil. A place called Manaus. Since it will be evening when you land, we've arranged overnight hotel accommodation. All the details will be sent to your phones. In the morning, you're to return to the airport where a charter helicopter will be waiting to take you to base camp. Again, we will send the details to your phones."

"Got it," Decker said.

"Now, listen carefully. This is very important. You are to wait until you board the helicopter to open the encrypted file containing the coordinates of base camp. The pilot won't know where he's taking you until you provide him with that information." Hunt observed the two men with narrowed eyes. "You understand?"

"Yes. We understand," Decker replied.

"Crystal-clear, boss," Rory added.

"Good. When you get to base camp, you will provide the second set of coordinates—the ones that will lead you to the pyramid—to the leader of the Ghost Team. His name is Commander Ward. Do not share any of this information with anyone else."

"It goes without saying," Decker said.

"Excellent." Hunt smiled for the first time since Decker had entered his office. "Go down to the canteen. Eat a hearty breakfast. You'll need it. Both of you."

"Yes, sir." Decker stood up.

Rory followed suit.

Hunt reached down and pressed the concealed button under his desk. The office door locks disengaged.

They made their way out, but Decker stopped in the doorway and turned back toward his boss. "Sir?"

"Yes?"

"Is there something you're not telling us?" Decker couldn't shake the feeling this assignment was just a cog in a bigger narrative and that their lives may be in more danger than Adam Hunt was letting on.

Hunt met Decker's gaze with a cool detachment. "Mister Decker, what I'm not telling you could fill a football stadium."

"No, I mean about this assignment in—"

"I know what you mean." Hunt's eyes shifted to the right, over Decker's shoulder. "Close the door on your way out."

## 9

Seven hours after Rory McCormick stepped into Adam Hunt's office, he and Decker occupied the plush cabin of CUSP's Gulfstream jet. They were less than an hour away from landing in the Brazilian city of Manaus. A commercial flight would take almost eight hours to make the trip, but CUSP's state-of-the-art jet flew faster and higher, cutting the flight time down to under six.

Since it would already be evening when they arrived, Hunt had arranged overnight accommodation. The next day the helicopter would fly them three hours northeast to the base camp, where they would meet up with the rest of their team. After that, they would press into the unknown.

Rory sat opposite Decker. A thick folder sat open on a narrow desk in front of him, which he studied with singular intent. Earlier, as the jet made its way down the East Coast, they had chatted, catching up on all that had happened since Ireland. Since neither could talk freely about their previous assignments, the conversation had soon died out.

Now, as they neared the end of their flight, Decker observed his companion with interest. "You've had your nose in that file for more than three hours. Must be enthralling."

"Oh, it is." Rory pushed a pair of wire-frame spectacles higher on his nose. "This is everything I could dig up on the Cyclops."

"Want to share?" Decker asked. His own knowledge of the fabled beast came mostly from old Sinbad movies.

"I thought you'd never ask," Rory said with a grin. He closed the folder and turned to look at Decker. "What do you want to know?"

"Well, for a start, what exactly is a Cyclops. I know it was a creature from Greek mythology with a single eye in its forehead, but beyond that I'm fairly clueless."

"There actually isn't just one type of Cyclops, but three, depending on which ancient source you listen to," Rory said, his eyes sparkling with excitement now that he was talking about something he loved.

"The creature originated in Greek mythology but was later adopted by the Romans. In the original story they were three brothers called Brontes, Steropes, and Arges. They made the thunderbolt weapon for Zeus. Homer's Odyssey tells it a different way. They were a race of island-dwelling giants who liked to eat human flesh. One such beast kept Odysseus and his men captive in a cave for days, eating them two at a time. Eventually Homer's protagonist blinds the Cyclops, and tricks it into letting them escape. In another rendition, they were supposed to be the builders of Mycenae, the Bronze Age Greek city."

"So which one is it?" Decker asked.

"Well, if you believe the eyewitness testimony of Darren Yates, a bad-tempered giant with a hankering for human flesh would seem to fit the bill."

"Not what I hoped you'd say." Decker wondered what Adam

Hunt had gotten him into. "And apparently there's more than one of them."

"There would need to be if their race were to survive through the millennia."

"And the Egyptian angle?"

"That remains a mystery. But don't worry, we have an excellent Egyptologist on the team. If she can't figure it out, no one can," Rory said.

"You've worked with her before?"

"Twice." Rory's cheeks reddened. "I'm rather looking forward to seeing her again, to tell the truth."

"Are you really?" Decker couldn't contain a grin. "I take it there's something between you and this Egyptologist."

"I don't know if there's anything between us, but I hope there will be. The last time we were on an assignment together was in Luxor. We ended up trapped in a tent during a dreadful sandstorm. It was the best three hours of my life."

"I hope you're exaggerating."

"Well, maybe a little. But there was chemistry between us. We both felt it."

"How long ago was this?"

"A little over a year. It was a couple of assignments before Clareconnell."

"Did you keep in touch afterward?"

"We did at first. There were reports to write."

"And after that?"

"Not so much." Rory looked uncomfortable, as if this touched a nerve. "But that's okay. It wasn't like anything happened, and she's consumed with her career. Very single-minded. But I figured one day we'd end up working together again, and since the attraction is already there... who knows?"

"Sounds like you really like this woman." Decker turned in his seat to better face Rory. "Would you like some advice?"

"I don't know. When we were in Egypt, I emailed Colum for advice. He wasn't helpful."

"I'm surprised about that," Decker said. "Colum strikes me as the kind of guy who doesn't have much trouble with women."

"He doesn't." Rory sighed. "That's the problem. What works for him would get me slapped in the face."

"Surely not."

"You think? He's an ex-Army Ranger with the scars to prove it. He has muscles on top of his muscles. I spent my youth playing Dungeons and Dragons and now I scrabble around in the dirt for a living."

"It isn't all about physical appearance," Decker said.

"No. But it helps." Rory looked defeated. "Maybe I shouldn't bother."

"Look, I don't know this woman. I've never met her. But I did spend time with you in Ireland, and you're so much more than just a guy scrabbling around in the dirt. You faced down Grendel, after all. If you want my advice, just talk to her, and take it from there. Don't force it. Get to know her, and if she seems receptive, tell her how you feel."

"I guess."

"And don't forget, we're about to travel into the heart of the Amazon to do battle with the Cyclops. Even the ancient Greeks thought that was pretty heroic."

"Don't remind me about what we're doing." Now Rory looked queasy. "Every time I think about it my stomach churns. I don't know why Adam Hunt keeps putting me on these assignments."

"Maybe he sees more in you than you see in yourself?"

"Or maybe he just doesn't like me."

"You could just quit and go get a job with the museum if you hate it that much."

"What? End up begging for grant money and donations again. No, thank you. Been there, done that. I might have to fight the occasional monster in this job, but at least I'm well-funded."

"Can't argue with that," Decker said, bemused.

At that moment, the pilot came over the intercom and announced that they were about to land. Twenty minutes later, the plane was on the ground and taxiing toward a private terminal.

## 10

It was early evening in Manaus, and the sun was inching toward the horizon, casting long shadows. The taxi that had picked up Decker and Rory from the airport sped through the narrow streets, past ramshackle apartment buildings and garish storefronts. Some stores were shuttered and adorned with graffiti, sprayed gang tags and street art crowding the dilapidated frontages one on top of the other in an unintentional mishmash that ended up looking like the work of a crazed surrealist painter. Other stores were open, their metal shutters rolled up to display brightly colored clothing hanging on racks and electronics sitting in glass cases. Yet more shops sold produce or liquor. Utility poles lined the sidewalk on both sides, masses of tangled electrical cables running in all directions with no sense of order.

A bicyclist with shopping bags strung on his handlebars appeared from an alley between two buildings and bumped over the curb, swerving into the road ahead of them.

The taxi driver leaned on his horn and let out a string of curses in Portuguese, then spun the steering wheel hard right to avoid a collision. Even so, he barely avoided clipping the bicycle's rear tire.

In the back, Decker steadied himself as the careening vehicle's center of gravity shifted. Beside him, Rory was gripping the taxi's grab handle for dear life, his knuckles white.

"Holy crap, where did this guy learn to drive?" Rory said, breathless. "I have a half-blind uncle who could do better than this."

"I take it you've never been in a New York taxi then?" Decker said, but even so he reached up and took a hold of his own grab handle.

"How far is it to the hotel, anyway?"

"Does it matter? I think we're about to break the land-speed record," Decker said.

As if to prove him right, the taxi driver swung the lumbering vehicle—an old Mercedes 300E sedan with three regular tires and one whitewall—around a tight corner and onto a road even narrower than the first, without bothering to use the brakes.

The tires squealed, and the back fishtailed.

Decker lost his grip on the handle and slid sideways into Rory, who grunted and shot the oblivious driver a thunderous look.

Decker pulled himself back to his own side and gripped the handle even tighter.

"It's a good job I don't get motion sickness," Rory said.

"Tell me about it."

The taxi reached another intersection and turned. This road was wider. A one-way thoroughfare with three lanes and cars parked on both sides. On their right was a wide-open grassed space with a monument in the middle. A street seller had set up shop at its periphery, under a multicolored sun umbrella next to the sidewalk. Helium balloons on thin ribbons bobbed in the breeze, struggling to break free of their moorings. A trap for parents bringing their children to play in the open space.

Another seller further along offered bottles of water from a red cooler.

The taxi driver pointed as they sped by. "Praça da Saudade. Oldest square in city."

"Is it walking distance to the hotel?" Rory said in a low voice. "Because I've had just about enough of this roller coaster ride."

"Walking. Yes, good," the taxi driver replied, apparently understanding only a part of Rory's question. "Great place to come in summer. Play frisbee. Kick soccer ball."

"I'll remember that."

"You play soccer?" The taxi driver asked, his eyes darting up to the rear-view mirror and observing his passengers. "I'm on best team in city. We win championship three straight years."

"No, I don't play soccer." Rory looked at Decker. "Do I look like the kind of person who would play sports?"

"I'm going with a no on that one." Decker watched the square slip by.

"My son play soccer," the driver said with a smile. He pulled down his sun visor and pointed to a picture attached with a rubber band. The photo showed a smiling boy, perhaps ten or twelve years of age. He was posing on a sports field with a foot resting on a soccer ball. "He made school team last year. Was very good."

"Was?" Decker asked, looking at the photo. "Does he not play anymore?"

The driver shook his head. "Not since the illness. He has… what do you call it…" The driver searched for the right word. "Seizures."

"Oh. I'm sorry to hear that." Decker said.

"It is life." The taxi driver shrugged.

Praça da Saudade was behind them now. The green space was replaced by more buildings. A café stood on the corner, and beyond that another vacant storefront, it's pulled down silver shutters one more blank canvas for the graffiti artists. A cluster of mopeds stood parked under a tree at the edge of the sidewalk. Another street seller had found enough space in between the vehicles to set up shop. Phone chargers and umbrellas hung from a makeshift rack. The proprietor sat on a kitchen chair in a vacant parking spot, reading the newspaper.

"Are you seeing a doctor about the seizures?" Decker asked at length.

Paulo nodded. "We are on waiting list to see specialist. If we had money, we could pay and see doctor right away, but we cannot afford that. We rely on state medicine, which is free."

"How long have you been waiting?" Decker asked.

"Six month. The specialist is in Rio de Janeiro, so my wife took him there. She has been living with cousin in Del Castilho neighborhood. Not good part of city. I worry about them."

"She can't bring him back here until the appointment?"

The taxi driver shook his head. "We do not know when it will be. If there is an opening, we must be ready."

"What's your son's name?" Decker asked.

"Caio. It means happy."

"How much does it cost to see the specialist right away?" Rory asked, his demeanor toward the driver softening.

"Much money. Five thousand real. We cannot pay so we wait. I am afraid. Caio's seizures get worse."

"That's awful. I'm sorry," Rory said.

"It okay. My problem. I will deal with it." The taxi driver weaved around a city bus and turned onto a wide avenue. Here the buildings were larger. They were also in better repair. Then, opposite a second square which also contained a monument, he swooped to a stop in front of a large five story building and turned to face them. "Casa Amazonia." He pointed out the window. "Hotel."

The taxi driver left the car idling and jumped out. He went to the back of the vehicle and opened the trunk.

He pulled their bags out and deposited them on the sidewalk

as Decker and Rory exited the cab. "You want me to take luggage into hotel?"

"No, thank you. We'll be fine," Decker replied, taking his bag.

"Sure, sure. Forty-five real for the ride." He grinned and held out his hand.

"A bargain," Decker said, opening his wallet. He took out two banknotes, a fifty and a ten real, which he handed to the expectant driver.

"Thank you very much." The man grabbed the notes and quickly pushed them into his pocket, then turned to leave.

"Hang on." Decker stopped him.

"You need ride somewhere else?"

"No." Decker shook his head. "What's your name?"

"My name is Paulo."

"And your son's name is Caio."

"Yes. That is right." Paulo looked confused.

"Stay right where you are. I have something to give you." Decker knelt beside his travel bag and opened a side pouch. He removed a wad of tightly wrapped bills secured with a rubber band. He counted them quickly, keeping a small amount for himself, and then offered the remainder of the wad to Paulo. "Here."

"What is this?" Paulo eyed the money warily. "You already pay your fare."

"This isn't for the ride. This is for Caio's tests. Five thousand real."

"No. No." Paulo shook his head vigorously and backed away. "I cannot take."

"I insist," Decker said. "We can afford it, and you need to take care of that boy."

"Are you sure?" There were tears in Paulo's eyes.

Decker nodded.

"Will you just take it?" Rory said. "We're sure."

"Okay, then." Paulo reached out and took the money. He

CRYPTID QUEST | 61

looked at it for a moment as if he couldn't believe it was really in his hands, then he stepped forward and hugged first Decker, then Rory. "You don't know how much this mean to me."

"I have an idea," Decker said.

"I am in your debt," Paulo said. He handed Decker a card with a telephone number on it. "You need taxi again, or anything else, you call me. Any time. Day or night. I help."

"We'll keep that in mind," Decker promised.

"Good." Paulo slammed the trunk, then retreated and hurried back around the cab. "Thank you again, my friends. Thank you." He climbed in and gave them one last wave.

Rory slung his bag over one shoulder. He watched the taxi pull away, then turned to Decker. "That was a nice gesture."

"Seemed like the right thing to do." Decker started toward the hotel lobby.

"Exactly how much is five thousand real?" Rory asked.

"A little under a thousand dollars."

"That's most of our walking-around money."

"I kept about five hundred real. It should be enough."

"Let's hope."

"And don't forget, we have credit cards, too." Both Decker and Rory carried plastic in the name of Clayborne Petro-Chemical, a shell company CUSP used as cover. It allowed them to spend without attracting undue attention or leaving a trail that could be linked back to CUSP. Even the names on the cards were aliases.

"I know," Rory said. "How are you going to explain our charitable contribution on the expense report?"

"Easy. I'll tell the truth." Decker opened the hotel's wide glass door and stepped into the lobby. "Not even Adam Hunt is heartless enough to raise hell over such a good cause. We'll be fine."

"I hope you're right," Rory said.

"Me, too," Decker replied. Deep down, he knew he was.

## 11

The Casa Amazonia hotel was one of the more upscale establishments in the city of Manaus. The lobby was large, with marble floors and sumptuous sitting areas scattered among columns with intricate carvings that punctuated the wide double height reception area. A sense of grandeur that hearkened back to the romance of the Art Deco twenties pervaded the space, albeit faded.

Decker approached the registration desk and gave their names. Five minutes later, electronic key cards in hand for the pair of rooms Hunt had reserved for them, he and Rory were riding the elevator to the third floor. They were only staying one night. After breakfast the next morning, they would head to a private airstrip on the west side of town. From there a ninety-minute helicopter ride would bring them to base camp. But for now, Decker was looking forward to a hearty meal and a good night's sleep.

"It's eight o'clock local time," Decker said, glancing at his watch. "Let's drop our bags in the room and find something to eat. I don't know about you, but I'm starving."

"The sandwiches we ate on the flight didn't hold you over?" Rory said, chuckling.

"Not so much."

"I have no clue what the cuisine is like around here. You got anywhere in mind?" Rory swiped his key card and waited for the door lock to disengage.

"I figured we'd stop at the concierge desk on the way out and see what they recommend." Decker unlocked his own room and pushed the door open. "Let's take fifteen minutes to freshen up and we'll head down."

"You got it." Rory stepped into his room, then turned back to Decker. "You're not going to make us take another taxi tonight, are you?"

"Wasn't planning on it." Decker grinned at his companion before crossing the threshold into his own room. "See you in fifteen."

Rory nodded and disappeared from view.

Decker closed the door and surveyed his accommodation. It was as plush as the public area of the hotel. A king-sized bed with crisp cotton sheets and full pillows stood against one wall. A flatscreen TV faced it on the other. A table with two upholstered chairs was placed near the window. The city beyond sparkled with a thousand twinkling lights now that night had fallen.

Decker deposited his travel bag on the bed, then crossed the room and pulled the shades. He went back to the bag and took out a fresh shirt, then went into the bathroom with his toiletries bag. Ten minutes later, feeling more like himself and wearing the clean shirt, he left the hotel room and knocked on Rory's door.

∽

The concierge desk stood next to the hotel bar, on the far side of the lobby opposite check-in. The concierge himself was a thin man in his early forties, with black hair slicked over his scalp. A goatee clung to his chin, making his already long face look even more so. But he was only too happy to help Decker and Rory and suggested several nearby eateries ranging from dubious street carts to a restaurant he claimed was Michelin starred. All were within easy walking distance, he assured them.

After a moment of consultation, Decker and Rory decided to split the difference and chose a reasonably priced restaurant recommended by the concierge for its local flavors. The place was named simply Vivo, which was, apparently, the Portuguese word for alive.

They took down directions and left the hotel. Ten minutes later they arrived at the restaurant. They were given the option of either sitting inside or dining on a large patio area that fronted the building. The patio overlooked Praça da Saudade, the square their taxi driver pointed out to them earlier. It sat across the road and was now lit up with streetlamps that illuminated the square's pedestrian walkways. They decided to dine on the patio and enjoy the view, not to mention the cool breeze that had sprung up now the sun had set.

Rory picked up a menu and studied it. "I'm not sure what any of this stuff is," he said with a furrowed brow. "Everything is in Portuguese."

"You don't speak the language?" Decker said with a laugh.

"No. Do you?"

"Not a word." Decker turned the menu over and found the drink options. This much he did understand, recognizing both Heineken and Peroni on the beer list. When the waiter arrived, he ordered a Heineken, and Rory followed suit.

Turning the menu back over, Decker explained to the waiter that neither of them spoke the language and asked for a recommendation.

"You should try the Pirarucu de Casacu," the man said in accented but impeccable English. "It really is very good. A local delicacy."

"Yeah, I've had delicacies before," Rory said, wary. "It usually means I end up eating something gross."

The waiter laughed. "You like fish?"

"Sure. I like fish." Rory nodded.

"Then you will like Pirarucu."

"What is it, exactly?" Decker asked.

The waiter pointed to a picture on the menu. "This is what it looks like. Pirarucu is a giant fish local to the Amazon basin. It's extremely delicious. We take the salted fish and combine it with fried bananas and sautéed shoestring potatoes. If you're looking for a flavor of the Amazon, this is it."

Decker to Rory. "What do you think?"

Rory shrugged. "It's that or we ask this guy to translate everything else on the menu, and I'm hungry."

Decker looked up at the waiter. "In that case, sold. We'll both have the fish."

"Very good." The waiter grinned and scribbled their order on a notepad. "I'll bring your drinks," he said before turning and departing back inside the restaurant.

Decker sat back and watched cars pass by on the road in front of the restaurant while he waited for his beer to arrive. A young couple walked arm in arm in the square, their heads bent close to each other.

"This isn't so bad," said Rory. "Even the hotel is nice. Much better than the places Hunt normally books for me."

"I'd reserve judgment until we see base camp tomorrow, if I were you." Decker's gaze wandered toward the restaurant. The waiter had reappeared carrying a silver tray, upon which were two glasses and a pair of green beer bottles. He made his way toward them, weaving through the tables occupied by other diners.

A squeal of tires distracted Decker. He glanced toward the road and saw a black SUV stop at the curb. When he looked back, the waiter was almost upon them. He reached the table and lifted one of the glasses. As he did so, there was a popping sound and the tray jumped from his hand, sending the remaining glass and two beer bottles crashing to earth where they smashed, spewing frothy amber liquid in all directions.

Then Decker noticed the waiter, and the crimson stain swiftly spreading across his previously white shirt.

The man stayed upright for a moment, a look of startled disbelief on his face, and then his knees gave way and he crumpled to the ground.

## 12

A gunshot. Decker recognized the popping sound instantly. He also saw the two black-clad men wearing balaclavas who jumped from the SUV holding a pair of long-barreled handguns.

The patio dining area erupted into a cacophony of screams and panicked shouts. People dove to the floor. Others fled in terror, diners, and restaurant staff scattering in all directions in uncoordinated panic.

The gunmen were still advancing, oblivious to the surrounding chaos.

Decker's instincts took over.

Grabbing Rory by the back of his collar, he yanked the startled archaeologist out of his chair and to the ground while at the same time pulling the metal patio table over to create a barrier between themselves and the shooters. He reached to his left side out of habit, hand looking for the service weapon that would have been strapped in its shoulder holster if he were still a cop. Then Decker remembered he wasn't armed.

He wondered if the table would stop a bullet, doubted that it would. Especially at this range. In answer, he heard a sharp smack, and a hole burst open in the metal tabletop inches from his head. He felt the searing heat as a bullet whizzed past his ear.

Another sharp pop.

From somewhere close by, there was a pained grunt. A woman in a yellow floral dress dropped in her tracks, spinning sideways and almost crashing into their table shelter as she fell.

"We have to get out of here," Decker said to Rory, aware that if they didn't move soon everyone else on the patio would have either dispersed in terror or be dead. "When I say go, turn and run as fast as you can toward the restaurant. Whatever you do, don't go inside. There's an alley to the building's left. Aim for that and keep going. Don't follow a straight line. Weave as you run and whatever you do, stay low. It will make you a harder target."

"What about you?"

"I'll be right behind. Just do as I say."

Another bullet slammed into the table, splitting the air between the two men. Cats might have nine lives, but Decker knew that he and Rory didn't. The next bullet would probably kill one of them.

"You ready?" Decker asked.

Rory nodded but said nothing. His face was ashen.

Decker took a deep breath, prepared himself, and said, "Go."

Rory didn't need to be told twice. He pushed off, keeping himself bent low and dodging left and right through those diners that hadn't yet gotten clear of the patio.

After Rory left, Decker gripped the edges of the table and stood up, heaving it as high as he could with protesting muscles.

The two gunmen were only about ten feet away, their weapons extended and trained on Decker's location. Another second and more bullets would come his way. He hoisted the table aloft and brought his arms forward, letting go at the apex of his throw. The heavy piece of furniture didn't have as much momentum as he hoped and clattered to the ground well short of the armed men. But it made them react. The pair jumped back and sideways, trying to avoid the briefly airborne table.

That was all Decker needed.

He turned and sprinted after Rory, jumping over the prone waiter, who was obviously dead and laying in a growing pool of his own blood. He ran a zigzagging course toward the alley, careful to avoid any pattern of predictable movements even as more bullets flew.

He reached the alley and powered forward, ducking out of sight just as another bullet smacked into the concrete corner of the building, sending shards of masonry flying in all directions. As he entered the alley, Decker risked a glance backwards.

One gunman had turned and was sprinting back to the SUV. The vehicle had pulled up onto the sidewalk, with the engine revving in anticipation of the man's arrival.

The second shooter was continuing toward the alley.

Decker sensed what they were trying to do. Knowing the lay of the land better than he and Rory, they would attempt to trap their targets, with the still advancing gunman covering one end of the alley and the SUV racing around to block the other. They wouldn't stand a chance of escaping the alley and disappearing before the SUV showed up. Then he saw the metal door set into the wall ahead on the right. It gave him an idea.

Rory was several feet in front, but he wasn't as quick as Decker, who caught up easily and placed a hand on his companion's shoulder.

"That door. It's our only chance," Decker said, breathless, as they drew close. "Hurry."

"This is crazy," Rory said over his shoulder, but he picked up his pace anyway, somehow finding an extra spurt of speed.

They reached the door, and Decker gripped the handle.

It didn't open.

"It's locked," Rory said, glancing back down the alley toward the front of the restaurant. "We should keep going."

"No. If we do, we are dead." Decker banged a fist on the door. Three heavy thuds.

From the corner of his eye, he saw the shooter enter the alley and level the gun at them. He tensed, realizing they were out of options. Waiting for the bullet to smack into him.

But before their pursuer could get off a shot, the door swung inward to reveal a confused man dressed in a chef's white uniform. Behind him was the restaurant's kitchen, still running despite the chaos outside. Apparently, they hadn't yet gotten the message.

Decker pushed the confused restaurant worker backwards past the door, dragging Rory with him. "Run. As fast as you can."

"What are you going to do?" Rory asked.

"There's no time to explain. Just go." Decker gave Rory a shove, then stepped sideways behind the open door.

The chef watched Rory flee, obviously confused, then decided he didn't want to wait around to find out what was going on. He turned and ran, shouting at his coworkers to vacate as he went.

Decker stood silent and concealed behind the door. He counted off the seconds, judging how long it would take the gunman to reach the kitchen. He kept an eye on the crack between the door and the frame, that glowed yellow thanks to a lamp mounted on the outside wall above the door.

When a dark shadow fell across the gap, blocking the light from the overhead lamp, Decker put a shoulder against the door and drove it closed with all the force he could muster.

The gunman was caught off guard, half into the kitchen with his weapon extended ahead of him. He squealed with pain as the door slammed into his arms, crushing them between the door and the frame. He let go of the gun and it clattered to the floor.

Decker pressed his advantage, opening the door, and slamming it a second time, and then a third in quick succession before the now unarmed man had a chance to withdraw.

Pulling the door open a fourth time, Decker stepped out from behind it and gripped the injured man, pulling him quickly inside the kitchen and driving him toward a nearby cooktop, upon which sat a large pot full of bubbling liquid.

Decker propelled the gunman forward, slamming him into the pot, which toppled sideways and spilled its contents.

The man screamed as burning liquid scalded his face and arms. Decker dragged him back and slammed him down a second time. His head bounced off the cooktop with a resounding crack and his body went limp.

Decker let the unconscious man slip to the ground and turned back toward the door. The gun still lay there, its barrel lengthened thanks to a chunky black tube attached to the front. A suppressor, inaccurately known as a silencer even though it only muted the gun's discharge.

Decker scooped up the weapon, then frisked the man, finding two full magazines in his jacket pocket. Sixteen more bullets. These he kept. He didn't, however, find any identification on the shooter's person. Not that he expected to.

Then, fearing more assailants might be close at hand, Decker took off after Rory and the terrified kitchen staff. He wasn't sure what just happened, but he knew one thing. This assignment had just gotten a whole lot more dangerous.

## 13

Decker caught up with Rory in the restaurant's main dining room. It was strangely empty, with half-eaten meals sitting on abandoned tables and unfinished drinks lining the bar. Music was playing, a little too loud now there was no conversation or clink of cutlery.

"You made it," Rory said with obvious relief. "I thought they might have gotten you."

"Come on, we have to keep moving." Decker took Rory by the arm and led him toward the front of the restaurant, past the abandoned host station.

The restaurant's doors stood open. Beyond the patio area was a scene of devastation. Upturned tables and toppled chairs were strewn around as if a miniature whirlwind had come through. Items of clothing, coats and jackets abandoned by diners, lay crumpled on the ground. But it was the people who hadn't made it out that filled the scene with horror. Decker counted at least six bodies, including their waiter, who lay sprawled on his back with sightless eyes staring up into the humid Brazilian night.

Decker felt a pang of remorse. He was sure the killers had

come for himself and Rory. Even if he didn't know why. These innocent people ended up caught in the crossfire, straying in the path of bullets even as they tried to escape. He took in the scene quickly, evaluating the danger, then decided there were no gunmen remaining at the front of the building. The black SUV had sped away to cut off their escape route. It wouldn't be long before its occupants realized what had happened to their companion. But they wouldn't be back here, he knew. Because now Decker could hear the wail of sirens as the local authorities responded to the scene. Within minutes, this entire area would be swarming with cops.

If he and Rory were still here when the police arrived, they would be taken into custody for sure, especially since he was carrying a weapon used in the attack. And even if they could convince the authorities that they were not responsible for the massacre, red tape would keep them locked up long after they should have met the helicopter and flown to base camp where the rest of their team waited. Including a contingent of gun toting ex-soldiers. Now, Decker was glad for Hunt's prudence. He had a feeling the armed escort would prove necessary.

"Looks like the coast is clear," Decker said to Rory. "Let's move before local law enforcement arrives."

"Where are we going?" Rory asked. "Back to the hotel?"

"Not yet." Decker was sure that whoever just tried to have them killed was also watching the hotel. This was not some spur-of-the-moment act of violence. The men were well-trained and knew how to handle themselves. They were also, he suspected, not acting alone. There was organization behind their assault. "We need to find a set of wheels and get out of the immediate area."

"How are we going to do that?"

"Not sure yet." Decker stepped out of the restaurant and started across the patio, moving toward the grassy expanse of Praça da Saudade. He realized the gun was still in his hand. He unscrewed the suppressor and put it into his pocket, then pushed the weapon into his waistband and covered it with his shirttail. Running around the streets with a pistol in plain view was a good way to get yourself shot.

As they reached the road and crossed, the first police car came into view, turning onto the street several blocks distant. At least five more followed behind. From the other direction Decker heard ambulances, the tone of their wail different from the approaching cops. Not that there was much the paramedics could do. He suspected those left on the patio were beyond saving.

"Hurry." Decker pushed Rory along, and they entered the square.

The archaeologist pushed his glasses back up on his nose and stumbled forward as they ran down a wide central pathway that led to the monument in the middle.

Behind them, the first police cars arrived at the scene. Shouts went up and doors slammed. Decker kept Rory moving forward, aware that the cops would turn their attention to the surrounding area just as soon as they realized what had happened.

They reached the other side of the square. The road wasn't busy, and they barely had to slow down. After waiting for one lumbering delivery truck to pass by, the pair sprinted across the street. Decker scanned their surroundings at intervals, looking for the black SUV and its murderous occupants. But they were nowhere in sight. Having discovered that Rory and Decker had escaped, they probably decided discretion was their best option, given the circumstances. But that didn't mean it was now safe. The gunmen could appear again at any time.

"Do you actually have a plan or are we just running aimlessly?" Rory asked, as Decker led him into another alley between two dilapidated buildings.

CRYPTID QUEST | 75

"I have an idea that might turn into a plan if we're lucky," Decker said. "Does that count?"

"You're not filling me with confidence." Rory sounded winded. He was slowing down, too. He reached out and grabbed Decker's shoulder. "Hold up. I need to catch my breath for a moment."

Decker looked around. The alley was not a good place to stop. But he didn't want to end up carrying an exhausted Rory either if they ran into more bad guys.

"Fine," he said. "We'll stop, but only for a few minutes."

"Deal." Rory leaned against the alley wall and sucked in air, bent double. He looked at Decker. "Do you have any idea who those guys are?"

"Not a clue." Decker wished he did, because then they would know what they were up against, and why. "But I know we need to keep moving."

"We can't just keep going aimlessly."

"We aren't going to." Decker took out his phone, which worked almost anywhere and was untraceable. Any calls he made were secure too, all thanks to CUSP.

"Who are you calling?"

"The only person who can help us," Decker said, dialing a number from a business card he'd removed with the phone. After two rings, a familiar voice answered the call. It was Paulo, the taxi driver who had picked them up from the airport.

Decker told him what they needed, and where they were, then ended the call. He turned to Rory. "You ready to move yet?"

"I think so."

"Good. Because now we have wheels."

## 14

Decker led Rory to the other end of the alley, which came out on a wide three lane one-way street with shuttered and closed businesses on both sides.

"We need to look for a church," Decker said, glancing around.

"Huh?" Rory sounded perplexed. "I wouldn't mind a little divine intervention right now, but do you really think praying is the best course of action when we're being chased by a bunch of armed men who want to kill us?"

"I don't want to go inside and pray," Decker said. "That's where we're meeting Paulo. He said it would be an easy landmark to find because of the steeple."

"I see something that looks like a church down there," Rory said, pointing to a large white building a couple of blocks east. "Maybe that's it."

"I don't see anything else that looks like a church." Decker set off toward the building at a fast pace.

Rory hurried to keep up. "Of all the people in the world, why did you have to call that crazy taxi driver? He's almost as dangerous as those gunmen."

"Who else would you have me call?" Decker asked. "We're in an unfamiliar city, and we don't know anyone."

"What about Adam Hunt? He must have contacts."

"Maybe. Maybe not. But think about it. No one except CUSP knows we're here."

"You think Hunt or someone else in CUSP sent those men to kill us? That doesn't make sense."

"I don't think CUSP had a hand in this, but I do think that someone within our organization is feeding information to persons unknown."

"A mole."

"Precisely. It makes sense. We've been under surveillance since the minute we landed."

"Then how do you know we can trust the taxi driver?"

"I don't," Decker said. "But he was one of several taxis waiting at the curb when we left the airport. He couldn't have known we would choose his cab. Not only that, but if he was in on this, he could've just driven us somewhere remote and had us shot without needing to send armed men into a public place."

"I still think we should call Hunt and tell him what happened."

"Not yet. I trust Adam, but we don't know if someone around him is compromised. And don't forget, although our phones are secure and can't be externally tracked, I'm not sure if that level of security extends to our employer. A rogue operative inside CUSP might be able to pinpoint our location once those goons that attacked us back at the restaurant report their failure."

"Then we should turn them off," Rory said, reaching into his pocket and taking his phone out.

"I'm not sure that would do us any good," Decker said.

"Why not? If the phone's turned off, it won't communicate with cell towers anymore."

"These aren't ordinary phones. And even if they were, we

shouldn't assume that simply shutting them off will stop someone at CUSP from tracking our location. The National Security Agency can find a phone even if it's not on. It would be foolish to assume our own employer doesn't have the same capability."

"So why haven't we ditched them already?" Rory looked uncomfortable now. He glanced around, as if he expected to see the black SUV barreling toward them.

"Because there isn't anywhere safe to do so. We can't allow these phones to fall into the wrong hands."

"We destroy them."

"Too risky," Decker said, as they drew close to the church.

"What can we do, then? I don't want to walk around transmitting our location to whoever they send after us next."

"You won't have to." Decker spotted a familiar car at the far end of the street, speeding toward them. He steered Rory across the road to the church, where they stopped. "Our ride is here."

"Yay." Rory watched the taxi pull up to the curb with a sour expression. "This evening has turned out so great. We haven't had anything to eat because a pair of homicidal maniacs wearing masks shot our waiter, then tried to kill us, and now we're about to get into a car with the worst driver on the face of the planet."

"A driver who's probably saving our lives right now," Decker said, pulling the taxi's rear door open and motioning for Rory to climb in. After the archaeologist complied, he went around the car and climbed in the other side.

Paulo turned to face them, looking between the front seats. "My friends, it is good to see you again."

"Wish I could say the same." Rory clipped his seatbelt.

"Did you get what I asked for," Decker said.

"Sure, sure. I got them." Paulo grinned, handing Decker two small screwdrivers. "Easy to do. Found these at the taxi depot in the repair of bay."

"Perfect," Decker said, taking the screwdrivers.

"What are those for?" Rory asked.

"Hang on." Decker unlocked his handset and accessed the encrypted partition on the phone's hard drive. He used a retina scan to unlock the file containing the coordinates of both their base camp, and the pyramid structure. He studied them, committing the string of numbers to memory, then activated a purge of the phone's drive, wiping the data, along with everything else on the unit.

"Now your phone." Decker held his hand out.

Rory complied.

Decker activated the suicide app on Rory's phone and burned that hard drive too. But he had to go one step further. He took one of the small screwdrivers and inserted it into the first of a pair of holes that sat on each side of the charging port. "The only way to guarantee we won't be tracked is to remove the batteries. I asked Paulo to find us a couple of precision screwdrivers. One with a Torx head and the other flat. I figured the taxi depot would have them because they need to repair the radios and such in their cabs."

"Smart thinking." The fear on Rory's face eased a little.

"Thanks."

After removing the screw from the second hole, Decker inserted the flat screwdriver between the phone's case and the screen, then pried them apart. He lifted the screen out of the way and quickly unclipped and removed the internal battery. A minute later, he'd done the same to his own handset. He handed Rory his phone back, along with the extracted battery. "All done. Now we can't be tracked."

"And we can't make any more calls, either." Rory returned the phone to his pocket.

"An inconvenience, but a necessary one." Decker leaned forward and tapped Paulo on the shoulder. "Take us back to the hotel."

"Sure." Paulo swung the wheel and sped away from the curb.

Rory looked at Decker. "I thought you said we couldn't go back to the hotel."

"I did, but we still need our travel bags. I don't know about you, but I have no desire to spend this assignment wearing the same clothes every day."

"How are we going to do that? The minute we walk inside that hotel they'll spot us if what you said is true."

"That's why we won't be going in there," Decker said with a wry smile. "I have a better way to get our stuff."

## 15

Decker looked out the taxi window and studied the Casa Amazonia. They were parked across the road from the upscale hotel next to a bar from which throbbing Latin music played at levels that must surely have been contributing to hearing loss for those inside. They had picked this spot deliberately. Anyone surveilling the hotel for Decker and Rory's return would not give the taxi a second glance, assuming it was there to collect some reveler too drunk to make their own way home. Especially since Rory hunkered low in the back seat, out of sight.

"I don't see any suspicious persons," Decker said, scanning the valet parking attendants at their podium and occasional guests that wandered in and out of the building. "But it doesn't mean they're not in the lobby."

"Or maybe there's no one waiting for us at all," Rory said. "We could just walk in there and get our own stuff. Or better yet just spend the night in a comfortable bed instead of hiding out here."

"You want to wake up with a gun pointed at your face?" Decker finished studying the hotel's exterior and slid down out of sight next to Rory. "If we spend the night here, there's no way we live to see the morning."

"I know. Doesn't mean I have to like it." Rory adjusted his glasses, which had somehow survived the attack on the restaurant patio and subsequent chase. "What's your genius plan for getting our gear?"

"That's where our taxi driver comes in," Decker said. He looked at Paulo. "You think you can handle it?"

"Go to your rooms and get bags?" Paulo grinned. "Easy as cake."

"It's pie," Rory said. "Easy as pie."

"Hey." Decker nudged Rory. "Don't correct the man when he's about to put his life in danger so you can have clean skivvies."

"I am in and out in a Jiffy." Paulo shifted the car into park but left the engine running. "What are the room numbers?"

"Three twenty-six and three twenty-seven." Decker held his hand out toward Rory. "Give me your room key."

The archaeologist rummaged in his pocket and came out with a key card, which he handed to Decker.

Decker took the card and handed it to Paulo along with his own. "You good with this?"

"Sure, sure." Paulo nodded and opened the driver's door. "I am quick. Stay here."

"Be careful, too," Decker said. "We don't know who attacked us, but they mean business. They won't hesitate to take you out if they realize what you're doing."

"Do not worry about me. I can handle myself. I grew up in a shantytown out by the free-trade zone. Very bad place." Paulo flashed a toothy grin and closed the cab door before jogging across the street toward the hotel.

Decker watched him enter the lobby and then reached into his pocket. He removed the gun taken from the man he'd incapacitated in the restaurant kitchen and examined it. He screwed the suppressor back onto the barrel. "This is an unusual weapon for a person to be carrying here in Brazil."

"What do you mean?" Rory peered at the gun with a look of disdain on his face.

"The gun isn't western. It's a Makarov PB, sometimes used by the Soviet army, and the weapon of choice for the FSB. This particular model was made specifically for them."

"FSB?" Rory's eyes widened. "Aren't they the successors to the KGB?"

"They are, indeed."

"You think Russian intelligence is behind this?"

"Actually, I don't. I think it's more likely that this gun was acquired on the black market. It's also possible that the men who attacked us are Eastern European. The upheaval in that area over the last few decades has displaced a lot of bad actors. They could be mercenaries hiring themselves out to the highest bidder."

"In other words, we still don't know who they are."

"Pretty much." Decker checked the magazine. There were still five bullets left. He wondered how many of this gun's other bullets were responsible for the bodies back at the restaurant. He pushed the thought from his mind.

"That barrel you screwed onto the front of the gun," Rory said. "It's a silencer, right?"

"Suppressor. Silencer is a misnomer. This reduces the sound when the gun fires, but it does not eliminate it."

"That's why we could still hear the gunshots."

"Correct." Decker nodded. He turned the gun over in his hand and examined the frame above the grip. He ran a finger along, noting the rough metal there. "Definitely a black-market weapon. Serial number has been filed off. They knew what they were doing, too. Like how much metal to remove. There isn't even a hint of the number left."

"What does that mean?" Rory asked.

"It's untraceable. No way to know when this gun was manufactured or who it might have been assigned to."

"How do you know so much about this stuff?" Rory was staring at the gun. "I wouldn't know the difference between that thing and a water pistol."

"I spent years working for NYPD, most of it in the Homicide Division. We saw a lot of unusual guns. The first time I came across a pistol like this one was at the Manhattan penthouse of a Russian oligarch. He'd said some stuff the Soviets didn't like and believed he would be safe in the USA. He was wrong. FSB agents tracked him down and made sure he wouldn't be able to say anything ever again. They made it look like a suicide, of course. When we arrived at the scene, a Makarov was lying next to the dead man."

"But you figured out he didn't kill himself."

"We suspected it. Even had security footage of the probable killers entering the building. It was easy to ID them. The FBI kept meticulous files on all the personnel operating out of the Russian embassy. Problem was the men were traveling on diplomatic passports. The hit was state-sanctioned. We couldn't touch them, and they got away." Decker had been watching the hotel's main doors ever since Paulo disappeared inside. Now he saw the taxi driver emerge carrying a pair of bags. He started across the road, stopping briefly as a car sped past, then continued toward the taxi.

Behind him, two more men exited the hotel, dressed in smart charcoal gray suits.

Decker stiffened.

They could be a couple of businessmen looking for a cab to the airport, or they might be going out in search of a restaurant serving late-night fare. But he didn't think so. There was something about them that didn't feel right. The way they glanced around, furtive and on edge. As if they were summing up their surroundings.

Decker rolled his window down, intending to shout a warning to Paulo. But before he even had it halfway, the two men reached into their jackets and pulled out sleek black pistols, which they aimed at the retreating and oblivious taxi driver.

## 16

Decker didn't wait for the men to gun Paulo down in cold blood. He had the Makarov in his hand. He aimed it to the left of the two gunmen, toward the valet podium, which was currently standing unmanned. It was close enough to make his point, but still a safe distance from any innocent bystanders.

He pulled the trigger.

The gun kicked, almost causing him to fall backwards thanks to his bad shooting stance in the back of the taxi. The bullet did its job, though. It smacked into the podium and sent the two startled gunmen diving for cover. They took shelter behind the concrete columns that held up the hotel's portico.

A middle-aged woman in an evening gown was exiting the lobby carrying a small lapdog. She quickly turned and retreated inside. People scattered in all directions. Someone screamed.

Halfway across the road, Paulo stopped and turned, wondering what the commotion was.

"Don't stop," Decker shouted, waving toward the confused taxi driver. "Get in the car, now."

The two gunmen were regrouping. They stepped out from their concealment. Decker sent another bullet their way. It took a chunk out of a column close enough to make the nearest gunman flinch and scurry backwards.

Paulo was on the move again. He dashed across the road's last two lanes and pulled the taxi door open, throwing the bags onto the front passenger seat and diving in even as one of the dark-suited men got off a shot of his own. The bullet punched through the taxi's door and buried itself into the side of the driver's seat, inches from its target.

Paulo let loose with a string of curses in Portuguese and slammed the car into gear, then spun the steering wheel before accelerating away with a screech of tires.

Decker turned and looked through the back window in time to see the black SUV come streaking up and collect the gunmen. As soon as they climbed in, it shot forward, almost hitting a sleek black limousine that was trying to pull under the portico out of the way. Then the SUV gave chase.

"They're coming after us," Rory said, his voice rising in pitch. "Don't these guys ever give up?"

"The evidence would appear to suggest not." Decker wished he could call Adam Hunt for backup, but knew they were on their own. Besides, he'd disassembled their phones to make sure the men currently chasing them couldn't track their whereabouts.

"Don't worry," Paulo said, swinging the wheel hard and steering the speeding taxi down a side street. "I make sure they won't catch us."

"How are you going to do that?" Rory asked, watching the SUV accelerate toward them. "They're gaining on us."

"I have excellent idea." Paulo reached toward the taxi's two-way radio and unhooked the mic. He spoke quickly, then listened to the reply, then spoke again.

Decker and Rory exchanged glances, unable to understand him.

From behind them, the roar of the SUV's engine got louder.

It was a much newer vehicle than their own aging cab, and it was only a matter of time before it caught up with them.

Decker looked down at the gun in his lap. He had three bullets left, plus the two magazines he'd stripped from the man in the restaurant kitchen. He didn't want to waste ammo. It was turning into a long night, and they might need every bullet they could get.

He risked another glance backwards. The black SUV had gained ground. Decker couldn't see inside, but there must be at least three men, including the driver. They would all be armed. He wondered where the police were. After the shooting in the restaurant, they had arrived in no time at all, but now the streets were quiet. Even though Decker had fired two shots back at the hotel, he couldn't hear sirens. That was a bad sign. It meant that whoever was pursuing them had enough clout to sideline local law enforcement.

Paulo reached an intersection and took a left, then pushed the vehicle's accelerator to the floor, coaxing every ounce of speed from the old Mercedes.

"We will lose them soon," the taxi driver said, glancing back over his shoulder toward Decker and Rory. "You will see."

"Not sure how we're going to do that," Rory said, turning to look at their pursuers. "If anything, we're about to get caught."

"Just wait." Paulo turned his attention forward again.

They were coming up on a large two-lane rotary now. A monument on a pedestal rose from the center island. Paulo entered the traffic circle and shifted into the inside lane, slipping behind another white Mercedes with a taxi sign on the roof.

Decker turned to see what the SUV was doing. It was about to enter the rotary, but then slammed on its brakes as a third identical taxi appeared from the left and cut it off. The taxi then fell in behind their own vehicle.

"What's going on?" Rory's gaze shifted between the taxi in front of them and the taxi at their rear.

"Reinforcements," Paulo said with a grin.

The SUV had entered the rotary now and was speeding toward them. Paulo picked up the radio handset again and started talking fast. A moment later, the cab ahead of them shifted into the right lane and slowed down.

Paulo sped up and let the taxi behind fill in the space, creating a rolling roadblock.

The SUV changed lanes, then changed back again.

Yet another white Mercedes appeared, merging onto the rotary from their right. Now there were four similar taxi cabs ahead of the SUV as the cars completed a full circuit of the traffic circle.

Paulo barked more instructions into the radio and the cabs shifted places, changing lanes and positions like a crazy automotive version of the shell game. Then, after one more quick exchange, the four cars split up, and each took a different exit off the rotary.

Decker watched the SUV make another trip around, clearly confused. The only way the gunmen could identify their own vehicle was if someone inside had written down their license plate. But he suspected they hadn't thought to do that, which left a one in four chance of the gunmen picking the right vehicle.

Decker held his breath as the SUV approached their exit, but then it cruised on past and took the next one, following one of the other taxis into the night. They were safe, at least for now, and it was all thanks to Paulo's quick thinking.

## 17

Decker watched the fading red glow of the SUV's taillights as it followed one of the decoy taxis. After the vehicle had driven off into the night, he turned to look at Paulo. "That was a fancy maneuver, back there. I'm impressed."

"But where did those other taxis even come from?" Rory asked. "I radio my boss," Paulo replied. "He has many cabs just like this one."

"Well, I'm glad he agreed to help," Decker said.

"He believes there is too much crime here, just like me." Paulo had slowed the cab to a more moderate speed now. "It makes us look bad. He also doesn't like criminals shooting at his taxis."

"Please thank him from us when you see him next." Decker unscrewed the suppressor from the gun and put them both out of sight.

"I'm happy we escaped with our lives," Rory said, "but what are we going to do now? We haven't eaten yet and we have nowhere to stay tonight."

"I don't know, yet." Decker was hungry too. But stopping for food would be risky. Once the men in the black SUV realized

CRYPTID QUEST | 91

they were following the wrong vehicle, they would circle back. And they might not be the only ones looking for Decker and Rory. Who knew how many other operatives their unknown enemy had in the city?

"No worries, my friends. I take care of that too," Paulo said. "We go to a safe place now where you can eat and sleep."

Decker leaned forward. "Where do you intend to take us?"

"We will visit with my sister, Aline. She lives outside the city. We hide there tonight, and I take you where you want to go in the morning."

"Works for me," Decker said. He looked at Rory. "You down with that?"

"Unless Paulo's sister is going to shoot at us, I'm just dandy with it." Rory forced a smile.

"Excellent." Paulo slapped the dashboard. He reached for the FM radio and turned it on, then fiddled with the chooser. "We should have music to pass the time, it will take us an hour to get there."

Decker glanced at his watch. It was almost eleven at night. By now they should have been back at the hotel and climbing into their comfortable beds instead of driving through the darkness as hunted men. He leaned back and closed his eyes as the heavy beat of a Brazilian rock band filled the car.

In the driver's seat, Paulo hummed the tune for a while, then started to sing in an off key yet strangely melodic voice. If their close call and the bullet hole in the side of his taxi upset him, he didn't show it.

## 18

It wasn't long before they left the lights of the city behind and were speeding down a two-lane carriageway with dark forest on one side and a plateau of cleared land on the other. Piles of stacked tree trunks stripped of their foliage sat near the road.

Paulo pointed as they zipped by. "They clear rainforest here to build more slums. Too many people come looking for work in free-trade zone. It is sad. Manaus used to be a great city, but now it is exploited by foreign corporations who only care about profits."

"Why doesn't your government stop it?" Rory asked.

"A good question, my friend." Paulo turned onto a narrow side road with cracked and potholed asphalt.

Decker saw the outline of small dwellings on both sides, some of which had faint light glowing from within, while others were dark and seemingly abandoned. They followed the road for several miles, bumping along over the uneven surface. Between the broken asphalt and the taxi's bad suspension, Decker felt like his bones were being jarred out of their joints.

Just when he thought the trip would never end, Paulo pulled the taxi up in front of a small house built of blocks. A tin roof jutted out from the front of the building, creating a small overhanging porch with a dirt floor that fronted an equally dusty sidewalk. A red moped stood at the curb in front of the house. A cooler was strapped on top of the rear fender with bungee cords.

Paulo killed the taxi's engine and turned to face his passengers in the back. "This is my sister's house. I called her when I was getting your stuff from hotel. She is expecting us. No bad men will come here."

"Thank you for helping us," Decker said after they had exited the taxi and grabbed their travel bags from the front seat. "I don't know what we would have done otherwise."

"It is no problem." Paulo motioned for Rory and Decker to follow him. "Come."

Paulo's sister, Aline, was waiting when they reached the front door. She opened it and then unlocked a wrought-iron security door to allow them inside. She looked at Paulo and said something in Portuguese.

He nodded, answered her, and then turned to Rory and Decker. "My sister does not speak English, but she welcomes you to her home. She has made us food if you are hungry."

"I'm starving," Rory said. "Actually, I went past starving right around the time those goons were chasing the taxi. I'm not sure there's a word for how hungry I am now."

"What's on the menu?" Decker asked.

"She make us galinhada. Our grandmother's recipe. Delicious."

"Do I want to know what galinhada is?" Rory said.

"Does it matter?" Decker was already following Paulo and his sister to the back of the shack, where there was a small kitchen area with a wooden table and four chairs in the middle.

Paulo glanced back over his shoulder. "It is chicken and rice cooked in a pot. It also has pequi. That is a fruit from rainforest. You will like."

"I hope so. I don't do well with ethnic food," Rory said. But even so, when Aline handed him a bowl with a generous serving, he settled at the table and dug straight in. After a couple of mouthfuls, he looked up, surprised. "Hey, this is really good."

Paulo beamed with pride. "I told you. Old family recipe."

After that, they ate in silence. Both Decker and Rory allowed Aline to serve them second helpings, which they consumed with almost as much gusto as the first. They washed it down with a lemonade concoction made with limes and sweetened with condensed milk.

Afterward, when they had finished their meal, Aline spoke quickly to her brother, before picking up their bowls and taking them to the sink.

Paulo slapped the backs of the two men. "Come along. My sister says you look tired. I show you the room where you will sleep."

They followed the taxi driver down a short corridor and into a room not much bigger than a walk-in closet. The only furniture was a set of bunk beds and a small nightstand under a window with iron bars on it.

"I am sorry it is not like the Casa Amazonia," Paulo said. "But you will be comfortable."

"I'm sure we will," Decker said. "And thank you again for the hospitality. Please also thank your sister."

"Sure, sure." Paulo nodded enthusiastically. "I leave you alone now. In the morning I take you wherever you want to go."

Decker dropped his bag on the floor next to the nightstand. "Is there a bathroom where we can freshen up?"

"It is first door on right in hallway." Paulo hesitated in the doorway, looking between the two men. "You need anything else?"

"No." Decker shook his head.

"Okay." Paulo retreated into the corridor and disappeared back toward the kitchen. From somewhere inside the building a radio was playing, and they could hear Aline washing dishes even though it was past midnight.

Decker tested the mattress on the top bunk and found it to be agreeably plush. He rummaged in the travel bag for his toiletries case and headed toward the door. "You can take the bottom bunk. I'll take the top. I'll be back soon."

"Sure." Rory nodded and pulled the covers aside on the lower bunk.

Decker went to the bathroom and cleaned his teeth. He splashed water on his face, then returned to the bedroom. When he stepped inside, Rory was already asleep on the bottom bunk with a sheet draped around his shoulders. He was snoring.

Decker undressed, then he turned off the light and climbed up onto the top bunk. Soon he was asleep, too.

## 19

Decker awoke to a rooster crowing so loudly he thought it must be in the room with him. He sat up, forgetting he was in a bunk bed, and almost cracked his head on the low ceiling.

"What is that terrible noise?" Rory said from the bottom bunk. "It sounds like the alarm clock from hell."

"You never heard a rooster before?" Decker swung his legs off the bed and clambered down the ladder to the floor.

Rory sat propped up on his elbows, looking bleary-eyed. "I grew up in Boston. We didn't have roosters. We had garbage trucks and snowplows to wake us up. It's just more civilized."

"Well, where I come from, we had roosters aplenty. Not to mention every other kind of poultry you could think of. There was even a chicken that used to walk through the local coffee shop and lay eggs in the plant pots outside."

"This place must be like a homecoming to you, then."

"Not really," Decker said as he got dressed.

He stepped toward the door. "I'm going to see if our friend, Paulo, is awake yet."

"Sure." Rory climbed from the bed and grabbed his travel bag. "What time is it, anyway?"

"Early. A little after six."

"No wonder I still feel tired. Couldn't we have set that rooster to go off an hour later?"

"Not sure it works like that," Decker said with a laugh, then stepped out into the corridor and closed the bedroom door.

He made his way to the kitchen, where Aline was already fussing around.

When he entered, she looked around. "Olá."

"Hello." Decker went to the front of the house and peered out through the window. The taxi was still parked where they'd left it the night before. The narrow road was empty with no sign the gunmen in the black SUV had found them. Even so, he didn't want to take any chances. They would need to be careful. When he turned to go back to the kitchen, Paulo appeared.

He shot Decker a quizzical look. "You check the coast is clear?"

"Yes." Decker nodded. "Those guys that chased us last night meant business. I don't want to bring that down on your family."

"It will be okay." Paulo motioned for Decker to follow him back into the kitchen. "They won't find us here. Even if they ask at taxi depot, it is still safe. No one there knows I have a sister. Not their business."

"I hope you're right," Decker said. "Regardless, I would like to leave as soon as possible. We've chartered a helicopter to take us to into the Amazon. It will be waiting for us."

"You sure it's safe?" Rory asked, entering the kitchen. "What if those goons know about the helicopter. They could be waiting for us."

"Already thought of that. Hopefully it's all good, but I have no intention of just strolling blindly into a trap." Decker turned to Paulo. "Are you ready to go?"

"You want to leave now?" Paulo exchanged a look with his sister. He said something to her in Portuguese, and she replied, shaking her head vigorously. He looked back at Decker. "Aline says you must have breakfast first. Cannot travel hungry. Eat, then I take you."

"That's very generous of her, but the longer we stay here, the longer you're both in danger," Decker said. "Like I said, I want to be in the air as quickly as possible."

Aline slapped a hand on the table. She looked at Decker and said something he didn't understand.

Paulo laughed. "My sister says it will offend her if you do not eat before you leave. There is time, I promise. Airport is less than an hour away."

"Surely we can stay for breakfast," Rory said. "It would be rude not to."

"Alright," Decker said, against his better judgment. But at the same time, he didn't want to upset their host. To Paulo, he said, "You win. We'll have breakfast here, but then we leave straight afterward. Understood?"

"Yes, yes. I understand." Paulo spoke to his sister, and she went to work, fussing about the kitchen and preparing a breakfast of ham and eggs. Less than fifteen minutes later, they were sitting at the table, eating heartily.

"This is good," Decker said, digging into his food. "If we weren't in such a hurry, I might decide to stay here for a few days just for this cooking."

Paulo grinned and translated Decker's complement for his sister, who beamed with pride. Then he looked back toward Decker with a concerned look on his face. "I am not prying, but why were men with guns chasing you, anyway?"

"I wish I knew," Decker said between bites.

"You do something bad?"

"No." Decker scooped up a piece of ham and mopped egg yolk with it before popping it into his mouth. "But I think it might have something to do with our job, and why we came here."

"You are going deep into Amazon jungle, right?" Paulo asked.

"Yes." Decker nodded. "But I can't share more than that."

"It is a secret, yes?"

"Yes."

"I understand." Now it was Paulo's turn to nod. "A word of warning. The jungle is wild place. Easy to get killed. You should reconsider. I don't want you to get hurt, or worse."

"We don't have a choice," Decker said. "People are depending on us. Lives are at stake."

"What if the gunmen follow you to jungle?"

"I don't know," Decker said. This thought had been on his mind since the night before. The men in the black SUV, or whoever they worked for, would not give up, he was sure. He pushed his empty plate away. "Now, I think it's time that we left."

"Sure." Paulo stood up. "You get your bags, and I meet you at car."

"Hold up a moment." Decker took out his wallet and opened it. He removed the last of his bank notes and handed them to Aline. "For your trouble."

Aline's eyes flew wide. She counted the notes, then talked excitedly to her brother.

Paulo listened, then turned to Decker. "My sister says she cannot accept this. It is too much. Five hundred real."

"Is not too much," Decker said. "If I had it, I'd give her more. You're risking your lives for us. Tell her it's the least we can do."

Paulo bit his lip thoughtfully, then relayed the message to his sister.

She studied Decker for a moment, then came around the table and gripped him in a vice-like hug.

Decker waited for the grateful woman to release him, then put a hand on Paulo's shoulder. "Let's go."

"Sure, sure. I get my keys and meet you at the taxi." Paulo scurried off.

Decker noticed Rory looking at him. "What? You going to give me a hard time about the expense report again?"

Rory merely shrugged. "Not at all. I was just thinking it's a shame we can't take Paulo with us. He's proved pretty useful so far."

"Yeah. I'm not sure his sister would like that." Decker started toward the bedroom. "Come on, let's get our bags and get to that helicopter. I can't wait to meet this mysterious Egyptologist woman you're too afraid to ask out on a date even though you shared a moment in a tent during a sandstorm."

"I'm not afraid to ask her out," Rory said, hurrying along behind Decker. "I'm afraid she'll say no. That's much worse."

## 20

It took Paulo less than forty-five minutes to make it to the airport, which he declared was a personal record. When they arrived, he followed the perimeter road, ignoring the commercial passenger terminal, and took them to an FBO on the far side of the airport instead. FBO stood for Fixed-Base Operator. It was the same private terminal that CUSP's own jet had used the previous day. That aircraft was long gone, having flown back to the United States after dropping them off. Now they were here to meet the helicopter for the last leg of their journey to base camp.

When they parked, Paulo turned to face Decker and Rory, who were in the back. "See. I get you here on time, just like I promised."

"Thank you," Decker glanced around the parking lot, looking for the black SUV. There was no sign of it. If the killers were here, they used a different vehicle. He looked back at Paulo. "One more thing…"

"Yes?"

"I know it's a lot to ask, especially after all you've done, but can you wait here? Just until we confirm the helicopter hasn't been compromised."

"Sure. Sure. I wait right here," Paulo said. "I want to make sure you leave safely."

"I appreciate that. Give us fifteen minutes. That should be enough time," Decker said. "If it all looks good, we'll be back for our bags. If we don't return it means the gunmen found us and we're dead. In that case, I want you to get as far away from the airport as possible. Understand?"

"Sure, sure." Paulo nodded. "I wait fifteen minutes. No longer."

"Good." Decker climbed out of the cab. Together he and Rory approached the terminal, which was really nothing more than a square building constructed of concrete blocks that sat between two large aircraft hangars.

There was only one person inside, lounging behind a scuffed and worn counter. A bored-looking man in his sixties with a deeply lined and tanned face. He was wearing a Panama hat and blue tie-dye shirt, which made him look more like a lost tourist than an airport employee.

The waiting area was hardly plush. Three rows of hard plastic seats occupied the center of the room. A soda vending machine stood against the wall opposite the counter. Faded posters advertising rainforest helicopter tours and ecotourism trips dotted the walls.

When they entered, the man looked up with watery eyes.

"No tours until this afternoon," he said in heavily accented English.

"We're not here for a tour," Decker said. "We chartered a helicopter to take us into the Amazon."

The man observed them with disinterest. "I don't deal with private charters. Tour bookings only."

"No problem," Decker said. "Do you know where we can find our charter?"

"You will want the hanger," The man replied. He was chewing something Decker had assumed was gum, but now he turned his head to one side and spit a wad of mushy brown tobacco into a garbage can. When he turned his attention back to them, a bead of tobacco juice clung to his lower lip, threatening to dribble down his chin. He licked it away and swallowed before speaking again.

"How do we find this hanger?" Decker asked.

The old man nodded toward the door next to the counter. "Go through there and follow the corridor. When you get outside turn right and you'll be there. Can't miss it. Big doors."

"Thanks." Decker turned to leave, then checked himself. "Has anyone else shown up here this morning?"

"Sure." the old man nodded. "Couple of bad looking hombres. I sent them back there already."

"And they were looking for our flight?" Decker felt his gut clench. It appeared he was right to be cautious.

Again, the old man shrugged. "Don't know. Said they were with the charter company. Something about a pre-flight maintenance check."

"Are they still here?" Decker asked.

"Probably. Didn't see them leave."

Decker looked at Rory, then started toward the door. "I have a bad feeling about this."

"Then why are we still going to the hangar?" Rory asked as they stepped into the corridor and followed it airside.

"To make sure." Decker pulled the door open, and they stepped out into the bright sunshine. "For all we know, they really are technicians."

The hangar's main doors stood open, and Decker could see the nose of a helicopter within. He approached slowly, motioning for Rory to stay silent now.

When he reached the doors, he stopped short and peered around the corner. There was a man standing near the helicopter. He wore green overalls with a pair of pilot's wings pinned over the left breast pocket. He watched for a while, but the pilot appeared to be alone. There was no sign of the technicians the old man told them about, and no indication anything was amiss. Even so, Decker's sixth sense—his cop intuition—was jangling.

Rory tapped him on the shoulder and whispered. "You see anything?"

"No." Decker didn't know why, but his unease was growing. Something didn't feel right.

Then he saw what it was.

The pilot lifted his hand and sucked on a cigarette. He blew out a stream of smoke as his hand dropped back to his side.

Decker turned to Rory. "The pilot is smoking."

"So?" Rory shrugged. "Who cares? At least he's not chewing tobacco and spitting it out in front of us."

"You don't understand." Decker risked another look around the corner toward the helicopter. "No pilot would smoke in a hangar so close to an aircraft."

"In the United States, maybe. You're forgetting where we are."

"I don't think so," Decker said, spotting movement out of the corner of his eye. A second man emerged from further back in the hangar, also wearing an overall, although this one didn't have pilot wings. What it did have was a dark stain on the front that looked very much like blood. But it was the gun in his hand that confirmed Decker's suspicion. A Makarov PB just like the one he'd taken from the man in the restaurant kitchen the previous day.

Decker turned to Rory and ushered him backwards towards the waiting room. "We need to leave, right now."

"Those goons from yesterday?"

Decker nodded grimly. "And they killed our pilot. This is a trap."

## 21

"They killed our pilot?" Rory hurried to keep up with Decker as they rushed back through the FBO waiting room and out into the parking lot. "That's awful. What are we going to do now?"

"I don't know yet." Decker started toward the taxi. "But as I suspected, it's not safe here."

"Do you think they have someone watching the parking lot?"

"Unlikely. They wouldn't want to lose the element of surprise if we spotted them."

"What about the old guy in the waiting room?" Rory asked. "Was he in on it, too?"

"Doubtful." Decker shook his head.

As they drew close to the taxi, Paulo looked up. "You are back."

"We need to leave, right now."

"Your flight no good?" Paulo asked.

"No. Those men that chased us yesterday killed the pilot. They were waiting to murder us, too."

"Where you want to go, then?"

"I don't know," Decker admitted. "We need to find another way into the Amazon."

Paulo was silent for a moment, then he motioned for them to jump back into the cab. "Come along. I have idea."

"He'd better not be planning to drive us all the way to base camp himself," Rory said to Decker as they climbed back into the cab. "I'm not sure how much more I can take riding around in this taxi. I'd say the suspension is shot, but I'm not sure it has any."

"Hey, it's better than being dead." Decker leaned forward and tapped their driver on the shoulder. "Where are you taking us?"

"You will see." Paulo put the car in gear and steered out of the parking lot. He turned left onto the airport's perimeter road and sped away.

Decker twisted in his seat and looked through the rear window. The road behind them was empty. No one was following, which meant the gunmen were still back at the hanger. It would be a couple of hours before the killers realized they were waiting in vain. But it would all be for nothing if they couldn't find alternative transportation.

But Paulo came to the rescue once again.

He followed the road until they came to a set of gates in the perimeter fence about as far from the airport's commercial terminal as it was possible to get. One gate was open, sitting askew on its hinges. Beyond this was a small parking lot and a concrete pad surrounded by another chain-link fence. Within sat an aging helicopter with the name *Rainforest Sky Tours* written in fading paint along the copter's tail. There was no waiting room or hanger here.

Paulo pulled beyond the gates and stopped short of the helicopter. He got out and banged on the top of the cab for Decker and Rory to follow.

"I find you new ride," the taxi driver said as Decker climbed out. "What do you think?"

Rory circled around from the other side of the taxi. He

stared at the helicopter in disbelief. "I think I'd rather take my chances with those gunmen back there."

"It is fine," Paulo said. "I bring people here all the time to take tour. No crashes yet."

"He's not filling me with confidence," Rory said to Decker.

"We'll be fine." Decker gave the road one more glance, just to make sure.

When he looked back, the helicopter's side door was open, and a thick-set woman dressed in blue jeans and a white polo shirt was striding toward them. She had long black hair pulled into a ponytail and wore no makeup. Decker guessed she was in her mid-thirties.

"Paulo. My man. You bring me more victims... I mean tourists," she said in a West Coast accent.

The pilot was American, which surprised Decker. "We're not tourists. We want to charter your helicopter to take us into the jungle."

"Charter?" The woman looked at Paulo. "You know I don't do private charters. Strictly sightseeing tours."

"These are my friends," Paulo said. "They are in much trouble. Need to escape danger. Please, Cathy."

"Great. Like that's going to convince me." The woman looked at Decker. "What did you do, rob a bank?"

"Nothing like that. We're archaeologists," Decker said, fudging the truth. "We need to get to our base camp to meet the rest of our group. It's very important. Will you help us?"

"Why would a couple of archaeologists be in trouble?"

"It's a long story," Decker said.

"We made a discovery and rival archaeologists want to steal it from us," Rory said, stepping in. "It's a professional hazard."

"Rival archaeologists, huh?" The pilot said. "Doesn't sound that dangerous to me."

"Will you help us, or not?" Decker was losing patience. He couldn't be sure the two guys at the hangar were the only people looking for them. Their pursuers might appear at any moment, realizing Decker and Rory had rumbled their plan, and the helipad was too open. They wouldn't stand a chance if bullets started flying.

The woman looked at Paulo. "You vouch for these guys?"

"Yes. I vouch for them." Paulo nodded. "They good people."

"Fine. Where is this place you need to get to, and how far?"

"I have the coordinates memorized," Decker said. "I'll give them to you when we're in the air. It's about a hundred and sixty miles from here."

"Yikes. That's right on the edge of my range. Pretty much a full tank of fuel there and back." Cathy thought for a moment. "There room to land?"

Decker nodded. "Our colleagues took a chopper out there a few days ago."

"Fine." Cathy made a tutting sound. "Two thousand dollars, US."

"You're kidding me," Decker said, raising an eyebrow.

"Hey, that's the friends and family rate. Take it or leave it."

"We don't have that kind of cash," Decker said. He had given all their cash money to Paulo and his sister. He had no intention of asking for any of it back, especially given Paulo's need.

"You got a credit card?" Cathy asked. "I'm flexible."

"I do, but we can't use it," Decker told her. Even though their credit cards were issued under false names and couldn't be traced back to CUSP, that didn't mean someone inside their own organization wasn't watching to see if the cards were used. "Too dangerous. We're travelling under the radar."

"Ain't that a pickle." Cathy shook her head. "I'm not sure what Paulo here told you, but I'm not a charity."

"What about this?" Rory slipped a watch off his wrist and offered it to her. "Collateral until we get back. Upon our return, we'll be able to pay you everything you want. We'll even give you twenty percent more for your trouble."

Cathy looked at the watch. "Why would I take that?"

"It's a Tissot," Rory said. "Automatic movement. Exhibition case. Turn it over and look at the back. It's glass. You can see the inner workings. I paid over fifteen-hundred dollars for it."

"That's still five hundred bucks short. And used, I bet that watch isn't worth half what you claim."

"Come on. Cut us a break. Like I said, we'll make it right once we get back."

"I don't work on promises," Cathy said, but even so she took the watch and examined it.

"Take this, too." Paulo dug into his pocket and removed the wad of money Decker had given him the previous day. He held it out to the pilot. "Here. For you."

"Wait." Decker said. "That cash is for you. We'll find another way if necessary."

"I agree." Cathy gave the taxi driver a stern look. "There's no way I'm taking one single penny of your money, Paulo. You need everything you can get your hands on for that kid of yours down in Rio. Put it away, for heaven's sake."

"So, you will take them for the watch?" Paulo asked, hopeful.

"Haven't decided yet." Cathy rubbed her chin, still looking at the watch.

"You will do this for me, please?" Paulo said. "I help you when the Red Militia want to use your helicopter for drug smuggling. I make them go away. You help me, we will be even."

"Aw, hell. I was wondering when you'd bring that up."

"Does that mean you will do it?"

"Sure. Against my better judgement, I might add." She fixed Paulo with a deadpan stare. "But we're even now, okay?"

"Yes, yes. We are even." Paulo nodded.

The pilot looked at Decker and Rory. "Come on then, your sky limo awaits." Then she turned and started back toward the helicopter. "But I'm keeping the watch until you pay me."

Decker picked his bag up and turned to Paulo. "Thank you."

"No worries, my friend. You stay safe and find me when you get back."

"We will," Decker said. "And keep your head down. You might have made some dangerous enemies in the last twenty-four hours."

"I can handle that," Paulo said with a wave of his hand. "No worries."

"I have a feeling that you can," Decker said, then he followed the pilot toward the helicopter, with Rory a step behind. Ahead of them, a hundred and sixty miles distant, base camp waited.

## 22

The helicopter took to the air and banked left, circling once around the pad before flying northeast toward the green expanse of jungle on the horizon. Below them, standing next to his taxi, Decker saw Paulo watching with one hand above his eyes to shield them from the sun. He raised the other and waved. Then the helicopter's steep turn blocked him from view.

Once they were flying high, and on their way, the pilot spoke. Her voice was audible over the thrum of the helicopter's engine thanks to the headsets they all wore. "We haven't been properly introduced yet. I'm Cathy."

"John Decker. My colleague is Rory McCormick."

Rory raised a hand. "Hey. Nice to meet you."

"Pleasure's all mine." Cathy glanced back toward them. "I don't want to know what trouble you guys have gotten yourselves into. Not my business, even though your story about rival archaeologists is clearly bunkum. Just answer me one question, is it going to put me in danger, too?"

"Probably not," Decker said.

"Well, that's comforting. You could try to be a little more definitive."

"Just being truthful." Decker looked down at the landscape below them. The city had slipped away and now they were flying over a sea of green. To their right, he could see the weaving line of the Amazon River. "You're not from around these parts. How did an American end up flying tourists around down here in Brazil?"

"Sometimes I ask myself the same question," Cathy said. "I did two tours of duty with the United States Air Force. That's where I learned to fly these birds. Spent four years in Afghanistan. Wasn't much fun. After I left the Air Force, I bought this helicopter tour business and came down here on a whim. Thought it would be an adventure. Turns out that it was, but not in the way I imagined."

"The Red Militia?" Decker asked.

"Yup. They started as a street gang and turned into a drug cartel. They tried to strongarm me into flying for them, ferrying drugs back and forth. It got pretty hairy for a while."

"And Paulo helped you get rid of them?" Decker suspected the taxi driver was savvier than he first appeared, but his intervention between an American helicopter pilot and a Brazilian drug cartel indicated a deep connection to the criminal underworld. Decker wondered what lay concealed in the man's past.

"If it hadn't been for him, I probably wouldn't have lasted a year down here. The previous owner of this business had a nice little side hustle that he didn't tell me about. When the cartel came calling, I was completely clueless. Saying I wouldn't run drugs didn't exactly endear me to them either. If Paulo hadn't intervened, I would have probably ended up with a bullet in the back of my head."

Decker and Rory exchanged looks. Paulo was more than he seemed.

"How did he get them off your back?" asked Decker.

"Beats me. He said to lie low for a couple of days, that he

CRYPTID QUEST | 113

would handle it. After that, they never bothered me again. Paulo's been one of my best friends down here ever since. I can't say for certain, and he doesn't speak about it, but I get the impression he was involved in some bad stuff during his youth. He grew up in the slums. People there either fight their way out or they sink. Often, the way they choose to escape their poverty is not entirely legal."

"They never came back?" Decker asked. "The Red Militia?"

"Not since Paulo intervened. Now he feeds me a steady supply of tourists. I take them up, show them the jungle, or fly down the Amazon River for a few miles. It's not going to make me rich, but it pays the bills. I tried to pay him a cut of the proceeds, a kickback for bringing me so much business, but he won't take it. I think he views me as his responsibility since he saved my hide."

"Yeah. That sounds like our taxi driver," Decker said. "He could have bailed when he realized we were trouble, but instead he went out of his way to help. He even took us to his sister's house and let us stay there overnight."

"He's a good guy," Cathy said. "He makes Manaus a better place, that's for sure."

Decker nodded in agreement. "Have you ever thought of returning to the States?"

"Sure. On and off. But I have a life here now. It's not perfect, but nowhere is. And I like it."

"Which is why I hope you'll listen to what I say next," Decker replied.

"That sounds ominous." Cathy glanced back toward him. "Is this where you admit that the archaeologist story is a bunch of phooey? That you're really on the run from Interpol, or you just assassinated some world leader?"

"Nothing so dramatic. But if the men who are chasing us find you, it could be trouble. You were right about one thing. The story we gave you is not totally accurate, although there is a grain of truth. My colleague here really is an archaeologist."

"Dammit. I thought as much." Cathy grimaced.

"Do you have somewhere to go for a few days, some place safe until this blows over?"

"You mean do I have a place to hide."

"Pretty much." Decker nodded. "I know it's a huge imposition, but you're a part of this now, even though I hated getting you involved. Your life could be in danger."

"Wouldn't be the first time. I can handle myself."

"Not against these people. I'm serious. You need to drop off the grid."

"Fine," Cathy said in a resigned voice. "I know where to go. I have a friend in Itacoatiara. Lives on the edge of the jungle. About as off the map as one can get. I'll fly directly there and land at the local airport. There should be enough fuel left after I drop you off."

"How far is it from Manaus?" Decker asked.

"About a hundred and ten miles as the crow flies but given our heading it's actually closer to fly there from your destination. I'll hang out with my friend and keep my head down."

"Good." Decker felt relieved.

"You owe me though. Big time. If I'm in hiding I won't be making money."

"I'll make it up to you."

"I'm going to hold you to that."

"I expect nothing less." Decker lapsed into silence. Beside him, Rory was peering out the window, studying the jungle as it slipped by below.

Decker sensed every passing mile, grateful for the distance they were putting between themselves and the gunmen. The attempts on their lives had left him shaken and concerned. It proved there was more to this assignment than just rescuing a reality TV production crew who'd gone in over their heads. Someone had gone to great lengths to stop Rory and himself. He wondered what their attacker's end goal was, and how much danger he and Rory were still in. He also worried about the team at base camp. The gunmen might know its location if there was a mole within CUSP. Had something bad already gone down there? If so, what new danger were they flying toward? Having disabled the cell phones, he and Rory had been unreachable since the previous evening. A lot could have happened since. Decker felt his gut tighten. They had escaped a bad situation back in Manaus, but a worse one could be waiting at their destination.

## 23

They arrived at base camp a little over an hour and a half after departing Manaus. Their pilot, Cathy, circled twice, looking for the best place to set the helicopter down. It relieved Decker to see that everything looked fine. A row of small tents was set up on one side of a large clearing. There were also a couple of larger tents and a staging area stacked with crates. A fire pit occupied the central plateau between the tents. Decker could see a couple of people moving around. They did not look like a threat, but he wouldn't be sure until they landed. The gunmen at the FBO hanger in Manaus had disguised themselves using coveralls, one of which was no doubt taken from the slain pilot. They had been lucky to avoid being ambushed there. Decker could not be sure this wasn't a similar trap, although his gut told him they were safe.

That intuition proved correct when the helicopter touched down, and they climbed out. Several people emerged from one of the large tents to watch the helicopter's approach, and one of them, a burly man wearing head-to-toe camo with a rifle slung over his shoulder, now broke off and hurried across the clearing to meet them.

"You guys must be John Decker and Rory McCormick," he said as he drew near them. "My name is commander Joel Ward. I'm in charge of security around here."

"That's us." Decker shook the man's hand, then looked past him toward the assembled group near the tents. He counted four more men in military garb among the bystanders, all armed with rifles. Each one also carried a Sig Sauer P226 sidearm in a holster at their hip. These must be the Ghost Team operatives CUSP had sent to protect them. After their experiences of the last twenty-four hours, it was a welcome change to encounter armed men who weren't shooting at them.

"Everyone good here?" Cathy asked from the helicopter's open door. "If I'm not needed anymore, I'll be on my way."

Decker looked at Ward. "Everyone good?"

Ward shook his head. "We are all tiptop."

Decker turned to the helicopter pilot. "Looks like your job is done."

"Roger that." Cathy glanced around the clearing. "Have to say, I'm glad you guys are camping out here, and not me."

Ward observed her with steely eyes. "I've bedded down in worse places. Spent some time in Bagram. That was a dusty hellhole."

"You were in Afghanistan?" Cathy asked. "What branch?"

"Marine Corps. You?"

"Air Force. Spent six months in Bagram."

"Nine for me," Ward said. "Then another six in Delaram. That was worse."

"I bet it was." Cathy glanced back toward the cockpit. "I'd better get this bird back in the air. It's a long flight back."

"Take care," Ward said, saluting her.

"Back at you, Commander." Cathy returned the salute. "Try not to get eaten by anything out there in the jungle."

"That's the plan." Ward shifted stance and hitched the rifle higher on his shoulder.

Cathy looked at Decker. "Pleasure meeting you guys. I hope the trouble that found you in Manaus doesn't follow you here."

"Me, too," Decker said. He and Rory moved back, as far out of the copter's wash as possible.

Cathy stepped back into the helicopter and pulled the door closed. A moment later, the rotors started spinning faster, kicking up a small cloud of dust. The aircraft took to the sky and banked, passing over the clearing and turning as it gained altitude.

Ward looked at Decker. "What did she mean by trouble following you?"

"It's a long story," Decker said. "I'll fill you in once we get settled, but suffice to say, we aren't the only ones with an interest in whatever those TV people found in the jungle. Someone knew we were coming, and they tried to kill us. We were lucky to get out of the city alive."

"I don't like the sound of that," Ward said as they walked back toward the waiting group. "I'll expect a full briefing as soon as you're ready. Don't want to be caught off guard."

"You've got it." Decker looked around the group. Apart from the soldiers, he counted three other people, none of whom he recognized. "I think it's time for some introductions."

"In that case, let me be the first to welcome you to our little home away from home." A large red-faced man with a shock of unruly ginger hair stepped forward. He wore a khaki shirt ringed with sweat. "My name's Tristan Cook. You've probably heard of me. I'm kind of famous."

Decker glanced at Rory, who shrugged. "Sorry. The name doesn't ring a bell."

"Really? I had my own show on Discovery a few years back. Almost won an Emmy. *Bigfoot Babies—The Hunt for Offspring.* I have a crypto podcast right now. Has sixty thousand subscribers. I'm also a regular contributor on the Travel Network show, *Places People Forgot.*"

CRYPTID QUEST | 119

"Crypto?" Decker asked. "Like in the digital currency?"

"No. Cryptozoology. Finding elusive animals that aren't supposed to exist."

"You ever found any?" Rory asked.

"Came close a few times." Cook grinned. "You must have seen my show. Everyone has. Almost won an Emmy."

"You said that already."

"Did I?"

"Yes. And I don't watch a lot of TV," Decker said. "What exactly are you doing here?"

"Network asked me to come along," Cook replied. "Thought I might be of help. I've been on my fair share of expeditions to the Amazon."

"If you work for the Travel Network," Decker said, "you must know Darren Yates. The presenter of Cryptid Quest."

"Yeah. I know him. Can't say I like the man. Bit of a poser. Publicity hound. Shouldn't have been running around the Amazon jungle if he didn't know what he was doing. It's no wonder he got lost."

"He didn't exactly get lost." Decker glanced at Rory. "How much do these guys know?"

"Beats me," Rory said, shrugging.

"If you're asking if I know about the Cyclops, then yeah. Doesn't mean I think it's real. Probably just Yates trying to drum up publicity for his little show. I bet he has a nice camp set up somewhere out in the jungle, and he's just waiting it out until there's enough media attention, then he'll reappear and hog the limelight. I mean, come on. A freaking Cyclops? He could have tried a little harder. Loser."

"Hey, Tristan, you're the one hogging the limelight right now." A man of slight build with a thin face and hooked nose stepped forward. He looked at Decker. "I'm Hugh Henriksen. I'm a senior producer on Cryptid Quest. I know everything about the show and the special we were filming here." He turned his attention back to Cook. "And for the record, Tristan, no one is faking anything. We might have fatalities out there. I'd ask you to show some decorum."

"Yeah, whatever." Cook waved a hand toward the producer, then turned and walked back toward the tents.

Decker watched him go. "He's going to be fun to work with."

"I wouldn't worry too much," Henriksen said. "He likes to spout off, and he can be a pain in the rear, but he's a professional, deep down."

"I'm surprised you're defending the guy," Decker said. "Didn't sound like you liked him much."

"I don't. Can't stand the man." Henriksen chuckled. "But that doesn't mean he's not good at his job. Besides, the network sent him, so I'm stuck with it."

"Why exactly do your employers want that guy here?" Decker asked. "My superiors agreed to your presence in an advisory capacity because you know the show and what the crew was doing here, but I don't see a role for him."

"To host the special, of course."

"I thought Darren Yates, your missing talent, was hosting that."

"No." Henriksen shook his head. "Not that special. The *new special*. The one on this expedition. It's going to be a single-camera observational documentary. Most of the shots will be taken hand-held by Tristan himself, almost like found footage. We're calling it *Life or Death-Rescuing Darren*."

"No, you're not." Decker shook his head. "No filming. If I see one peek of a camera, there will be hell to pay. Understood?"

"Now hang on—"

"I'm serious." Decker cut the producer off. "None of my team gave consent to be on camera. The agency we work for has strict protocols regarding protecting our identities. You so much as take one unauthorized photo and you'll be pondering your mistake from a prison cell."

"You can't do that."

"Try me." Decker gave the man a stone-cold stare. "And make sure you relay the message to your colleague, too."

"This isn't over." Henriksen spun on his heel and marched off.

Apart from Decker and Rory, only the four soldiers were left. They looked uncomfortable.

"That was a bit harsh," Rory said.

"You want to be on TV?"

"No." Rory shook his head. "Still threatening to toss him in prison?"

"Maybe it was a bit heavy-handed," Decker admitted. "But I want to nip this in the bud. Last thing we need is our faces all over some half-baked reality show."

"You do realize we have no authority to sling people in the slammer, right?"

"Yup." Decker nodded. "But he doesn't."

"Fair enough." Rory smirked.

"Now. Let's continue the introductions." Decker glanced around. "Someone is missing. Where's your Egyptologist?"

"I'm right here," a female voice said from behind the soldiers.

Decker turned toward the newcomer and saw a slim woman dressed in jeans and a white cotton shirt. She had long brown hair pulled back into a ponytail and intense blue eyes that sparkled in the sunlight. She was walking toward them from one of the large tents.

Rory grinned and stepped up beside Decker. "John, this is—"

"Don't bother," Decker said, interrupting Rory as the woman drew close. "Her name is Emma Wilson."

"You know her already?" Rory looked between them, confused.

"Yeah." Decker felt like the clearing had gotten suddenly small and claustrophobic. "We've met."

"Really, John?" Emma smiled and cocked her head coyly. "We've met… That's how you'd describe our relationship?"

"That's exactly how I'd describe it," Decker said in a low voice. Then, with his travel bag in hand, he turned his back on her and headed toward the nearest tent. He didn't look back.

## 24

"How quickly can you be ready to move out?" Decker was standing in one of the two larger tents, which served as both a mess hall with plastic tables pushed together for dining, a kitchen, and a small operations area for the Ghost Squad team. Right now, the only other person in the tent was Commander Joel Ward. "The longer we stay here, the greater danger we are in."

"First thing tomorrow morning," Ward said. Decker had already briefed him on the events in Manaus and the attempts on their lives. "We'll head out at sunrise. You have the coordinates of the pyramid, I assume."

"Yes. My phone is toast, but I memorized them. I'll write them down for you."

"Good. But wait until morning. The less people who know our destination ahead of time, the better. Including me."

"When did CUSP become so paranoid?" Decker asked.

"Just following orders."

"I don't like the idea of staying here tonight," Decker said. "I'd rather leave today."

"No can do." Ward shook his head. "It's already early

afternoon, which means the earliest we can leave today is around 4 PM. That only gives us a few hours of daylight before we would need to stop again. We can't travel after dark in the Amazon. Far too dangerous. Even if we leave in the morning, it's still a two-day trek to the fortress."

"Fair enough," Decker said. "But if we must stay here tonight, I want a guard posted at all times. By now those gunmen back at the hangar will have realized we evaded them."

"And if there really is someone at CUSP working against us, those men that came after you might know the location of this camp, despite all our precautions."

"I think it's unlikely. They tried to kill us in Manaus for our phones. I'm sure of it. They wanted the coordinates. Both sets. If they already knew where we were, they would have come here by now, killed us all, and continued on to the pyramid."

"But we can't be one hundred percent certain." Ward rubbed his chin. His eyes narrowed in concern. "We'll need to be alert."

"Speaking of which," Decker said, "how well do you know the rest of the men in your unit?"

"I would trust them with my life," Ward said. "I served alongside two of them in the Marines. The rest have been in my Ghost Squad unit since CUSP recruited me."

"You're sure their allegiance lies solely with us?"

"None of my men have been compromised, if that's what you're asking." Ward's voice was calm, with no hint of offense. "But I understand why you want to know. So would I, under the circumstances."

"I'm pleased you see my point of view, because I have to be sure," Decker said. "It's no good posting a guard if all we're doing is putting a fox in charge of the henhouse."

"You won't find any foxes under my command." Ward glanced out through the tent's open flap toward Rory, who was standing near the fire pit, hands in his pockets, staring out toward the jungle. "What about him?"

"Rory?" Decker followed Ward's gaze. "He's one of the good guys. I worked with him on an assignment in Ireland. I trust him."

"Good. And the others?"

"Same goes for the Egyptologist, Emma Wilson. I can't vouch for the explorer, Tristan Cook. Never met the man before today. He looks harmless enough, not that it means anything."

"I agree," Ward said. "I'll be keeping a close eye on him for the time being."

"Good idea."

"Have you spoken to Adam Hunt yet?" Ward asked. "Reported the events in Manaus?"

"No." Decker shook his head. "Phones are out of action. I disabled them so the gunmen couldn't track us. Took the batteries out. I'm not sure it would be a good idea to put them back together."

"You could use the satellite phone." Ward nodded toward the Ops table and a chunky handset. "Whoever has been trying to kill you must surely have realized by now that you escaped, despite their best efforts. They probably know that you came here, too. You have nothing to lose by calling Hunt."

"That's true," Decker said. "But I'm not sure that he can be of any help."

"He can start looking for double agents inside CUSP. That's a start."

"It might also put his life in danger. These people are not playing around."

"That's not your call to make, and we need to know that the people we work with have our backs."

"That's true. I just hate to think that anyone in CUSP would be our enemy." Decker didn't relish calling Adam Hunt with the news that an unknown enemy had infiltrated their organization. But what choice did he have? "I'll make the call this afternoon."

Ward nodded. "While you do that, I'm going to put the camp under twenty-four-hour guard until we head out tomorrow. I'll assign six-hour shifts throughout the night, with two men on each watch. No one will get past us."

"Don't underestimate them," Decker said. "They only sent two men after us back in Manaus, but that doesn't mean there aren't more."

"If there are, we'll be ready." Ward turned and left the tent.

Decker watched him go. The last few days had been full of surprises, not least of which was the reappearance of Emma Wilson, a woman he'd expected never to see again. It brought back a flood of memories, some good, and others not so much. After the incident with the Cult of Anubis, the two had become close. He hadn't meant to, but Decker found himself falling in love. Then she left, ripping a hole in his heart. It was unfair. It was cruel. At least it felt that way to him. And now, here she was again. Coming into his life as if she sensed he had moved on. That he was happy again. He wondered what confluence of circumstances allowed fate to toy with him so. But mostly, he wondered what she was doing working for CUSP and if Adam Hunt knew their history when he sent Decker down here.

But those answers would have to wait.

There were more pressing issues. Like staying alive. Commander Ward had thought Decker should report the events in Manaus to Hunt. But the more he thought about it, the less he felt inclined to make that call. What if the mole wasn't some random underling working against CUSP from the inside? What if it was Adam Hunt himself? After all, the man knew their movements and had the means and opportunity to send killers after them.

Decker considered this for a long minute. Then he discarded the idea as hogwash. If Adam Hunt wanted him and Rory dead, there had been plenty of opportunities to achieve that goal before this. Besides, why would Hunt send them down here to investigate the pyramid, only to order hitmen to kill them the minute they arrived? The answer was simple. He wouldn't. Still, that didn't mean Decker was looking forward to the phone call. Unfortunately, that wasn't a good enough reason not to do it. With a sigh, Decker picked up the satellite phone and dialed.

25

Night in the Amazon brought with it a darkness Decker had rarely seen in his life. Surrounded by jungle, and without even a hint of light pollution, the sky was a coal black expanse broken only by the shimmering arch of the Milky Way that soared above him like a billion fireflies trapped in the ether.

Decker stood at the edge of the clearing with his back to the fire pit, within which flames leaped and danced, sending bright orange embers spiraling up into the humid Amazonian air. The air was redolent with the fragrance of the jungle. A thousand varieties of tropical plants from dazzling orchids and passion flowers to brightly colored bromeliads. And above all this, the lingering smell of roasted meat cooked on a spit over the open fire.

It reminded him of summer camping trips with his dad when he was a kid, back before his mother died and everything went to hell. Until he remembered where he was, and the danger they were all in.

A voice spoke up behind him. "Decker?"

He turned to find Rory lingering a few feet away, his hands

clasped in front of him, fingers tightly interwoven. The man looked uncomfortable. "Hey. What can I do for you?"

"I just wanted to clear the air." Rory took a step closer.

"Why?" Decker asked. "I wasn't aware there was anything wrong."

"It's about..." Rory hesitated. He looked around, ringing his hands. He turned back to Decker and took a deep breath. "It's about Emma and what I said to you on the plane when we were flying down here."

"What of it?"

"Look, if I'd known there was a thing between the two of you, I wouldn't have spoken up."

"There's nothing between us," Decker said. "I can assure you of that."

Rory continued, as if he hadn't heard. "I mean, how was I to know the pair of you were already acquainted? That you'd... Well, you know." He laughed nervously. "What are the odds, right?"

"Rory." Decker raised his voice. "I already told you, there's nothing between us. We're ancient history. If you like Emma Wilson, she's all yours. Actually, you'd be doing me a favor."

"Oh. I see. You're not mad at me then?"

"No reason to be mad at you. If I'm going to be mad at anyone, it will be her."

"Guess she really messed you up, huh?"

"You could say that." Decker turned back toward the rainforest. "What you said on the plane about Emma being consumed with her career was not wrong. Single-minded doesn't even begin to cover it. The minute an opportunity popped up she left without a word of explanation. Couldn't wait to get out the door. Despite what she said, I was nothing more than an entertaining distraction until something better came along."

"You know that's not true, John." Instead of Rory, this was a female voice, and one that Decker recognized all too well.

He turned around. "What are you doing here, Emma?"

"You mean right now?" Emma was standing with her hands pushed into the pockets of a pair of khaki shorts above tanned, long legs. She still wore the white shirt, but with the top two buttons undone to reveal a hint of cleavage. "I thought I'd come over here and clear the air."

Decker shook his head. "I don't mean right at this moment. What are you doing down here, in the Amazon, working for CUSP?"

"I imagine I'm doing the same thing as you." Emma looked at Rory, who was standing mouth agape. He had the appearance of a gazelle caught between two lions. "Would you mind giving us a moment?"

"I'd love to," Rory stammered, and then beat a hasty retreat toward the fire pit where the rest of the team sat drinking hot cocoa, boiled in a pot over the open flames, and talking among themselves.

"I think he has a crush on me," Emma said, her mouth widening into a thin smile. "How do you think I should handle it, John?"

"Don't change the subject." Even from several feet away, Decker picked up the jasmine and citrus notes of her perfume rising above the forest scents. He recognized it right away. Hermès Calèche. The same as she'd worn during their brief but intense relationship. He marveled at the fact that she'd bothered to bring perfume all the way into the jungle.

"I'm not trying to change the subject." Emma closed the gap between them. She reached out and touched his arm.

"Don't." Decker pulled away. Her perfume was stronger now, overpowering his senses. He could feel the heat of her body through the sweltering tropical air. For a moment, the years melted away as if they had never been apart. He shook the feeling off. "Is this why you left me? To join CUSP?"

"Would you believe me if I said no?"

"What do you think?" Decker had often thought of what he'd say to Emma if they ever crossed paths again, especially in those lonely first weeks and months after she left him. He'd imagined this conversation and how it would go, but he never dreamed they would meet again under such unusual circumstances or in such a strange and deadly place. The realization that he was going to be near her for at least the next several days tempered his anger, if only because he realized that now was not the time. "Why didn't you tell me where you were going?"

"Come on, John. You know the answer to that."

"Do I?"

"You must work for CUSP now, too, or you wouldn't be here. Maybe if they'd recruited us both at the same time, things would've been different. But they didn't, and I wasn't allowed to tell you anything." Emma's eyes grew wide. "But look at us. We're together again."

"What are you trying to say?" Decker asked.

"I think you know very well what I'm saying." Emma reached out and put a hand on his shoulder. Their bodies were so close now that Decker could feel the swell of her breasts against his chest. "I don't need to keep secrets anymore. Not from you."

"That's enough." Decker took her arm and pushed it aside. He stepped back.

A strange look passed across Emma's face. She gazed up into his eyes for a second, perhaps hoping to find some softening of his demeanor. Her mouth moved as if she was about to say something, but no words came out. Instead, she turned on her heel and marched toward the fire pit, then kept going, skirting the rest of the group. A moment later, she disappeared inside one of the small tents without so much as a backward glance.

## 26

Decker lay in one of the small tents pitched in a semicircle around the fire pit. It was early in the morning, a little after three o'clock, and base camp was quiet. Above him, on the tent pole, hung a battery-operated lamp set on low, giving off just enough light to fill the tent with a yellow glow that allowed them to see, but not enough to disturb their sleep. To his left, Rory was curled up on a bedroll. An occasional snore proved he was fast asleep.

Decker wished he could do the same.

Emma had been on his mind ever since their conversation earlier that evening. She hadn't changed one bit. If he was single, it would be too easy to fall for her wiles all over again. Except he remembered the way it ended the first time he'd gotten ensnared by her. But one thing bothered him more than anything else. He had not mentioned Nancy. He wondered why that was. The simple explanation, the one he'd been trying to tell himself all night, was that it was simply none of Emma's business. But deep down he knew there was another, less innocent explanation. He didn't want Emma to know because he still felt there was unfinished business between them, and even if he didn't intend to do anything inappropriate, he couldn't quite slam the door. Not yet.

He closed his eyes and willed himself to fall asleep. They would have a tough hike into the jungle tomorrow, and he would need all the rest he could get. But it was no use. He pulled on a pair of jeans and a T-shirt, then unzipped the tent's mosquito net and pushed the flap back, crawling out into the clearing.

A fire still burned in the pit, the flames smaller than they had been but kept alive by a couple of medium-sized logs, no doubt to dissuade any nocturnal predators that might think about strolling through camp looking for an easy meal.

At the edge of the clearing, he saw a pair of figures. Two members of the Ghost Team keeping guard. They walked a slow circuit around the clearing, moving in opposite directions until they passed one another and repeated the lap. He felt safer knowing they were there.

"Couldn't sleep?" A voice spoke in the darkness to his left.

Decker turned to see Commander Ward standing near the ops tent, an M4 Commando short-barreled rifle at his side. "Not so much. Can't turn the brain off. What's your excuse?"

"Just doing my job. The reason everyone else can sleep soundly in their tents is because people like me are out here watching over them."

"You're not going to be much good to us tomorrow, if you haven't slept." Decker sauntered over to the commander. "I'm sure your men can handle look out duties."

"I'll turn in soon." Ward leaned against a tent pole with his arms folded. "There's a changing of the guard at 4 AM. I'll probably stick around for that, then catch some shuteye."

"Any sign of unusual activity?" Decker asked, eyeing the dark silhouette of trees that surrounded base camp.

"Not so far. Had a helicopter flyover earlier, but I doubt it was looking for us. It was too high and only circled back once.

My guess is the Brazilian military doing a sweep of the area looking for gold and drug smugglers who prefer to travel under the cover of darkness. Probably equipped with thermal and night vision."

"They must have seen us, then."

"More than likely. But we don't look like smugglers. For a start, we're not trying to hide our location. They're more interested in finding unusual activity like people moving at night to avoid detection."

"And you're sure it wasn't the men who came after us in Manaus?" Decker asked. He didn't know if any of the gunmen could fly a helicopter, but they certainly had access to one, having killed the pilot of Decker and Rory's charter.

"Can't be one hundred percent sure." Ward shook his head. "But it's likely your attackers already know the location of our base camp and would prefer stealth over a brazen flyby. Besides, I recognized the engine noise. Pretty distinctive if you know what to listen for. It was a Black Hawk. I'm guessing that whoever we're dealing with wouldn't have access to hardware like that."

"I hope not," Decker said. "I'm pretty sure those guys in Manaus had some military training, but I don't think they were current armed forces."

"Exactly."

"On the other hand," Decker said, his eyes shifting down to Ward's semi-automatic rifle, "CUSP isn't a military organization either and look at the toys we have."

"That's different," Ward said without elaborating. "Speaking of CUSP, did you brief Adam Hunt?"

"I spoke to him."

"And?"

"He wasn't as alarmed as I expected. Although it's hard to tell with Adam. He plays it pretty close to the vest at the best of times."

"You think he's already aware of a mole inside the organization?"

"He didn't say, but his muted reaction would lead me to that conclusion." Decker wondered how much Adam Hunt was keeping from them, and why. He didn't like being sent into the field without full disclosure, but he also knew that compartmentalization was a necessary evil. High as he was, there was probably sensitive information and codeword-classified operations that even Hunt was not read into. Need to know went with the territory. If another organization was actively working against CUSP—and given his experience months before with Thomas Barringer on the submerged research station, Habitat One, Decker suspected as much—then compartmentalization of information would become even more important. "Until we can discount such a scenario, we should all watch our backs."

"I've been watching my rear for decades," Ward said. "In this line of work, it's a healthy habit to acquire."

Decker nodded slowly. He yawned. "I'm done. Time to hit the sack again."

"Probably a good idea." Ward observed his men still following their circular route around the periphery of the camp. "I'm not far behind."

"Goodnight." Decker made his way back to the tent.

In the distance, the sky flickered briefly white before falling back into darkness. The telltale sign of a far-off thunderstorm. He hoped it wasn't coming their way.

He bent low and opened the tent's flap, then unzipped the mosquito net. He moved to enter, then froze.

Curled up on Decker's bedroll inches from Rory's head, and visible in the lantern's dim light, was a slender, pale green snake that observed him with beady black eyes.

## 27

"Whatever you do, don't make any sudden moves." Commander Ward peered into the tent toward a frightened Rory. "That's a forest pit viper. Extremely venomous. You do not want it biting you."

"Really?" Rory said through clenched teeth. "You need to state the obvious?"

"How aggressive is that thing?" Decker asked. He was standing to one side, holding the tent flap open with one eye on the snake and the other on Ward.

"About as bad tempered as you ever want a snake to get," Ward replied. "One bite could cause bleeding from the nose, mouth, and eyes, throwing up, and loss of consciousness. Of course, by the time you pass out it will be a relief, I'm told that the pain is quite intense."

"Can you just get rid of it?" Rory said. "I'm not sure how much longer I can stay still."

"You have a plan?" Decker asked.

Ward removed his pistol from its holster at his waist. "Only one way I can think of to handle this."

"You're not going to fire that gun into the tent, are you?"

Rory asked, his voice trembling. "Because there's not a lot of room in here, and I would really prefer not to get shot."

"Does he always complain this much?" Ward asked Decker.

"Not all the time," Decker said.

"Hey," Rory said. "I'm not complaining. I just think it would be better if one of you reached in and grabbed it, instead of turning the tent into a shooting gallery."

"Trust me, this is the best way to handle the situation," Ward said. "We try to grab that thing… it will probably bite you before we even get close. Then it'll bite us."

"All right. Fine. Just make sure you don't miss."

"Hasn't happened yet." Ward dropped back into a shooting stance. "But there's a first time for everything."

"I'm sure he won't miss," Decker said, seeing Rory's expression. "But you might want to close your eyes for this."

Rory squeezed his eyes shut.

"Here goes." Ward aimed his pistol at the snake and squeezed the trigger.

The boom was deafening.

The snake's head exploded in a gory spray.

The body coiled tighter upon itself.

"It's still alive." Rory opened his eyes and jumped up with a scream. He scrabbled off the bedroll and almost toppled forward in his haste to exit the tent.

"It's not alive," Ward said, reaching out and helping Rory to his feet. "It's just a death spasm."

"Well, whatever it is, I'm not sleeping in that tent again tonight." Rory batted a piece of snake from his cheek with a shudder. "No way."

Decker reached in and grabbed the snake's headless body. When he lifted it out, Rory took a hasty step backwards, almost falling over a guide rope.

"Easy there," Ward said. "It can't hurt you anymore."

"I hate this place," Rory said. "Just once I'd like to have an assignment that didn't offer multiple ways to get killed."

"Boy, you're working for the wrong organization." Ward shook his head. He holstered the gun and looked at Decker. "You going to get rid of that, or you are thinking of making a wallet out of it?"

"Hey, what's going on here?" The sound of the gunshot had woken Emma. She climbed from her tent and approached them.

The explorer, Tristan Cook, trailed behind, rubbing sleep from his eyes. The soldiers on guard duty looked their way but continued pacing the perimeter. Their commander clearly had things under control, so they didn't feel the need to intervene. The other two soldiers had come running and now stood behind Ward, guns at the ready.

"Nothing to see here, everyone." Decker held up the snake carcass. "Just a little visitor to our tent."

"My goodness." Emma looked shocked. "That's a pit viper."

"Not anymore," Decker said. He walked between the tents and tossed the snake's remains as far into the understory as he could.

"I need a shower," Rory said, as Decker returned to the front of the tent. "I'm covered in snake's head."

"Don't be so dramatic," Ward said. "It's just a couple of chunks."

"I'd still like to wash it off."

"There's a ten-gallon solar shower with a privacy screen over near the supply tent," Emma said. "Don't expect the water to be too warm at this time of night though."

"Thank you." Rory reached gingerly into the tent and pulled a towel from his travel bag, then stomped off toward the shower area.

"Well, if the excitement is over, I'm going back to bed." Cook wiped the sweat from his forehead with a white handkerchief, then ambled off toward his tent.

Decker dragged his bedroll out and shook it to remove any lingering pieces of snake. Toward the top, through the fabric, was a bullet hole. There was a matching hole in the ground cloth. The offending slug must have buried itself in the earth beneath the tent after dispatching the snake.

He threw the bedroll back inside and stood with hands on hips. "What I want to know is how that snake got in there."

"Maybe it slithered in when you left the tent," Ward said.

"Doubtful." Decker shook his head. "I zipped the mosquito net and closed the flap."

"It's the jungle. You'd be surprised what can get into the tents." Emma looked at Decker. She grinned playfully. "If you don't want to bed down in there again tonight, I have room."

"You should make that offer to Rory," Decker said, stone-faced. "I bet he'll take you up on it."

"Well, this is uncomfortable. Maybe the two of you should have your passive aggressive fight some other time?" Ward said. He stepped around the tent, studying it. At the back, he stopped. "In the meantime, I think I've found how that snake got in."

"Really?" Decker went to the back of the tent. "How?"

Emma followed along; the grin wiped from her face now.

"Through there," Ward said, pointing.

All three looked down toward the tent's rear wall, and the neat five-inch-long slit cut into it. More than enough space to sneak a deadly serpent into their tent while they were sleeping.

## 28

They broke camp early the next morning after a quick breakfast, during which Commander Ward gave a stern talk regarding the obstacles and dangers they would face as they pushed into the forest on their two-day trek to the pyramid.

Rory sat listening with a look of increasing apprehension on his face. Decker could tell the archaeologist wished he were anywhere but about to penetrate one of the world's most dangerous expanses of wilderness.

Decker's thoughts were more focused on the events of the night before, and the snake's appearance in their tent. He hadn't voiced his suspicions, but he didn't believe the rip in the tent was an accident. Someone had made the small slit deliberately to allow the snake's entry while they slept. He didn't know when the sabotage had occurred, but suspected that it was earlier in the evening while the group sat gathered around the fire pit. But there was no way to tell which one of the eight people already at base camp when he and Rory arrived might be responsible. People were coming and going throughout the evening, grabbing drinks and food from the mess area, retreating to their tents, or answering the call of nature. Any of them could have done it.

It was only by good fortune that Decker had risen, unable to sleep, and decided to stretch his legs in the middle of the night. Were it not for that, one or both of them would likely have suffered a debilitating and possibly fatal bite from the highly venomous pit viper.

How the snake had arrived in their tent was another mystery. Simply slicing a hole in the canvas would not be enough. The snake must have been placed close enough to guarantee its entry. That meant someone went to extraordinary lengths to handle a dangerous serpent and position it thus. Not a task for the faint of heart. And they did it without alerting the sentries Ward had posted to keep them safe during the night. Decker knew this because the commander had questioned them at length already. Either they hadn't seen the perpetrator, or one of them was hiding a secret.

The whole incident made Decker feel uneasy. It was a completely different tactic to the blunt force assault he and Rory had barely survived in Manaus. It also showed that the rot within CUSP ran deeper than he'd previously suspected, reaching one or more members of their own team. This made the trek into the jungle even more dangerous and would require them to be on the alert for further attempts to sabotage the expedition.

Now, after packing up their tents and heaving pounds of equipment and supplies onto their shoulders, the group entered the jungle, following in the footsteps of the Cryptid Quest film crew.

It was slow going, only made a little easier by the path already hacked through the undergrowth by the previous party to make this trek. Even that meagre trail was already growing back in.

They walked single file, alert for snakes and spiders that

could drop from the trees or strike their ankles without warning. Commander Ward insisted they stop at frequent intervals to catch their breath and regroup. During these gratefully received respites, they sipped small amounts of liquid from water bottles to stay hydrated in the brutally humid tropical heat, and mopped sweat from their brows.

After one such pause, Emma, who was walking toward the back of the line, ahead of the two soldiers who were bringing up the rear, pushed her way past Rory and Tristan Cook.

She drew level with Decker and walked alongside him for a few minutes, as if she were waiting for him to initiate a conversation, before giving in and speaking up. "Nothing to say to me?"

"Nope." Decker kept his eyes forward and watched the back of the soldier in front of him. At the head of the line, he could see Commander Ward moving forward with his M4 slung over one shoulder as he chopped and slashed at the encroaching forest with a long-bladed machete.

"You were never this quiet when we were together. You had an opinion on everything."

"I still have an opinion. I just choose not to share it with you." Decker finally glanced at her. "And believe me, you probably don't want to know what I'm thinking right now."

"Look, I get it. You're angry with me…"

"No. I left angry behind three years ago along with the hurt. What you're seeing now is indifference."

"Has it really been three years?" Emma's shoulder brushed his as they walked. "Doesn't feel like that long. I always meant to come back you know. Eventually."

"I waited for six months. If you intended to come back, there was ample time to do it."

"You waited for me?" Decker thought he sensed a tinge of sorrow in Emma's voice. "That's so sweet."

"Foolish would be a better description."

"John, don't say that." Emma looked at him. "I got busy. You know how it is with CUSP. They were sending me all over the world and wouldn't allow me to tell anyone what I was doing, or why. After a while I didn't even know how to come back. But I never stopped loving you."

Decker's heart skipped a beat. He hadn't heard those words from her in so long and didn't think he would ever hear them again. After she left without so much as a goodbye, he'd convinced himself that her love was a sham. Nothing but a cruel lie uttered in the height of passion. Now he suspected they were something else. A get out of jail free card for her guilt. Maybe she had really loved him. Or not. None of that mattered now, because he was with Nancy and that was the love he could count on. Still, he wondered if a small flame still burned somewhere deep within for the alluring Egyptologist with whom he once thought he could spend the rest of his life. He didn't like that, though. Not at all.

"John?" Emma touched his shoulder, snapping him from his thoughts. "I wish you'd say something. Anything."

"I don't know what I'm supposed to say." This much was true.

"You could start by saying you never stopped loving me, either."

"Is that what you want to hear?" Decker stepped over a thick log that had fallen across their path. Without thinking, he took Emma's hand to steady her as she climbed over.

"When I found out that you'd joined CUSP, I had this fantasy that you would seek me out, eventually."

"Even if I'd wanted to, how could I do that?" Decker said. "I didn't even know where you'd gone or why. You never told me. And it's not like CUSP provided me with a staff directory."

"I know. But we're here together now." Emma was still holding Decker's hand. "Even if you won't admit there's still any love between us, at least say you're pleased to see me."

"Maybe I'm not pleased to see you." Decker extricated his hand from hers. He felt the sudden emptiness where their palms had pressed together moments before.

"Oh." Emma sounded momentarily taken aback, then she gathered herself together again. "Well, I'm pleased to see you. And until you tell me I should do otherwise, I'll keep on trying to undo the damage to our relationship."

"Suit yourself," Decker said. "But just so you know, there is no relationship. Not anymore."

"We'll see," Emma said in a quiet voice. But Decker could tell that his words had hurt her. And he hated the satisfaction he derived from that. He thought about Nancy, waiting for him back in Maine, and in that moment, he almost turned to Emma and told her why they could never again be together.

But before he got the chance, Commander Ward brought the tired group to a halt. "Okay, people. End of the line for today."

They were in a small clearing among the trees next to a fast-running stream with crystal-clear water that weaved through the jungle on its way to the region's namesake river. In the middle of the clearing, Decker saw the remains of a recent fire pit with dirt shoveled over the ashes, and disturbed ground.

They had found the original film crew's overnight camp. Now, apparently, it would also be theirs.

## 29

They made camp near the stream and built a fire as night approached. Emma sat across from Decker and cast him the occasional furtive glance but made no attempt to engage in conversation beyond the bare minimum.

Dinner was ready to eat meals, also known as MRE's. These lightweight freeze-dried packages of food were light to carry and nutritious. Each person carried enough for a one-week round-trip journey.

Commander Ward tested the water from the stream and determined that it was safe to consume. They used it to rehydrate their main courses and heated these in a pot over the fire. The ration kits also came with a cookie and a sachet of powdered cocoa, which they all drank before turning in for the night.

Rory and Decker shared a tent again. Earlier that day Decker had patched the hole through which the snake had entered to prevent any further critters from finding their way in while the pair slept. It concerned him that one of their group might be working with the gunmen who attacked them in Manaus, but commander Ward was adamant that no further incidents would occur on his watch. To this end, he assigned his men to guard the camp in four-hour shifts, two at a time.

The night passed as promised, without excitement. If there was a double agent in their midst, they did not reveal themselves.

The next morning, they ate breakfast—more freeze-dried rations—packed up their tents and continued upon their way. The going was rough, the forest closing in around them on all sides as if it were trying to stop their forward progress. Commander Ward took the lead again, chopping and cutting his way through the thick, almost impenetrable vegetation.

After a grueling seven hours on their feet, they heard rushing water. Soon after, they emerged from the trees to find themselves standing at the edge of a precipice that dropped vertically into a massive green jungle below them. The tall cliff face continued for as far as they could see in both directions, curving around as if it might continue in a full circle and meet itself somewhere over the horizon. A tumbling waterfall some distance away to their right crashed over the rim and fell out of sight.

"Unbelievable," Rory breathed, stepping carefully toward the ledge, and peering over. "Just look at the forest down there. It goes on as far as the eye can see. It's like a whole tropical ecosystem sitting inside a giant bowl in the earth."

"Do you think the film crew went down there?" Emma asked, peering across the treetops in awe.

"I'd say it's a fair bet," Ward said. He pointed toward a rope system tied off onto tree trunks near the rim and hanging over the edge. "I don't see any other way that rig could have gotten here."

Decker walked to the ropes and tested them. He went to the rim and looked over, noting that the rope went all the way down. "These ropes are solid. We can use this to get to the forest floor below."

"Are you sure that's a good idea," Emma said. "I understand we need to find the missing film crew, but don't you think we should exercise a little caution. After all, they could have climbed back up, but they didn't. Whatever happened was so cataclysmic that it prevented even one of them from escaping. If we go down there too, we could end up trapped and unable to retreat just like them."

"We aren't going down. At least, not tonight," Decker said. He studied the land near the edge of the precipice. It looked flat and solid, with little sign of edge erosion. The trees were thinner here too. "We'll set up camp right here at the top of the cliff. We should be safe from whatever befell the original film crew up here."

"I concur," Ward said, nodding his agreement. "We occupy the high ground. Easily defensible against threats from that jungle down there and we leave ourselves a quick line of retreat should it become necessary."

"And the pyramid?" Rory asked, looking out over the dense and sprawling jungle below them.

"Tomorrow morning I'll lead an expedition down the cliff," Decker said. "We'll make reaching the pyramid our goal and look for survivors along the way. We know they descended down the cliff from here and what their objective was, so we'll be retracing their steps."

"A risky plan, but probably our only reasonable option," Ward said. "I try to avoid walking into unknown situations. But there's nothing to be gained by staying put. We can't learn anything from up here on top of the cliff. We have no means of assessing the situation remotely and no knowledge of the landscape ahead of us. There is only one viable way to get the answers we need and find those missing people."

"My thoughts exactly," Decker replied.

Ward nodded. "According to the lidar data, the pyramid is

less than five clicks from our current location so we should have no trouble hiking in and out during daylight."

"Excellent," Henriksen said. "I know you said no cameras, but I'm hoping you will make an exception in this instance. That jungle down there is TV gold, and if we do find survivors, I want it all on film."

"You're staying right here," Decker said, looking at Henriksen and his production company colleague, Tristan Cook. "Both of you."

"Like hell we are." Cook's cheeks puffed out and his nostrils flared. "You have no authority over us."

"I thought we'd already gone over this once," Decker said, wearily. "This is not a civilian expedition and I say no cameras. This is not up for debate."

Cook looked like an angry pufferfish. "You're just going to leave us sitting up here while you have all the fun?"

"If you call entering a hostile jungle and risking our lives fun, then that's exactly what I'm going to do." Decker glanced at Ward for help, but the stoic commander appeared content to let him take the flak. At least for now. "We have no idea what's down there. I'm not risking civilians."

"What about those two?" Cook asked, waving a hand toward Emma and Rory. "I suppose you're letting them go along, and they're civilians."

"True. But they are also experienced operatives who know how to handle themselves. You people are not."

"I beg to differ."

"Really?" Decker raised an eyebrow. "Is that why your original production crew are unaccounted for and probably dead?"

"Well…" Cook looked flummoxed. "That's not… I mean…"

Check mate.

Decker resisted the urge to smile. "I rest my case."

## 30

"We should set up camp." Commander Ward glanced toward the wide expanse of sky soaring over the forest beyond the cliff, and a line of dark clouds that were gathering on the distant horizon. "We've only got a couple of hours' good daylight left, and it looks like there's a storm coming in. I don't want to be caught in the open when it gets here."

"Me either," Decker said. "If everyone pitches in, we can be finished in under an hour."

"Alright, people." Ward fixed the group with steely eyes. "You heard the man. Let's get this done."

The group jumped into action. Even Henriksen and Cook, who were clearly still mad, did their part. Soon tents were set up between the trees, and there was a fire pit ringed by small boulders gathered from the surrounding land. When the storm came, if it did, the fire pit would be useless, but until then they could beat back the approaching night and keep the upper jungle's more mundane predators at bay.

Afterward, with an hour of daylight left, and the storm clouds still sitting out on the eastern horizon, Emma approached Decker. "I'd like to look around if that's okay with you. Explore a little along the cliff."

"I'd rather keep everyone together," Decker replied. "At least for tonight."

"Please?" Emma stepped close to him. She looked up into his face. "Tomorrow we'll be going down the cliff and hiking to the pyramid. I would be shocked if that structure is all that's hiding in this jungle. There might not be another opportunity to explore up here. Why waste the last of the daylight?"

Decker met Emma's gaze, just for an instant. But then he looked away, uncomfortable with the way those deep blue eyes still made him feel. Not any current desire, but something else. A fleeting impression of what might have been if she hadn't left. The ghost of emotions he'd thought long since put to rest. And memories too. The way those same eyes had looked up at him during the heights of passion and intimate moments that had become their shared, if distant, history. In the end he agreed to her request, mostly because he didn't want to remember. He had another life now, and deep down, he sensed the threat his old flame posed to that life. But he wasn't willing to let her go alone. "I'm coming too."

"Sure." A faint smile played over Emma's face, just for a second. "I'd like that."

"And we're bringing a member of the Ghost Team." That way, he wouldn't have to be alone with her.

Emma shrugged. "You're the boss."

She turned—her long hair sweeping across her shoulders as she did so—and started toward the edge of camp. "No time like the present."

They struck out toward the waterfall, following the cliff's edge. Decker went first, with Emma in the middle, and a member of the Ghost Team bringing up the rear, his M4 semi-automatic at the ready. Decker didn't think there were Cyclops or other such creatures prowling the clifftop, but there were still jaguars, boa constrictors, and other dangerous animals lurking in the gloom between the trees.

They walked for twenty minutes, before Emma cried out. "Look. What's that?" She pointed toward the tree line ahead and hurried forward.

At first, Decker didn't see anything out of the ordinary, but then he spotted the object that had gotten her so excited. A shape that looked like a tall, flat-faced rock covered in foliage. It sat near the cliff edge, between two trees.

As they drew closer, he realized it wasn't a rock at all. At least not in a conventional sense. It was too angular and perfectly positioned, as if it had been carved and placed there deliberately.

"This isn't natural. I'm sure of it." Emma ran forward and tugged the at vines and foliage, exposing the oddly shaped rock's face. She looked at Decker, grinning. "Just as I suspected. There's writing on here. Carvings."

"Let me see." Decker stepped forward and helped remove the remaining forest growth clinging to the object.

The rock wasn't a rock at all. It was a six-foot-tall stele. An upright stone slab that had been set into the ground. It reminded Decker of an oversized gravestone except that the writing covering the surface wasn't put there to commemorate some poor departed soul, he was sure. This was not a burial site. For one, the ground was much too hard given their location near the cliff—solid rock with only a thin layer of soil and detritus. Then there was the writing itself. Egyptian hieroglyphics.

"This is incredible." Emma could barely contain herself. She reached out and ran a hand over the stela's weathered surface. "It must have been here for millennia."

"Can you decipher it?" Decker asked, circling the rock. The hieroglyphics were only on one side, facing the jungle. The back was rough-hewn and unfinished, as if the long-dead stonemasons who carved it just chipped the granite slab out of bedrock and flattened only the surface they wished to write upon.

"I think so." Emma studied the stela, lips moving silently as her finger traced the three columns of glyphs from top to bottom and left to right. At length, she stepped back. "Fascinating."

"Well?" Decker asked impatiently. "What is it?"

"A warning," Emma said. "It's an ancient warning."

"Would you care to be more specific?"

"Sure. Keep in mind I might not get this perfect, but it will be close enough." Emma started from the top again and moved downward, following the columns as she read. "To all who may come, be warned. Beyond this place lies the meeting of the two lands, where the beasts from the realm of the Gods are free. Take care all who enter here."

"The meeting of the two lands?" Decker repeated. "I wonder what that means?"

"Your guess is as good as mine," Emma said. "She looked out over the jungle beyond the cliff. "Maybe we'll find out tomorrow when we go to the pyramid."

The Ghost Team soldier had been loitering a few feet away, scanning the jungle warily. Now he tapped Decker on the shoulder. "Sir? The sun will be setting soon, and we don't want to be out here after dark." He pointed toward the horizon. The dark clouds were closer now. "Not to mention that storm. It's still coming our way. We should go back."

"Sure." Decker nodded. He looked at Emma. "You good?"

"Hang on." She took a compact digital camera from her pocket and snapped off a few pics. "I want to document this."

"Make it quick." Decker folded his arms and waited.

Emma stepped back and snapped a few more photographs from further back, then turned to him. "All done."

"Great." Decker placed a steering hand on her back. "Let's go."

31

As darkness settled over the Amazon, they lit a fire and ate MRE's for dinner. Afterward, Commander Ward assigned his men to guard duty while the rest of the group sat around the fire and discussed the following day's plan.

"I'd like to get to the pyramid as soon as possible," Emma said, "after seeing that stela back there, and those hieroglyphics, who knows what we'll find next. I can't believe the Egyptians made it this far, especially since there's no record of them making any transatlantic crossings. The Egyptians weren't much of a seafaring nation for most of their history, especially during the Old Kingdom. They mostly used their ships to transport goods up and down the Nile River."

"What about Thutmose and Rameses?" Rory asked, as he sipped a mug of cocoa from his MRE pack. "They both understood the importance of a navy. Rameses used warships to his advantage in his conflict with an invading force called the Sea Peoples. They had already destroyed the Hittites and wanted Egypt's wealth."

"That's true," Emma said, nodding. "But the Egyptian force

was mainly composed of riverine vessels, which they used as platforms for their archers, whereas their opponents had what we would today call tall ships. In the confined space at the mouth of the River Nile, the more ponderous, larger craft of the Sea Peoples didn't stand a chance. But that's all a far cry from sending their ships across the Atlantic Ocean. Remember, these were single masted open vessels powered by up to forty oarsmen. They just weren't built for that kind of journey."

"Which they clearly made," Rory said. "I'm more interested in how they wound up here with the Greeks."

"I guess we'll find out in the morning."

"Speaking of which," Henriksen said, glancing toward Decker over the leaping flames. "Have you given any more thought to what we talked about earlier?"

Decker took a swig of cocoa. "What did we talk about?"

"You know." Henriksen rubbed the back of his neck, then swatted at a mosquito. "About us coming with you tomorrow. I'm hoping you've changed your mind."

"I haven't." Decker met his gaze.

"You're looking at this the wrong way," Cook said, chiming in. "What you seem to forget is that I'm a veteran explorer. This isn't my first trip to the Amazon. I'm sure we can come to an arrangement. Allow me to accompany you and bring my camera. I'll let you review the footage before we air it and veto anything you don't like. Sound fair?"

"I'd have to veto everything," Decker said. "I don't want myself or any of my team on film."

"Okay. How about a compromise. We'll blur your faces. The network does it all the time on crime shows when they're interviewing undercover guys or shy witnesses. We even blur other bits—if you know what I mean—on that series where they run around buck naked. It's easy."

Decker shook his head.

"But that's not—" Cook stood up and glared at Decker.

"I don't want to hear it." Decker cut him off. "I'm in charge of this expedition, and what I say, goes."

"I agree with Mister Decker," Ward said. "We're in hostile territory and already have one group of missing people. I won't allow a pair of untrained civilians to walk blindly into danger."

"Which brings me to my next point," Decker said. "This is not just a research trip. It's also a rescue mission. Our priority is to find that film crew and bring home any survivors."

"And recover their footage." This was Hugh Henriksen, the producer. "If you won't let us come with, that's the least you can do. We spent hundreds of thousands researching and filming this show. It's imperative we have every single frame they shot. We can't complete the season without it."

"Good to see you have your priorities straight." Decker shot the producer a withering look. "Has it occurred to you that your on-air talent might be dead?"

"Of course it has," Henriksen snapped. "I pray that they're still alive. But if they aren't, why waste good publicity."

"You think anyone is still going to want to watch your show if the entire production crew got themselves killed making it?" Emma asked, incredulous.

"Are you kidding me?" The producer let out a dry laugh. "The ratings will be better than ever. Why do you think people slow down to look at a car wreck? I'll tell you why. Morbid curiosity. The same reason folk will tune in for the show if Darren Yates and the rest of the team don't make it back. Human nature. The only thing better would be if there's actual video of their demise. With the gory bits blurred out, naturally."

There was a moment of shocked silence around the campfire.

Henriksen, perhaps realizing he'd said the quiet part loud, tried to backtrack. "Not that I'm wishing them dead, you have to understand. Nothing of the sort. Like I already told you, I hope we find everyone safe and sound."

"Yeah." Decker shook his head. "You keep telling yourself that."

## 32

The storm came rolling in a little after ten that night, driving everyone to their tents where they sheltered overnight as thunder rumbled and lightning split the sky. It was a violent maelstrom that pounded their camp with several inches of rain. The only upside was the wealth of fresh drinking water they collected thanks to Commander Ward, and the collection device he'd fashioned by lashing the corners of a trail tarp to the trunks of four trees. A small boulder placed in the middle of the tarp pulled the center down, almost to the ground, forming a rough bowl shape.

When the storm passed, there was plenty of clean water that they wouldn't have to test or boil before consuming. And with storms being a regular feature in the rainforest, they would have a steady supply for as long as they were here.

They used some of this water early the next morning to brew coffee, which they drank while eating more MRE's. Afterward, they prepared to descend the cliff.

Commander Ward took charge of that. He assigned two of his men to stay topside with Henriksen and Cook, who looked suitably put out but accepted their fate quietly, then gathered the rest of the team near the ropes they had discovered the previous day. The ones used by Darren Yates and the film crew the previous week.

He tested the ropes, checking they were tied off correctly and still safe, then clapped his hands to get everyone's attention. "All right, people. Time to do this thing. We brought harnesses and descenders with us for just this scenario. And we got lucky. The rope is already here, so we don't need to worry about setting up our own rappelling system. That will save a lot of time."

"Maybe we should find another way down," Rory said, eying the ropes.

"Negative." Ward shook his head. "It would take too long, and we might never find a path to the bottom. We use the ropes. Trust me, I'll get everyone down safely. This is what I do."

"You sure about that?" Rory asked, nervous. "I was never much good at climbing rope in school. Made me dizzy. I was more of a sit in the library and read type of person."

"Why does that not surprise me?" Ward asked, giving Rory's slight physique the one over. He grinned. "Don't worry. I'll show you what to do. It's all perfectly safe so long as you follow my instructions. And just to be sure, one of my men will be on the ground holding the ropes. If you slip, they'll be able to arrest your descent."

"You make it sound so easy," Rory said with little enthusiasm.

"It is." Ward said. "Like riding a bike."

"I was a late bloomer with that, too," Rory said.

"Hey. I'll go first," Emma said to him. "If a girl can do it, you should have no trouble."

"Great." Rory pulled a face. "You must think I'm a real wimp. To tell the truth, I don't like heights. Never have. Okay?"

"I don't think you're a wimp," Emma said. "Quite the opposite."

"Really?"

"Really!" Emma placed a hand on Rory's shoulder. "Otherwise, you wouldn't be working for CUSP. Weren't you on the team that caught Grendel?"

Rory nodded. "Along with John and a few others."

"There you go, then." Emma flashed a smile and stepped closer to the ropes, studying the setup.

"You going to be okay?" Decker asked, concerned.

"Sure." Rory nodded. He stood with his arms folded, peering at the precipice. "I'll be fine."

"That's the spirit." Decker slapped his friend on the back. "And just so you know, you really aren't a wimp by any stretch. In the last four days you've survived an all-out assault by hostile gunmen, a car chase, and a run-in with a poisonous snake. Now you're about to rappel down a cliff. Name me one wimp who could do all that?"

## 33

It took the better part of an hour to reach the base of the cliff. Two members of the Ghost Team went first, rappelling down one after the other as if it were nothing. Emma went next, and while she lacked the soldier's flair, proved to be more than competent. Then it was Rory's turn. One of the soldiers held the ropes from below. If he slipped and fell, they could stop his plunge. Despite his vocal complaints, the archaeologist managed a clumsy dissent with Ward shouting directions from above, and Emma egging him on from beneath. That left just Decker and Commander Ward.

With most of the team already below, they got to work lowering their backpacks, filled with water canteens, food, and survival gear, on a fresh rope that Ward had set up for just this purpose. They couldn't risk carrying the packs down on their backs, because the uneven weight would have made it even more dangerous to rappel.

When the gear was safely on the forest floor below, Ward instructed Decker to go next. He donned the harness, triple checked his equipment, and then stepped over the edge. Planting his feet on the cliff face, Decker inched his way down, keeping his body perpendicular to the rock. He fed the rope through the descender, keeping it tensioned, and continued like this all the way down until he felt the ground beneath his feet. One of the soldiers at the base helped him out of the harness and sent the gear back topside for Ward to use. Ten minutes later, the entire team stood at the base of the cliff and surveyed the unfamiliar landscape around them.

"Feels different down here," Emma said, studying the forest that stood less than twenty feet from the cliff face. The ground they now stood on was almost level—a gentle slope toward the tree line covered in shale and small rocks. "It's at least a couple of degrees cooler, and there's no breeze."

"No animal noises either," Ward said. "We should at least be hearing cicadas, howler monkeys, and birds. But there's nothing. It's like the entire forest is holding its breath."

"It's spooky." Emma took a nervous step backwards. "Why is it so quiet?"

"That's a very good question," Ward said. He stood, hands on hips, and eyed the trees. "And one that we might answer as we explore deeper toward the pyramid."

"The waterfall is about a mile to our right," Emma said. "I think we should follow the cliff until we reach it. According to the lidar imagery, the pyramid straddles the river. We can follow the riverbank all the way there. It will be safer than trudging through the jungle."

"I concur," Ward said. "The going will be easier too. Less foliage and vines."

"Sounds like a plan," Decker said, picking up his backpack and slipping it onto his shoulders. "Let's get moving. And keep your eyes peeled. I have a feeling there are some nasty things down here that we might not want to run into unprepared."

"Yeah, like a Cyclops," Rory said, giving the trees a nervous glance. He looked toward the commander and his two soldiers, at the semiautomatic weapons they carried. "Wonder how many shots from one of those it would take to bring such a beast down?"

"I'd rather not find out." Ward lifted his own pack onto his back and slung the M4 carbine over his shoulder. "As Mister Decker said, let's move."

# 34

The waterfall was even more impressive up close than from afar. It thundered over the cliff in a frothy, turbulent maelstrom. Beneath it, at the base of the falls, was a wide pool of dark water from which the river meandered into dense, almost impenetrable jungle.

Decker felt uneasy. They didn't know what lurked in the jungle, and their only means of escape were the ropes left dangling over the cliff a mile distant. But at least they were armed, which made him feel better.

The two soldiers and Commander Ward had their M4 carbines, and Sig P226 sidearms on their belts. Decker was packing the Makarov PB pistol—the one confiscated from the gunman back at the restaurant—although he didn't bother attaching the suppressor. There was no need. He still had two full magazines, which he carried in his pocket.

Emma hated guns and opted for a machete.

Rory remained unarmed, despite Ward's offer of a KA-BAR Fighting Knife—the preferred blade of the US Marine Corps. The Ghost Team leader deemed the blade safer than putting a gun in the untrained archaeologist's hands. But Rory refused,

CRYPTID QUEST | 165

looking at the weapon as if Ward were offering him a one-way passage to hell.

Decker took the lead, with one of Ward's men at his shoulder. The Ghost Team operative was late thirties, broad shouldered and tall, with a military style buzz cut and a square jaw. He looked every bit the Marine he once had been. Following behind were Emma and Rory. Ward and the other Ghost Team soldier protected their rear.

They left the waterfall behind and trudged along close to the riverbank. Decker used a compass to make sure they were on the correct heading. Ward had determined this the previous evening as they sat around the campfire using the coordinates Decker had provided him.

"What's your name, soldier?" Decker asked of the Ghost Team operative as they pushed deeper into the jungle, leaving base camp and the rest of the team far behind them.

"Kyle, sir," the man replied. "Kyle Garrett."

"You been with the Ghost Team long?"

"Yes, sir. Three years. Before that, I served under the commander in Afghanistan. When I finished my tour, he recruited me straight into CUSP." Garrett kept his attention focused on the surrounding forest, his eyes wandering in all directions, looking for any threat. "The commander had already left the service by then and was putting together his team."

"You like working for CUSP?" Decker asked. The questions sounded innocent enough, but he was digging to see if there was any flicker of untruth in the man's answers. Someone had sliced that hole in Decker and Rory's tent, and he didn't think it was Emma, or the production company man, Henriksen. Decker's gut also told him that the Ghost Team leader, Ward, was probably not their man. That left the four ex-soldiers and the explorer, Tristan Cook. Which of them was the culprit, Decker couldn't guess.

"I do, sir." Garrett nodded. "It pays more than the Marine

Corps. A lot more. Benefits are better too. Plus, they're not sending me to war zones for months on end."

"You don't need to call me sir," Decker said. "John will do just fine."

"Yes, sir…" Garrett hesitated, gave Decker a sheepish grin. "I mean… yes, John."

"That's better." Decker glanced backwards toward Rory. "You doing okay there, buddy?"

"I feel like a walking lunch buffet. Friggin' mosquitoes. I've been bitten at least a thousand times," Rory replied, batting away a large flying insect that had strayed too close to his face. "And I can barely see for all the sweat in my eyes. But apart from that, I'm just peachy."

"Not to worry," Decker said. "I'm sure it will be worth it when we get to the pyramid."

"How much further?" Rory asked. "I feel like we've been walking for days already. This tropical heat is killer."

"It's only been an hour," Decker said, checking his watch, a Marathon GSAR Military Issue. "But if the lidar coordinates are right, we must be at least halfway there."

"I hope so." Rory swiped at something that looked like a giant ant with wings. It buzzed around him for a few seconds, ignoring his attempts to move it along, then flew in a lazy circle around his head and up toward the tree canopy above them. "This place is full of-"

He never got to finish his sentence, because Garrett, who had taken the lead, held an arm up, fist closed. He motioned for the team to be quiet.

"What is it?" Decker asked in a whisper. "You see something?"

Garrett nodded. He motioned for them to follow him and stepped away from the riverbank, melting into the understory like a ghost thanks to the camo uniform he wore.

Decker and Rory followed, joining the soldier when he

crouched down behind a large bush with yellow berries hanging from its branches. Commander Ward, Emma, and the other soldier followed their lead and disappeared into the brush several feet distant.

The soldier put a finger to his lips, instructing them not to speak.

At first, Decker didn't understand what had spooked the soldier, but then he heard it, too. A rustle of leaves, and the crack of twigs underfoot. Something large was moving through the jungle behind them. He glanced to his right, glimpsed the rest of their group sheltering some distance away in the understory. He motioned them to stay concealed. Ward pulled a branch aside and flashed a thumbs up. He was aware of the danger.

When Decker turned his attention back to their own group, Rory was looking at the Makarov, pushed into the waistband of his khakis. Decker wondered if the archaeologist now regretted turning down the combat knife Ward had offered him. Not that a knife would do Rory much good, anyway. To use it, he would need to be in close contact with his attacker, and whatever was approaching them sounded too big to engage in hand-to-hand combat.

Decker reached down and slipped the Makarov out.

The sound was getting louder now.

Garrett had removed the M4 from his shoulder and now clutched it in a tight embrace across his chest. If need arose, he could swing it down and fire in a heartbeat.

Something moved off to their right.

A shape emerged from the understory. A large bipedal creature with leathery brown skin. It was hairless and tall, at least seven feet. A crude loincloth made of what looked like animal hide hung around its waist.

The creature lumbered toward the river and kneeled. It

reached out with enormous hands and scooped up water, which it slurped noisily.

Decker held his breath.

Next to him, Rory tensed.

Garrett silently lowered the M4 carbine and aimed it toward the stooped creature.

It lifted two more handfuls of drinking water, then climbed to its feet and stood erect, looking out across the river with its back to them.

The creature stayed that way for the better part of a minute, then lifted its head and snuffled the air loudly.

Rory nudged Decker, a perplexed look on his face.

Decker just shrugged. He didn't dare speak.

The creature lifted a thick arm and scratched the back of its neck with one meaty finger, then turned away from them and took a step back toward the jungle. But then it paused, sniffing the stirring breeze a second time as if catching a stray scent. It turned, and they saw its face for the first time, and the single large eye inset into a sloping forehead above a flattened and flaring nose.

Decker's breath caught in his throat.

A Cyclops.

Beside him, Rory let out a small whimper.

The creature sniffed one more time. Its single eye swiveled toward their hiding place. Its chest puffed out and it let forth with a loud and throaty roar. Then the Cyclops charged straight at them.

# 35

Their hiding place discovered, there was no longer any need for stealth. Garrett reared up and dropped back on one leg into a more stable shooting stance and adjusted his aim to compensate for the lumbering creature.

He pulled the trigger.

Decker flinched, expecting the triple report of the gun's three-round burst.

But nothing happened.

Garrett made a grunting sound and reached down, slapping the bottom of the magazine, then tried again.

Still nothing.

Decker glanced quickly right, toward the rest of their group, wondering why they hadn't opened fire. Ward was on his feet. His own M4 now slung over his shoulder. Had that failed to fire, too? And what about the other Ghost Team soldier?

Ward reached down and plucked his sidearm from its holster. He pulled the trigger. An empty click. Then another. He observed it in horror.

This gun had failed too. Which was impossible. Unless...

Decker didn't have time to contemplate the reason why.

The Cyclops was closing fast.

He gripped the Makarov with both hands and fired.

Once. Twice. Three times.

On the fourth pull, the gun clicked empty, but the creature kept coming. Either Decker's shots had sailed wide, or the outdated 9x18 ammunition's inferior stopping power had done no serious damage.

Either way, there wasn't time to reload, and the Ghost team's more lethal M4 weapons appeared to be out of action, at least for the time being.

Off to his right, Decker caught a flash of movement.

The Ghost Team soldier standing between Ward and Emma lunged forward, dropping the M4, and bursting from the understory toward the angry Cyclops. He held his pistol at arm's length and pulled the trigger several times, even though he surely knew it was pointless. Discarding the useless weapon, he let out a high-pitched battle cry and barreled into the charging creature, wrapping his arms around it in a brave attempt to buy his companions enough time to retreat.

Decker didn't squander the brave soldier's selfless act of sacrifice. Ripping his eyes away from the Cyclops and struggling ex-Marine, he barked a curt command. "Run!"

## 36

Decker, Rory, and Kyle fled into the jungle. Behind them, swiftly
cut off, he heard the dying cries of the Ghost Team soldier who
had sacrificed himself to buy them time. He didn't know what
had happened to Emma and Ward. In the initial panic of their
escape, the two groups had gotten separated, bolting in different
directions. He was worried but didn't dare circle back to find
them. The creature was already on their trail. But at least it was
following them, and not Emma and Ward.

They pushed through thick vegetation and creeping vines
that threatened to trip them. But there was no time for caution,
even though there was a high risk they would inadvertently
disturb some poisonous denizen of the Amazon, like a pit viper
or the dreaded Brazilian wandering spider- the world's most
venomous arachnid. Not to mention giant centipedes, dart
frogs, and a host of other creatures small and large that would
happily defend their territory against an invading human.

But none of these were as terrifying as the creature that
currently chased them. Decker could hear it crashing through
the underbrush in hot pursuit. Proof his bullets had only served

to further enrage the beast. And it appeared to be gaining on them.

"It's no use," Rory said through ragged breaths as they pushed deeper into the jungle. "We'll never outrun that thing."

"If you can think of a better plan, I'm open to suggestions," Decker said, pushing a large branch out of the way and ducking under it.

Garrett was bringing up the rear, even though Decker suspected he could easily have moved faster than his companions. He came level with Decker and spoke. "There's only one viable option. I'll create a distraction. Lure the beast away from you."

"No." Decker shook his head. "Too dangerous. We've already scattered once. I don't want to further fragment the group."

"It's that, or we all get killed," Garrett replied. "I don't love the idea either, but it makes sense. I'll lead the creature off, and the two of you escape in the other direction. We'll rendezvous at the pyramid once I give it the slip."

"What if it doesn't follow you?" Rory asked.

"Don't you worry about that. I'll make sure it knows who to chase." Garrett motioned toward the Makarov. "Give me your gun."

"This is insane," Decker said. "You'll get yourself killed. We need to keep moving."

"Just give me the damned gun," Garrett said sharply. "I'm trained for this. You worry about yourselves. Get out of here before we all end up dead."

"Very well," Decker said, although he had severe misgivings about further splitting up. But there was no time to argue. The creature was almost upon them. He put a fresh magazine in the gun, then handed over the Makarov, and one remaining mag. "For the record, I don't like this."

"Not too keen on it myself," Garrett replied. "Now, go."

"We'll see you at the pyramid." Decker pushed Rory ahead of him, away from the soldier.

Garrett nodded.

"Good luck." Decker turned and dashed back toward Rory, who was lingering several feet away, watching the jungle warily.


"We can't just leave him here," Rory said, as Decker rejoined him. "It's insane. The Cyclops will rip him apart."

"We don't have a choice." Decker gripped Rory's arm and dragged him along. "The man's doing his job. That's why Adam Hunt sent the Ghost Team down here."

"But-"

"It's our best chance." Decker let go of Rory's arm and was pleased to see that the archaeologist kept moving of his own accord. "We can debate the merits of our actions later, but right now we need to concentrate on staying alive."

From the jungle to their rear, Decker heard the pop, pop, pop of Decker's Makarov, followed by an angry bellow. Either the Ghost Team operative had wounded the beast or enraged it even further. Decker couldn't tell which, but he was sure of one thing. Garrett hadn't killed the Cyclops.

Rory had heard the shots, too. He risked a furtive glance back over his shoulder. "Do you think it got him?"

"Don't know." Decker steered the archaeologist back toward the riverbank. They needed to reach the pyramid, and the best way of doing that was to follow the weaving Amazonian tributary, since the lidar survey data clearly showed it was located directly upriver from their base camp. This was the only reason the anomalous structure had been so easily located by the film crew. Even though it was covered in thick jungle foliage, its position straddling the river and significant height meant the building wasn't totally concealed beneath the dense rainforest tree canopy. It stood out on the imagery, even to an untrained eye.

Decker pushed through the understory, hoping that his instincts were taking them in the right direction. Five minutes later, he was rewarded by the sound of rushing water, and soon they stepped out of the jungle onto the riverbank. He stopped and looked around, getting his bearings. They had emerged a good way upriver from their original location, where they first encountered the Cyclops. He looked back toward the trees, wondering if Garrett had successfully led the Cyclops away from them.

Rory stood near the riverbank. He bent over, hands on knees, catching his breath. He looked sideways at Decker. "Are we safe now?"

"Safer than we were fifteen minutes ago," Decker said, still scanning the jungle for any sign of pursuit.

"Do you think Garrett made it okay?" Rory asked.

Decker was about to say that he hoped so, but before he could speak, they got their answer. From somewhere deep within the crowded jungle, came a shrill scream, quickly cut off.

## 37

"You think that was Garrett, or one of the others?" Rory asked, his voice trembling. "It didn't sound like a woman, so at least we can rule Emma out."

"I don't know who it was." Decker's heart sank. Whoever it was, they were likely dead. "Let's keep moving."

"Are you sure we shouldn't go back to base camp and fetch help?" Rory looked back in the direction from which they'd come, even as Decker started along the riverbank in the opposite direction. "The rest of the Ghost Team is there. They have guns."

"I'm sure," Decker replied. "We agreed to meet Garrett at the pyramid. If he survived, he'll be heading there. The others, too, probably. Besides, I bet those guns at base camp don't work either."

"Speaking of guns, how could they all fail at once?" Rory asked, as they walked. "You think they were sabotaged?"

"I can't think of another explanation." Decker hated to think that the guns were deliberately tampered with. That confirmed a member of their team was a double agent. But it made sense after the snake incident. Someone had been trying to slow them up, probably to delay them long enough for gunmen to arrive and make sure they never went anywhere again. "Right now, we need to worry about surviving and reuniting with any members of the team that are still alive. We can deal with the rest later."

"Who do you think the saboteur is?" Rory asked, hurrying to keep up with Decker, who was moving fast. "One of the production company people, maybe?"

"I don't think so." Decker shook his head.

"Then a member of the—"

"Quiet!" Decker shushed Rory with a wave of his hand and came to a sudden halt.

The hairs on the back of his neck were standing up.

Something was moving off to their left, in the thickest part of the underbrush. He could hear rustling as it drew closer. His gaze swept across the landscape, looking for whatever made the noise. A moment later, a large Cayman came into view from behind a flowering bush and slipped effortlessly into the river with barely a ripple. It swam out a few feet and turned to observe them, beautifully concealed with only its eyes, snout, and the top of its back breaking the water's surface.

"Crap, that was close." Rory took an instinctive step backwards. He observed the scaly beast with a wary eye. "If you hadn't stopped us, we would have walked right into its path."

"We should be careful," Decker said. "If that's a female, she may have a nest around here. There could be eggs. If she thinks we're a threat to them, she could attack."

"Great." Rory looked at Decker. "Why couldn't you have kept that to yourself?"

"Just keeping us safe." Decker led them past the spot where the Cayman had entered the water. He kept the animal in view, aware that it could strike quickly and without warning. But the Cayman showed no interest in going after them. Instead, it moved further out into the river with a lazy swoosh of its tail.

Here, the bank curved as the river took a wide turn to the

left. Decker was relieved to be out of the Cayman's line of sight, but when they rounded the bend, he saw something that made him even more happy.

Rising out of the jungle was a pyramid shaped building, its four slanted triangular faces draped in thick carpets of foliage that gave it the appearance of a straight sided mountain. It spanned the river from one bank to the other, with a huge dark tunnel running through the middle to allow the water's passage. The opening reminded Decker of a submarine pen, with a wide base and a taller middle section that gave it the appearance of an upturned blocky letter T. He'd seen photos of such pens on the Internet after his experience on Habitat One with the sunken German U-boat had led him to browse the origin of the deadly Nazi vessel. But this was not meant for submarines. It was here thousands of years before such vessels even existed. So why did they build the pyramid over a tributary of the Amazon and put a steep walled tunnel through the middle of it? The answer, he was sure, lay somewhere deep within the bowels of the building. And he hoped they would find out. But in the meantime, they had a bigger issue.

Something else was moving toward them in the jungle, and this time he was sure it wasn't a Cayman.

"What's that?" Rory asked, looking around.

"I don't know," Decker admitted. He pushed Rory forward. "Don't stop."

"What if it's Garrett or the others?" Rory asked. "They might be looking for us."

"Doubtful. Whatever is coming, it's making too much noise," Decker said. There was no way anyone in their group would be crashing through the understory in such a reckless fashion. Even if they were injured. "My guess is the Cyclops."

"Just great." Rory quickened his step.

Decker looked around frantically. "We're too exposed out here. We have to get out of sight, and quickly."

"Hiding didn't do us much good last time," Rory said. "That Cyclops could smell us."

"Better than standing out here in the open," Decker said. They were close to the pyramid now. The building loomed over them, blocking out the sun. Decker saw a stone path leading into the dark tunnel beneath. Up close, it looked even more like a submarine pen, with vertical stonewalls lining the riverbank flanked by wide walkways.

Decker risked a glance back over his shoulder, just in time to see a familiar shape emerge from the trees on the bank behind them.

The Cyclops.

And this time it showed no interest in having a drink of water. There was only one thing on his mind. The two of them.

"Hey, over here."

Decker was startled to hear a female voice calling out to them. He turned and saw a slim woman with a cascade of tumbling brown hair standing at the entrance to the tunnel. She waved her arms above her head and gestured frantically.

"Hurry," she shouted. "You don't have much time."

And they didn't.

The Cyclops was already making its way toward them, loping along with an alarmingly fast gait. Its arms swung back and forth as it went. Its single eye fixed them with an unwavering stare.

"I think we should do as she says," Decker said quickly, pushing Rory toward the pyramid.

The archaeologist needed no urging.

Together they sprinted along the riverbank, while behind them the Cyclops thundered along, its heavy footfalls audible over the sound of rushing water to their right.

Decker didn't dare glance back now. Any such move would only slow him down, and they needed every second they could get. His lungs burned and his leg muscles ached. He expected powerful hands to grip him from behind at any moment, lift him into the air, snap him like a twig. But miraculously, they reached the gaping black hole in the pyramid's side and tumbled through into the gloomy interior.

The mystery woman was waiting for them.

No sooner had they reached her, than she turned and took off deeper into the tunnel, calling over her shoulder, "Follow me if you don't want to die."

## 38

They continued deeper into the tunnel with the mystery woman in the lead. Once they put some distance between themselves and the entrance through which they'd came, she slowed up and turned to face them. "This should be far enough. We'll be safe now."

"How do you know that?" Rory asked, glancing back over his shoulder.

"They don't like to come in here," the woman replied. She nodded back toward the entrance where the Cyclops stood, watching them but refusing to advance. "See?"

Decker watched as the Cyclops paced back and forth, frustrated but obviously afraid to venture further. It glared at them and bellowed in anger; the sound echoing along the tunnel and repeating eerily.

"How long will it wait out there?" He asked. The woman stood with folded arms. "They can be pretty single-minded. It will probably wander off by morning, though. If we're lucky."

"The morning?" Rory's face fell. "We can't stay in here all night."

"Then leave," the woman said. "Be my guest."

"Why can't we just walk all the way through the tunnel to the other side?" Decker could see another entrance in the distance, weak light spilling in.

"Because where there's one of those things, there's probably more. And they're smart. They might not want to come in here, but I bet you there's at least two of them waiting on the other side of the tunnel for us to do exactly what you just said."

"Come on," the woman turned and started walking further into the tunnel.

"Wait, you haven't even told us who you are," Decker said.

The woman glanced backwards over her shoulder. "I'm Cassie Locke, one of the co-presenters on Cryptid Quest."

"John Decker. My colleague is Rory McCormick. We came here to find your team, rescue any survivors."

"And not a moment too soon. I was starting to lose hope of ever being rescued. I'm so happy to see you guys."

"Don't mention it."

"Oh, I'm going to mention it. You're my hero's."

"I wouldn't speak too soon. We still have to get you back to base camp."

"Which won't be happening for a while," Cassie said. "In the meantime, we have to keep moving. It's not safe here."

"I thought you said the Cyclops wouldn't follow us inside here," Decker said.

"It won't, probably. At least it hasn't so far." Cassie was approaching a large archway built into the side of the tunnel. "But there are other things out there. Creatures just as nasty as that one-eyed monstrosity, and some of them aren't afraid of the pyramid. Believe me, I learned that the hard way."

"Like what?" Decker asked.

"All sorts of things. I've only run into a few, but I've heard enough strange noises in the jungle to know there's a whole lot of other terrifying beasts lurking out there." She paused, as if gathering her thoughts. "You ever been chased by a Hydra?"

Decker shook his head. "Can't say I've had the pleasure."

"Well, I have. Damned near got me, too. Reared up out of the river while I was collecting water. Scared the life out of me." Cassie looked back at them. "There will be plenty of time to talk about that stuff later. Right now, I'd rather get us to safety."

They were coming up on the archway. Decker noticed that the stone path they were now on turned at right angles and disappeared into this new tunnel. Flickering light spilled out onto the pathway, lighting up the entrance.

Cassie reached the corner and turned back toward them. When Decker drew level with her, he stopped short.

This new tunnel continued for about three-hundred feet before ending at a stone wall. There were torches lining the wall, their flames leaping high as they crackled and burned. But it was what sat in the middle of the tunnel that took Decker's breath away.

In front of them, sitting upright with its bow facing the rear wall in a waterless channel, was an immense ship of ancient design, a least a couple hundred feet long.

Decker and Rory exchanged astonished glances.

It was no wonder the tunnel resembled a U-boat pen, Decker realized, because it had been built for a similar purpose, albeit many centuries earlier. Unbelievable as it was, they were standing inside an ancient, covered dry dock complete with a sailing vessel that must be thousands of years old, and yet was in such good condition that it might have sailed here only yesterday.

## 39

"You've got to be kidding me," Rory said in an awed voice as he stared up at the ship in front of them. It sat upright in a deep dry dock, supported by thick wooden posts that braced the hull against the dock's vertical sides. Two hefty wooden gates, sheaved in what looked like copper, stood closed across the dry dock's entrance, holding the river water beyond at bay. Even after so many centuries, the mighty doors were still watertight. What looked like open pipes sat at intervals sticking out from the sides of the dock, no doubt part of the mechanism by which the sailors who brought the ship here pumped the water out, probably to work on the hull after a long sea journey. Or maybe because they knew they would be here awhile and didn't want to subject the ship to any more water damage than necessary.

Decker was momentarily dumbstruck.

Rory, not so much. His eyes glinted with the excitement of a kid on Christmas morning. "It's all so well preserved. Simply incredible."

"Isn't it, though," Cassie said, a slight smile lifting the edges of her mouth. "I was floored when I found it. Not that I had much time to stop and marvel right at that moment. I was also being chased by Typhon, or at least the creature from which the myth probably sprung."

"What's a Typhon?" Decker asked.

"A creature from Greek mythology," Rory said. "The offspring of Titans—pre-Olympian gods. A serpentine winged creature with the upper body of a man. He was the father of Cerberus, the multi-headed dog that guarded the gates of Hades. Not a pleasant monster to encounter."

"I can vouch for that," Cassie said. "It was the first creature we encountered here. Damned thing swooped down and took our producer, Evan Granger. Carried him off. I haven't seen him since, so I assume he's dead."

"There's more of my production crew out there, but I haven't seen them since the initial attack. I don't know if I'm the only one left, or if anyone else survived."

"If anyone else is left, we'll find them," Rory said. He was still gazing up at the double masted galley in wide-eyed wonder. "I can't believe this is here."

"Me either," Cassie agreed. "I mean, a pre-Christian Mediterranean trireme in the middle of the Amazon jungle?"

"Looks Greek," Rory said, walking along the stone dock to the front of the ship and peering up at the still visible red and white painted eye that adorned the curved bow.

"It's not quite a true Greek design," Cassie said. "For a start, there aren't any openings for oars along the vessel's sides. A classic trireme would have space for a hundred or more oarsmen. This one has none. It relies solely on sail power. I'm assuming that's because it was ocean going and would have needed a smaller crew to ensure their supplies lasted over such a long journey."

"Not to mention the rigors of traversing such a large and dangerous body of water," Rory said. "Oars wouldn't cut it and leaving all those open oar holes on the hull would be a recipe for disaster. One bad storm would flood the ship and cause her to sink."

"Exactly." Cassie nodded her agreement. "But here's the best part. There's Egyptian influence on this boat, too. I found hieroglyphics carved into the beams on the inside. I suspect the ship was a joint venture between the two civilizations."

"Which must date it after the eighth century BC," Rory said. "Somewhere around the rise of the Greek civilization at a point in history when the Egyptians were reaching the end of their run."

"I guess we know how the Cyclops arrived here," Decker said. "It came on one of these ships."

"Maybe. Maybe not." Cassie said. "For all we know the Greeks and Egyptians came here to get the Cyclops, and transported them the other way, back to Europe and Africa."

"You think?" Decker asked.

"It's a theory I've been mulling. Maybe they were harvesting these things for some reason, capturing them in the Amazon, along with a host of other nasty creatures that shouldn't exist," Cassie said. She glanced around nervously and motioned toward a crude gangplank leading from the dock up to the ship's deck. "Which is why we shouldn't linger out here. Not all the monsters that inhabit this jungle are shy about venturing inside the pyramid. The ship is safe enough, though. At least so far."

"Have you explored inside the pyramid, yet?" Rory asked, as Cassie led them toward the gangplank.

"No. There's an archway at the far end of the dock that leads into the building proper, but I've been more concerned with staying alive than exploring. Besides, after what I've seen lurking out here, who knows what may be deeper inside the pyramid."

"How did you survive?" Decker asked.

"It hasn't been easy," Cassie said. She started up the

186 | ANTHONY M. STRONG

gangplank. "If it wasn't for finding the ship, I'd probably be dead already. I was able to hide inside it, and the torches on the dock kept most of the critters away. I was able to light them with a box of matches from the emergency kit in my backpack. I was kind of surprised that they worked, to be honest. I figured the tar would be long since dried up. Guess I was lucky."

"And you kept them going all this time?" Decker asked as they stepped onto the weather deck. He looked around and took in the deck. The main mast rose into the gloom, its tip almost touching the top of the tunnel. The single sail was furled against the yard, although the fabric itself had clearly deteriorated over the centuries. Decker suspected it would disintegrate if unfurled. A smaller foremast stood further away, rigged to the bowsprit. Pieces of rope, the remains of ancient rigging, lay coiled on the deck where they'd fallen, probably rotten.

"I found more barrels of tar in the hold. Whenever a torch went out, I just removed and soaked it again. Honestly, the ship is like a time capsule. Museums would kill to get their hands on this thing." Cassie led them to a hatch, down a set of steep stairs, and into the ship.

"Still doesn't explain how you survived." Decker looked around as Rory clambered down behind him. They were now on a wide enclosed deck. The forward half looked like crude crew quarters, with cots lining the walls and a central living area that included long tables and benches. A brazier stood under a chimney that disappeared through the ceiling above to vent smoke from belowdecks. A fire burned within, illuminating the interior with a warming orange glow. The rear was partitioned into smaller cabins, but Decker could not see inside to determine their purpose. "What did you do for food and water?"

"I had a good supply of MRE's in my backpack. I was also able to scavenge more from Evan Granger's pack." Her eyes moistened with tears. "It was still where he'd left it before the creature got him, on the ground outside the pyramid when we were going to make camp."

"I see," Decker said.

"And I've been taking water from the river, like I said." Cassie nodded toward the brazier. "I boil it over the fire before I use it. I can't guarantee that will make it safe. But what choice do I have?"

"We tested the water," Decker said. "It was fine, at least further back by the waterfall."

"That's good to know."

"There must be another level below this one," Rory said, glancing around. "This deck is not high enough to account for the ship's size."

"There is." Cassie nodded. "That's where I found the barrels of tar. There's other stuff down there, too. Ancient weapons. Barrels of drinking water, although most of those have long since dried up. There are also the remains of foodstuffs. The storage area probably counts for about a third of the deck space. The rest of it is taken up with barnlike wooden pens that appear to have been used for transporting animals. The Cyclops and other creatures would be my guess."

"There are pens?" Decker's interest was piqued. "Can we see them?"

"Sure." Cassie said, heading toward the rear of the vessel. "I'll take you down there. Follow me."

# 40

They descended through a hatch in the floor and down a set of creaky wooden steps into the bowels of the ship. It was pitch black down in the lower hull, but Cassie had brought a flashlight with her, retrieved from her backpack. The beam did little to illuminate much except a narrow patch of dusty and cracked floorboards. When they reached the bottom, she swung the flashlight around. The beam picked up ancient crates, barrels, and even a cluster of amphoras that must once have held wine or olive oil, stored in tight formation near the curving outer hull. A few had cracked over the ages or shattered entirely, leaving shards of dull brown pottery on the deck. There were other items too. Coiled ropes, metal tools, and stacks of unrecognizable cloth that might once have been clothing. A heavy scent of decay permeated the air. Dust particles swirled around, disturbed by their footfalls as they descended into the lower recesses of the ship.

"The pens are over here," Cassie said, swinging the flashlight around so that its beam picked out the wooden pens built along the sides of the hull. Thirty of them in all. Fifteen on each side.

Decker stepped forward to examine the closest Pen. Made of

wood, it measured approximately four by eight feet. Some kind of ancient and cracking tar-based product covered the floor, no doubt to seal the wood boards beneath. There were no portholes or other openings, except for a heavy wooden door attached to thick iron hinges. The door stood open. Decker could see the latch mechanism, which included a hasp on the door's exterior, through which an iron locking pin could be inserted.

He stepped inside and studied the pen.

There were chains with shackles attached to the floor and hanging from the side walls. When the pen's door was closed, whatever poor creature was confined within would be trapped in pitch blackness, restrained, and unable to move more than a few feet in any direction. Given the origin of this vessel, that meant it would have to endure an entire ocean crossing chained in the dark. He felt a pang of sadness. It was barbaric.

He stepped out of the cell—because that's what this surely was—and took the flashlight from Cassie. He made his way down the narrow corridor between pens, shining the flashlight into each as he went. The last four were bigger, with even more chains than the rest. Whatever had occupied these pens was clearly larger and more powerful. He could see scratch marks on the wooden walls. Gouges that bore testament to the previous occupants' feelings about their captivity.

Decker heard Rory come up behind him.

"You think they kept the Cyclops in these pens?" Rory asked, peering over Decker's shoulder into one of the larger wooden stalls.

"Either that, or some other unfortunate creatures." Decker still wasn't sure if the ancient Greeks and Egyptians who operated the ship were bringing the creatures to the Amazon, or capturing and taking them away, back to their own countries. The answer, he speculated, might lie elsewhere within the pyramid structure.

"I wish Emma was here to see this," Rory said.

"Me, too," Decker replied. He wished he hadn't been so hard on her now. After all, their relationship had ended many years before, and any feelings he still harbored for the Egyptologist were nothing compared to the love he felt for Nancy. When they reunited with the rest of the team, he resolved to set the record straight and tell Emma that he was engaged.

If they reunited...

For all he knew, Emma and Commander Ward were dead, killed by the Cyclops, or some other nasty resident of this jungle. If that were the case, he would never get to tell her anything. He pushed the maudlin thought from his mind and returned to Cassie, who was waiting for them at the end of the short passageway.

"Creepy, isn't it?" She asked. "The people who sailed this ship here were up to nothing good."

"That much is a given," Decker replied, thinking of the heavy chains hanging from the walls of each pen. He gave the surrounding deck space another glance, hoping to find some other clue regarding the true purpose of the vessel. He came up empty. "And it begs the question, why is it still here?"

"And what happened to the people who were on board?" Rory added.

"Don't know, on both counts." Cassie took the flashlight back.

"Have you found any human remains since you've been here?" It was unlikely that the ship's crew had decided not to make the return voyage home of their own free will, so that left one alternative. Some unknown tragedy had befallen them. The supplies at the other end of the deck supported this conclusion. Even though it had long since rotted, Decker could still see the remains of stored foodstuffs. The crew hadn't consumed all the supplies they had brought with them. The most logical explanation was that they were not alive to do so. "Are there any bones or other signs of the crew?"

"No." Cassie shook her head. "But as I said before, I haven't explored the rest of the pyramid. The crew's remains might be there."

"Or they could be out in the jungle somewhere, buried under two thousand years of leaf litter and humus," Rory said. "If that's the case, we'll never find them. Needle in a haystack."

"I'm not sure it matters if we find them." Decker was heading back toward the stairs leading to the ship's upper level. "The fact of this vessel still being here speaks volumes about the fate of the crew. I'm sure they didn't stay voluntarily."

"I wonder why no one came looking for them?" Rory said, as they climbed back up.

"It's impossible to know if anyone came looking, or not given how many centuries have passed." Decker pulled himself out of the hatch and stepped aside to let the others up. "But we know one thing."

"What's that?" Cassie asked. She turned the flashlight off, no doubt to preserve the battery, and put it down.

"The creatures out in that jungle have been here for a long time. This is their home, and we are the interlopers. And if the Cyclops retained a race memory regarding the pyramid and this ship, we're in more trouble than I realized."

"Why is that?" Rory asked, his brow creasing.

"Because they won't want the outside world to know they're here, and the best way to protect that secret is to make sure we don't ever leave."

## 41

They sat around the brazier and ate rations from their packs. Decker was worried about the rest of their team, and he could tell Rory was, too. Ever since Cassie had brought them to the ship, Decker had held onto a hope that one or more of their lost companions would reach the pyramid and find their way in. But so far, that hadn't happened. He didn't need to look far to realize why. A couple of hours earlier, while it was still light, he'd risked a trip back along the tunnel toward the jungle. He was barely halfway there when a large, hulking shape appeared, silhouetted against the brightness of the tunnel's entrance.

A cyclops.

When he turned to make his way back to the ship, he noticed more dark figures skulking at the other end of the tunnel. Cassie had been correct. The beasts were waiting for them. He and Rory were trapped inside the pyramid, at least until the Cyclops gave up and went searching for easier prey. He only hoped that prey would not be his colleagues.

Rory had been sitting quietly while they ate, casting an occasional furtive glance toward Cassie. Now he mustered up the courage to speak. "What was it like?"

"What?" Cassie replied, scooping up the last of her meal from its foil packaging with a plastic fork.

"Being here all alone." Rory said. "You must've been scared."

"I saw that winged monstrosity carry off our producer. I heard my friends' dying screams in the forest." A haunted look passed across Cassie's eyes. "Hell, yes. I was scared. I still am."

"Is that why you didn't explore the pyramid?"

"Partly. I figured someone would notice us missing eventually and send help. The production company knew we were heading to the pyramid, so it made sense to stay here and wait. Especially since the Cyclops don't seem to like coming inside. That was fortuitous. Not sure what I would have done if they'd chased me in here. Probably ended up dead just like everyone else." Cassie crumbled her empty package and discarded it. "When I found the ship, I figured it was the best place to sit and wait. Then you guys came along just when I was starting to think I'd be stuck here forever."

"Are you sure the rest of your team is dead?" Decker asked.

"I know some of them are. Can't be sure everyone is, but no one else found their way inside the pyramid, and I don't see how they could survive out in the jungle." She looked at Rory. "What's your deal?"

"I don't follow." Rory shook his head.

"Well, your friend, John, looks like a guy who would go on a rescue mission into the rainforest, but you look more like a librarian."

"I don't look like a librarian," Rory said, indignant.

"Yeah, you do." Cassie smiled. "But don't get me wrong, it's not an insult. I just wondered what your gig is."

"I'm an archaeologist."

"He's also a mythology nut," Decker added. "If you ever spend time on a plane with him, he'll bore you to death with his theories about ancient civilizations."

"That is not true."

"It's so true. What about Ireland? You couldn't stop talking about Grendel and Norse warriors. You were positively glowing on the way down here talking about the Cyclops."

"He's exaggerating," Rory said. "I talk about other things, too."

"You don't have to defend yourself," Cassie said. "I love mythology. If I hadn't become a biologist, I probably would have gotten a degree in archaeology, or maybe ancient history."

"If you're a biologist, how come you're working on a reality TV series chasing impossible creatures?" Decker asked. "You don't strike me as the type."

"And what type would that be?" Cassie was still smiling, but now her lips were pressed tight together. She observed Decker through narrowed eyes.

"Well, we have a guy waiting for us back at base camp. Your production company sent him down along with some producer. He claims to have a show about finding baby Bigfoots." Decker paused. "Is that right? Or is *Bigfeet* the plural of Bigfoot?"

"Hmm. That's a good question." Cassie's smile widened again. "I'm not sure there is a set definition for the plural of the Bigfoot. Neither one of those options feels right, though. And bigfeet just sounds silly. I'm going to go out on a limb and say that the plural of Bigfoot, is simply Bigfoot."

"Got it." Decker was glad for the lighthearted banter. It distracted from his concern about Emma, Garrett, and the commander.

"Your guy back at base camp wouldn't be Tristan Cook, would he?"

"That's him. Kind of pompous and full of hot air."

"That's Tristan, all right." Cassie opened the packaged dessert that came with her MRE. A flattened wedge of blueberry muffin. "You think that just because I work on a TV show, I must be like him?"

Decker shrugged. "It's hardly the sort of work a serious scientist wants to do."

"It is exactly why I'm doing it. I tried the whole biology thing. Academia. Man, was it boring!"

"I'd kill for boring, right about now," Rory said. "Give me a nice tame dig outside Athens, or a newly discovered temple in Rome. That would be bliss."

"You're saying you'd rather be on some boring old dig than sitting here with me?" Cassie asked, a mischievous glint in her eye. "My feelings are kinda hurt."

"Oh. No. I mean…" Rory fumbled for words. His cheeks turned red. "That wasn't what I meant. I just—"

"Relax. I understand." Cassie look at Decker. "Is he always this easy to wind up?"

"Mostly." Decker nodded. His meal finished, he stood and stretched. He glanced at his watch. Several hours had passed since they first entered the pyramid. It would be dark outside now. He wondered if the Cyclops had left yet. "I'm going to take a walk. See if those creatures have given up on us yet."

"I bet they haven't," Cassie said. "After they chased me in here, they hung out for almost a full twenty-four hours. Persistent is not the word."

"I think I'll look, anyway." What Decker didn't say was that he hoped one or more of their missing group might have found their way inside the pyramid.

"Want me to come with you?" Rory asked.

"No need," Decker replied. "I won't be long. If nothing else, I'd like to know that our hidey-hole is safe before we bed down tonight."

"Sure." Rory's gaze drifted from Decker back to Cassie.

"Shout if you need us," Cassie said.

"Will do." Decker made his way to the steps and climbed up to the hatch. As he descended the plank toward the dock, he heard Cassie and Rory talking excitedly. He couldn't help but wonder if the archaeologist had found a new subject for his affections. And if so, that was probably just as well. Because Decker didn't want Emma to break his friend's heart, the way she had broken his own, all those years ago.

## 42

When Decker returned to the ancient ship, Cassie and Rory were in a heated conversation about Cyclops and how the mythology of the Mediterranean region related to what they had discovered in this region of the Amazon rainforest.

When Decker stepped inside, Rory looked up. "Any luck?"

"Still no sign of the others."

"Oh." Rory's face fell. "It's not looking good, is it?"

"No." Decker retook his seat around the fire.

"Cassie and I have come up with a theory about this place," Rory said, changing the subject, although Decker could see the worry in his eyes. "It might explain why the Cyclops are here."

"And all the other strange creatures, too," Cassie said. "I've been thinking it over for a while. I had a lot of time on my hands waiting for you guys to show up. Talking to Rory really helped make sense of my ideas. He really is very smart."

"He has his moments," Decker said, noting how Rory's cheeks reddened at the compliment.

"Like a librarian," Cassie said, grinning.

Rory snorted. "Funny."

"Enough with the flirting," Decker said. "What theory?"

"We're not flirting," Rory said.

"Sure." Decker couldn't help a smile. "Tell me what you've figured out."

Rory said, "Well, we haven't quite figured all of it out yet, but it's a start."

Decker nodded.

"I don't think they brought the Cyclops here from across the ocean." Rory licked his lips. "I think this is their home, and they were being captured and removed from it."

Cassie took up the narrative. "It makes sense. If these creatures were native to the European or African continents, there should still be a population of them living there now. On the evolutionary scale, a few thousand years is nothing. It's like the passing of a couple of seconds compared to the length of our own lifetime. Things just don't change that fast."

"Plenty of animals have gone extinct since man came on the scene." Decker pointed out. "What about the woolly mammoth and the saber-toothed tiger? The dodo was still hanging on not too long ago."

"That's true," Cassie said. "They killed the last Dodo only five hundred years ago. The bird lived on the island of Mauritius, where it had never experienced predation. When European explorers arrived, they hunted the animal to extinction for its meat."

"Same thing happened to the thylacine, better known as the Tasmanian tiger," Rory said. "That didn't go extinct until the twentieth century."

Cassie nodded in agreement. "But there's a big difference between hunting a small group of localized animals already on the brink of extinction and wiping out entire populations of more intelligent and diverse animals in such a way that they left no footprint on the fossil record."

"Maybe there were only a few to begin with," Decker said.

"Improbable. Every species needs a large enough population

to breed. Even if their numbers had dwindled by the time of the Greeks and Egyptians, these creatures should have been plentiful prior to that. Again, they should show up in the fossil record. And we're not just talking about Cyclops. There are all sorts of impossible creatures out there. Don't forget, A Typhon attacked us just after my team arrived here. Not to mention the Hydra that tried to eat me."

"That's another reason these animals can't have been brought here," Rory said. "There are creatures living in the river. They would be impossible to transport by ship."

"Okay," Decker said. "Let's assume you're right and this area of jungle somehow contains creatures not seen anywhere else on the planet. How did civilizations from half a world away know they were here?"

"I don't know," Cassie said. "But they did. The proof is right here. You're sitting in it. And here's the thing, creatures such as the Cyclops were not just limited to Greek myth. All sorts of cultures speak of one-eyed monsters. There are old tales from the Carpathian region of Central Europe. A creature called the Arimaspi, which supposedly had one eye in the center of its forehead. An ancestor of Genghis Khan called Duwa Sokhor similarly had a single central eye. The list goes on. The Kabandha of Hindu mythology. The Slavic Likho. The Serbian Psoglav. Then there are the giants of Philippine folklore called Bungisngis. Even the Irish had a one-eyed monster named Fachan."

"I'm not sure I'd count that one," Rory said. "The Fachan was also supposed to have one leg and one arm. When you think about it, that's almost comical."

"All right, but you get my point. For a creature that has no reference in the fossil record, it sure shows up in a lot of places."

"Coincidence," said Decker. "I bet most of these creatures vary wildly in description, except for the one common denominator of a single eye."

"True. But that can be attributed to the story changing through various retellings down the centuries as it became interwoven into each culture's mythology."

"Kind of like a historical game of telephone," Rory said. "The story changing slightly each time it's passed on until it bears little resemblance to the original."

"And at the heart of it all is the Cyclops, captured here and taken overseas." Cassie looked at Decker. "And that isn't the only creature that pops up in more than one culture. Take the dragon, for example."

"Or fairies," said Rory. "People think of them as an invention of Europe in the Middle Ages, but they're not. Irish folklore has the leprechaun. The Greeks had nymphs. Even the Samoans had a version of the fairy."

"What you're telling me, is all these fantastical creatures have a basis in fact," Decker said. "That over time different cultures took their memories of them and created the myths that got handed down over the centuries."

"I can't prove my theory. At least not yet," Cassie replied. "But yes, that's exactly what I believe. And I think in at least some of those cases, maybe even most of them, the original creatures came from this very spot in the rainforest."

"Still doesn't explain why the Greeks or the Egyptians would want to capture and remove them," Decker said. "Or what they were doing with them afterward."

"No, it doesn't." Cassie nodded. "But I bet the answer lies somewhere inside this pyramid, and now that you're here, I'm hoping we can find it."

"I don't think we have much choice," Decker said. "Not if we want to make sure history doesn't repeat itself. There are people out there, bad people, who would pay a lot of money to get ahold of a real live Cyclops."

"To use them as a weapon," Cassie said.

"Exactly."

"Then we might already have figured out what the Greeks and Egyptians were using them for." Cassie looked at the two men.

"Soldiers," Rory said. "Inhumanly strong, almost invincible soldiers."

## 43

Later that evening, Decker was standing on the weather deck, leaning against the railing, and looking out over the tunnel. Beyond the dry dock gates, he could see the river, its surface reflecting the dim light from the flickering torches along the dry dock walls.

"Hey," a voice said behind him. "What are you doing up here all alone?"

Decker turned to find Rory coming up behind him. "Nothing much. Just keeping an eye out."

"Still hoping Emma and the commander will show up, huh."

"Something like that." Decker nodded. "You left Cassie on her own down there?"

"I got the feeling she wanted a few minutes to herself. Girl stuff." Rory scratched his chin. "Actually, I'm glad we've got this time to talk."

"You got something to say?" Decker asked. Judging from the look on Rory's face, he did.

"We got interrupted before, when we were talking about Emma."

"And?"

"I've been thinking about what you said. About her being consumed with work. I know you have a lot more experience with her than I do, given your history."

"Look, Rory," Decker said. "Maybe I was too harsh when we talked before. Just because she abandoned me, doesn't necessarily mean she'll do the same to you. But at the same time, I'm not sure she's changed much. I'm not trying to put you off pursuing her, believe me. I'm engaged to Nancy and have no interest in Emma at this point. But I don't want you to get hurt."

"I appreciate that." Rory leaned on the deck railing next to Decker. "To be honest I'm not sure how much of a spark there really was between us. I probably imagined most of it. I haven't had many relationships, spent most of my life single. I'm just not that outgoing. Sometimes I get carried away."

"Don't be too hard on yourself," Decker said. "She's outgoing. Likes to flirt. I'm sure she didn't mean to lead you on."

"Yeah. You must think I'm pretty sad. A lonely and introverted archaeologist who can't tell the difference between friendly banter and serious romantic interest."

"I think nothing of the sort. And as for being introverted, you seem to be doing well enough down there with Cassie."

"Because we're talking about archaeology. It's my thing. Stray from the topic of conversation, and I'll clam up. Just watch me."

"Just be yourself," Decker said. "Do that, and you'll be fine."

"You think?"

"Sure. You're an interesting guy."

"That's nice of you to say. I appreciate it." Rory gazed out toward the river. "Do you think they're dead?"

"Emma and Ward?"

"Yes," Rory said in a small voice. "And Garrett."

"I hope not."

"Me, too," Decker said. "If they're not back by first light I'll go look for them, assuming the Cyclops has gone by then."

"I'll come with you."

"You don't need to do that."

"I know. I want to."

"Understood." Decker glanced back toward the hatch. "Come on, let's go back down below. We're not achieving much up here, and Cassie must be wondering where we are."

Rory nodded and turned away from the railing. "Thank you."

"What for," Decker asked as they headed toward the hatch.

"Trying to boost my confidence," Rory said. "I appreciate it."

"Anytime," Decker said. "And for the record, I think you deserve better than Emma."

"You know what," Rory said as they climbed back down the steps into the ship. "So do I."

## 44

Decker awoke with a start.

He glanced at his watch. It was the middle of the night, a little after three in the morning.

He looked around, wondering what had awoken him.

The interior of the ship was lit with a dull red glow, thanks to the smoldering fire still burning in the brazier. They had added extra fuel to this before bed-the splintered remains of crates found in the lower hold-because without it, there will be no light at all.

Next to him, Rory snored loudly. They were laying on two of the ancient cots last used by the sailors who brought the ship to the Amazon millennia ago. Decker was hesitant to use them at first, but Cassie assured him they were in good enough condition.

On the other side of the cabin, beyond the ebbing fire, Cassie lay on her own cot. He couldn't tell if she was asleep, but there was no movement, so he assumed as much.

He swung his legs off the cot and stood up, looking around. At first, he thought some stray creature might have wandered into their makeshift accommodation during the night, but everything appeared to be in order.

"What's going on?"

Decker glanced around to see Rory sitting up. "I don't know. I thought I heard something."

The archaeologist rubbed sleep from his eyes and yawned. "You know what it was?"

"No. I'm not even sure what I heard. It's quiet again now."

"Cassie said the Cyclops won't come in here, but that doesn't mean there aren't other things around."

"I know that." Decker wished he still had the Makarov PB. He looked around for a weapon, didn't see one. "I'm going to look outside the ship."

"What?" Rory's eyes flew wide with panic. "I don't think that's a good idea. You won't be able to see a thing out there."

"I don't have any choice," Decker said, eyeing the hatch through which they'd entered earlier, now closed and secured with a wooden door they had swung shut to guard against any unwelcome visitors taking them by surprise in the night.

Rory stood and watched Decker climb the steps and put his shoulder to the hatch door. Decker was about to push it open when Cassie came up behind them.

"Don't do that." There was a look of panic on her face. "It's still nighttime. There are things out there that you do not want to meet in the dark."

"Something woke me up," Decker said. "I need to make sure we're safe."

"Or you could just stay here until morning," Cassie replied.

"And then we would be sitting ducks if there really is something dangerous out there." Decker fixed her with a steely gaze. "Better to know now, than regret it later."

"Very well then. But I'm coming with you."

"Not a chance."

"I've been here longer than you. I know my way around." Cassie was defiant.

"Well, if the two of you are going out there, I'm not staying down here all alone," Rory said. "I've seen enough horror movies to know what happens to the person who stays on their own."

"This isn't a horror movie," Decker said.

"Really? Did you see what chased us yesterday?"

"Fair enough. We'll all go." Decker glanced around, then looked at Cassie. "I don't suppose you have any weapons handy?"

"Funny you should ask," Cassie said. She disappeared into the darkness at the back of the ship. A moment later, she emerged with three poles about six feet long. At the tip of each was a sharp leaf-shaped spearhead. She handed one to each of them. "I found these a few days ago when I was exploring the furthest regions of the ship."

"A spear," said Decker. "I would've preferred an M-16, but this is better than nothing."

"You're a few thousand years early for an M-16." Cassie chuckled. "But this will do some serious damage, believe me. And technically it's not a spear. It's a dory."

"Wow. I've only ever seen these on a dig, or in a museum," Rory said. "And most of the time it's just the spearhead and sauroter left."

"What's a sauroter?" Decker asked.

"It's the spike capping the rear end of the spear," Cassie said, pointing to a wicked-looking piece of metal at the bottom of the spear's shaft. "Here's a strangely pertinent piece of information. Sauroter is a Greek word. It translates as lizard killer."

"Seriously?" Decker raised an eyebrow. "Either that was a strangely prescient name, or they were using these things for more than poking enemy soldiers."

"Makes you wonder, doesn't it?" Cassie replied.

"It does, that." Decker felt the dory's weight, then turned to the door. "Ready to go?"

"Not in the least," Rory said. "But I'd rather see what's out there than spend the rest of the night wondering if something is going to come in here and eat me."

"My thoughts exactly," Decker said. He put his shoulder to the door and pushed, grunting with exertion as he heaved it open. "This thing weighs a ton. I can't believe you were opening and closing this all on your own."

"Didn't have much choice," Cassie said. "It was that or leave it open at night while I slept. There was no way I was doing that."

"Let's go," Decker said, turning his attention back to the job at hand. He climbed up onto the weather deck and waited for the others to join him.

Together, they descended the gangplank toward the dock. The torches that Cassie had placed into brackets along the dock were still burning, which surprised Decker.

Cassie must've noticed. "The torches are basically sticks wrapped in cloth. There are barrels of fuel in the ship's hold. It's still good. I don't know what it's made of, but it burns for days on end before I need to douse the torch again."

"Greek fire," Rory said under his breath.

"What was that?" Decker glanced toward him.

"Nothing. Just speculating." Rory held the spear in front of him with both hands. Despite his earlier reluctance to carry a weapon, he was not complaining about this one. He looked down the dock toward the archway. Beyond this was the passage carrying the river through the center of the building. "Looks like we're alone, after all."

"We'll see," Decker said. He started off down the dock toward the archway, clutching his spear.

When he reached the end, he stopped before turning the corner. He peeked around, expecting the tunnel to be empty.

But it wasn't. Three figures were running toward him, casting terrified glances back over their shoulders.

Decker recognized two of them. He felt a rush of relief. It was Commander Ward and Emma.

He stepped out and showed himself.

Rory turned the corner and let out a surprised gasp.

The pair kept running. They didn't slow down. Instead, they waved frantically.

"Move." Ward shouted. "It's right behind us."

"What is?" Decker saw nothing.

"Just do as we say," Emma said in a high-pitched voice. She sounded breathless. "Wherever you came from, we need to get back there."

"What are they running from?" Rory asked.

"Guys?" Cassie was looking at the water.

Decker followed her gaze and saw a V-shaped wake coasting behind Ward and Emma. It was gaining fast.

"What the hell?" Decker said, watching the rippling water.

"I think we should do as they say." Cassie backed up as Ward and Emma closed ground and almost barreled into them.

Decker decided they could discuss the matter later. He retreated, intent upon herding them all back to the ship. But in that instant, the water's surface erupted and three enormous heads appeared on long, writhing necks.

Emma screamed.

Decker's heart skipped a beat. "What are those creatures?"

"Not creatures, plural," Cassie shouted over the melee. "One creature, singular. A Hydra."

"Whatever it is, I don't want to be here anymore." Rory turned to run.

Two more heads shot from the water near the dry dock gates holding the fast-flowing river water at bay.

Then, as one, all five serpentine heads lunged toward them with an earsplitting, high-pitched screech.

## 45

Decker grabbed Emma by the arm and dragged her out of the way a split second before one of the attacking heads plucked her from the dock.

She let out a terrified shriek and stumbled backwards toward the dry dock.

Rory threw his spear at another head. The weapon glanced off the Hydra's thick scaly hide and fell, useless, into the water.

"We have to get out of its reach," Decker shouted above the creature's cacophony of angry screeches.

"It can't reach us in the dry dock," Cassie said. She began hustling everyone away even as the creature reached its multiple long necks toward them.

Decker stood his ground to buy the rest of the group some time.

He ducked quickly sideways to avoid a pair of tooth-filled jaws. They snapped at the space he'd just occupied.

Another head swooped in from the other direction, mouth open and ready to snatch him up. Decker jabbed at the creature with his spear, using its length to keep his arms far from danger. The spearhead found the creature's mouth and lodged in its upper palate. It flinched back, ripping the spear from Decker's hand.

The rest of the group was behind Decker now, moving toward the rear of the dry dock, beyond the creature's reach.

"Come on, man," Ward said, grabbing Decker's arm and dragging him backwards. "You can't fight that thing."

The creature reared higher out of the water, its body slamming into the dry dock gates. They shuddered and groaned but held firm.

A serpentine neck snaked into the tunnel and blocked Decker and Ward's retreat. The Hydra's head reared toward them. A pair of yellow eyes observed the two men with unblinking fascination. Then it swept sideways, knocking Ward off his feet.

Decker lunged forward, grabbing Ward's arms even as the creature closed its jaws on the commander's flailing legs and dragged him back toward the water where other heads waited, eager to tear him apart.

"No!" Cassie left the main group and rushed forward; spear held high. In the flickering light from the torches, her khaki shirt dirty and torn, face contorted in anger, she looked like some sort of avenging Amazonian warrior.

"Don't let go," Ward said, grimacing in pain as the creature bit down on his leg.

"Not a chance," Decker replied. He redoubled his efforts, gripping the commander's arms even tighter. But he could feel his grip slipping. He was no match for the Hydra's strength.

Then Cassie let the spear go with a mighty cry.

It sailed through the air, a six-foot-long sliver of wood and metal that looked puny compared to the monstrosity rearing above them. But then it hit home with a meaty whump, embedding itself in the attacking head's left eye.

A perfect shot.

The beast howled and recoiled, releasing commander Ward.

Decker dragged him backwards and helped him to his feet. He grimaced, keeping his injured leg raised.

The Hydra smashed into the dry dock doors a second time, trying to break through and follow the retreating group. Another head atop a long neck shot forward.

But Decker and Cassie were already backing up, supporting the injured commander between them.

The head gnashed at the empty space they had occupied moments before, but it could no longer reach them.

Decker breathed a sigh of relief and looked around, taking stock. The tunnel beyond the dry-docked ship's bow dead-ended in a wall built of enormous stone blocks. Inset into this was the archway Cassie had mentioned earlier, barred by a metal gate. All he could see inside was swirling darkness. He would prefer not to venture inside there unless absolutely necessary. Who knew what other horrors lurked within?

The Hydra, frustrated, pulled all five heads back and watched them silently, long necks undulating like a slithering nest of enormous snakes. Its heads swayed from side to side. The movement was almost hypnotic. Cassie's spear had dislodged from its eye and was nowhere to be seen. Decker could not tell how much damage the spear had done, but he hoped it was enough to keep the multi-headed beast at bay.

"What do you think it's doing?" Emma asked.

"Looks like it's trying to decide which one of us will taste best," Rory replied.

"It's already gotten a taste of me," Ward grumbled through his pain. "I sure hope it didn't like the flavor."

Decker glanced down at the commander's wound, where the Hydra had bitten down. His pants leg was shredded and bloody, and Decker could see puncture wounds in the skin beneath, but the man's foot was still there. This was a good sign. "It doesn't look too bad from here."

"Guys?" Rory pointed toward the Hydra. "I think it's giving up."

Decker looked back toward the tunnel's entrance. The creature was still waiting beyond the dry dock gates, but was now slowly descending back into the water. First one had disappeared beneath the surface, and then another, until only one remained. It watched them for a few moments longer. Then the Hydra gave one

last shrill shriek before the last head sank down and disappeared back into the river from which it had risen.

For a while the small group of bedraggled archaeologists and soldiers stood motionless, watching the darkness beyond the dry dock tunnel. Decker couldn't help wondering if the Hydra's swift exit was a trap to lull them into a false sense of security. Would it burst forth from the river and strike once they moved closer to the water?

"Well, that was fun," Emma said, even though the tone of her voice told Decker that she felt it was anything but.

"I was starting to think I wouldn't see you guys again," Decker said, looking at the commander and Emma. His gaze shifted to the third person. The man who'd arrived with them. It wasn't the soldier, Kyle Garrett. This was someone Decker didn't recognize. A well-built man in his early forties with a mass of tangled hair and several days beard growth on his chin. "Who's this?"

"Oh my God," Cassie said, stepping forward with a wide grin on her face. "I thought you were dead."

"Me, too, honey. Guess I'm harder to kill than you thought." His gaze shifted from Cassie to Decker. He held out a hand in greeting. "Hey there. Let me introduce myself. I'm Darren Yates."

46

---

It was four in the morning, less than an hour after a noise outside had awoken Decker. Everyone was sheltering back inside the ship, having decided the Hydra was gone, at least for now.

"Where's Kyle Garrett?" Commander Ward asked as Cassie worked on his leg while Rory held the flashlight so that she could see.

"Don't know," Decker admitted. "After the Cyclops attacked, he took off in a different direction. He led it away from us."

"The man saved our lives," Rory said.

"We heard three gunshots," Decker added. "After that, nothing. Either the Cyclops got him, or he's still out there somewhere."

"That's too bad." Ward shook his head. "How did he manage to get any shots off? Our guns weren't working."

"He took my gun," Decker said. "Or rather, the gun I took off one of those goons who was trying to kill us back in Manaus. Makarov PB."

"I see."

"Have you figured out why the guns weren't working?"

Decker asked. "I assume someone sabotaged them."

"They sure did." Commander Ward nodded. "I field stripped my weapon earlier this evening, hoping to get it working again. The firing pin was removed. Took me forever to get the damned bolt carrier group out. The cam pin rotated and jammed it."

"I have no idea what you're talking about," Rory said.

"The bolt carrier group allows the gun to fire semi-automatic." Ward let out a small grunt and jerked his leg as Cassie dabbed his wounded leg with an antiseptic wipe from a small first-aid kit she'd taken from her backpack.

"Hey, keep still." Cassie looked up at him.

"Are you almost done down there?" Ward asked in an irritated voice.

"I'll be done soon. I just have to finish cleaning the wounds and then I'll bandage it."

"How does it look?" Decker asked.

"Not great. There are some deep puncture wounds from that thing's teeth. But he'll live. At least as far as I can tell. I'm a biologist, not a doctor."

"Good enough for me," Ward grumbled. He looked back up at Decker. "The sabotaged guns confirm there's a traitor in our midst."

"Question is, who." Decker had already come to the same conclusion.

"Obvious answer is one of my men," Ward said. He didn't sound happy. "I can't imagine anyone else would know how to field strip an M4 and remove that pin, let alone do it to all the guns with no one noticing. Not to mention sabotaging our Glocks too."

Decker nodded.

"Except you," Ward said, watching Decker.

"Sorry to disappoint," Decker said. "But I've never field stripped an M4 in my life. Plenty of other guns, but nothing like that."

"Relax," Ward said. "I don't think it was you. Whoever did this to our guns also put that snake in your tent. I can't imagine you want to get yourself bitten by a pit viper."

"Unless he did it to distract attention," a voice said over his shoulder.

Decker turned and saw the TV presenter, Darren Yates, standing behind him. "I was sent down here to find you. You could try to be a little more grateful."

"Hey, I was just pointing out how you could avoid suspicion." Yates held his hands up in a gesture of submission. "I didn't say you did it."

"Darren, that's enough." Cassie glanced up briefly from her task, wrapping a bandage around Ward's leg. "Why don't you play nice? These people risked their lives to find us."

"And I'm very grateful," Yates said, grinning widely. "To tell the truth, I'm not sure how much longer I could have lasted out there on my own."

"Since you mentioned it, how did you survive out there?" Decker asked.

"Luck more than anything. After the attack on our camp, everyone panicked and ran in different directions. I ended up hiding in the undergrowth with my sound technician. Guy named Dan Weatherby. God rest his soul."

"Weatherby is dead?" Cassie looked up with tears in her eyes. "How?"

"The Cyclops. He tried to make a break for the cliff, climb up the ropes. The brute came out of nowhere and lifted him up like he was nothing. Ripped him limb from limb. Then it carried him off. At least the bits of him it wanted to keep. It was horrible."

"Oh." Cassie's face turned white. "I figured I was the only one left alive. I should be thankful that anyone else survived. But getting confirmation... Knowing that..." A sob racked her body, interrupting her speech. "I'm sorry. I know I shouldn't get so upset. Not while we're still in such a bad situation."

"Hey, it's okay." Emma kneeled beside the distraught woman. "Let it out. It's natural. You've been through a very stressful time."

"I was doing fine until now. Forcing myself to be strong. My survival depended upon it. But hearing about Dan... I mean, he was a nice guy. It's just so..."

"Sorry, Cassie." Yates looked sheepish. "I should have kept the details of Dan's death to myself. At least right now."

"It's okay." Cassie sniffed and wiped her eyes with the back of her hand. She pulled the bandage tight around Ward's leg and held it in place with a safety pin. She pulled what remained of his trouser leg back down. "All patched up. At least as good as I can do it. You'll need to get it looked at by a doctor if we... I mean, when we get out of here."

"Got it." Ward stood up and tested it, putting weight on his leg. He winced in pain, but managed to stay upright. "You did a good job. Thank you."

"My pleasure."

"You probably want to get a tetanus shot, too," Decker said. "Just to be safe."

"I think I'll be getting whatever jabs the doctor's offer me," Ward said. "Just to be doubly safe. Who knows what kind of germs were in that thing's mouth."

Decker turned his attention back to Yates. "You still haven't said how you survived for so long out there in the jungle."

"Is not much of a story, really," Yates replied. "After the Cyclops killed Dan, I turned and fled. I was terrified. Luckily, I didn't run into another one of those creatures. But I did find a falling down building out in the forest. An ancient temple of some sort. I crawled inside and hid. I stayed there for God knows how long, rationing the MRE's from my pack and drinking whatever small amounts of water I could catch in my hands when it rained. The temple roof leaked like a sieve. Not that I was complaining about that. I didn't want to step outside."

"That's where we found him," Ward said. "I think we almost gave him a heart attack. Poor guy thought we were a Cyclops."

"I've never been more grateful to see another human being in my entire life," Yates said.

Decker glanced at his watch. "I don't want to break up this little reunion," he said. "But since we've now patched up commander Ward's leg, we might want to get some sleep. It's still the middle of the night, and we're going to need our strength tomorrow."

"That's an excellent idea." Ward looked around the group. "But I don't want to leave us unguarded. I'll stay up and keep watch."

"There's really no need," Cassie said. "I've been living here for days and I've had no issues. The Cyclops are afraid to come into the pyramid, and I haven't seen any other creatures except the Hydra. Luckily, it gives up easier than the Cyclops do."

"Is my job to keep you all safe," Ward said. "I'll keep guard, anyway."

"How about a compromise," Decker said. "Why don't we drag one of the cots over by the door and you sleep there. That way if anything tries to open it and come in you can alert us."

"Well…" Ward didn't look convinced.

"If Cassie's been fine in here for so long, I'm sure we can survive one more night." Decker motioned to Rory for help with the cot. "I'd rather have you alert tomorrow when we really need it. You look exhausted."

"I can stand getting some shuteye. It was a long day and night out there in the jungle."

"It's settled then," Decker said, hauling the cot nearer the door with Rory's help. He yawned. "Now, unless anyone else has anything to say, I'm going back to bed for a couple of hours. We'll figure out our next move in the morning."

Without further argument, the group dispersed and found places to sleep inside the ancient ship. Decker returned to his own cot and lay back down. The wood in the brazier had mostly burned, but he didn't feel like going into the lower hold to retrieve more fuel, and it still gave off enough warm orange light for them to see.

He closed his eyes and was about to drift off when he felt movement. Someone had laid down next to him. A voice spoke near his ear. It was Emma.

"I'm sorry about how I behaved before," she said in a voice barely more than a whisper.

"Don't worry about it," Decker replied.

"Do you mind if I sleep here, near you?" She asked.

"Fine." Decker couldn't be bothered to argue. "Just don't snore."

"You already know I don't snore," Emma replied. "I just don't want to sleep on my own. I don't like this place. It smells old. Musty. A bit like that warehouse in New York where they…"

She let the sentence trail off, but Decker understood. It all felt so long ago. He wondered if her experience with the Cult of Anubis still haunted Emma. It wasn't every day that you got possessed by an angry God. He turned over and looked at her in the darkness. "There's something I have to tell you."

"What?"

"I'm with someone else. I'm engaged to be married."

There was a moment of silence. He could hear Emma breathing next to him.

Then she finally said, "I know. I'm sorry about that, too."

Decker didn't reply. He turned over and tried to sleep, but her words echoed inside his head. He knew what she was trying to say. In another reality where she made different decisions, stayed instead of leaving, it might have been Emma, not Nancy who walked down the aisle to marry him. Decker wasn't sure how he felt about that.

## 47

When Decker awoke early the next morning, Commander Ward's cot was empty. He took a quick headcount, confirming that the rest of the group were there, all asleep. Emma still lay next to him, which felt natural and strange, both at the same time. She didn't stir when he swung his legs off the cot and stood up.

Decker glanced around. The hatch leading up to the weather deck was open. Decker could see a faint patch of half-light against the cabin's darker interior.

He climbed up and saw Ward standing at the rail near the ship's stern. He was gazing out beyond the dry dock toward the fast-moving river as it flowed through the pyramid's high tunnel.

"I thought you were going to get some sleep," Decker said as he approached the other man.

Ward glanced around. "I did. For a few hours, anyway."

"What are you doing up here?"

"Just getting some fresh air," Ward replied. "That cabin down below is dark and musty. Not to mention stuffy."

Decker joined Ward at the rail. "You got any thoughts on our next move?"

"First thing I want to do is find my missing man." Ward glanced sideways at Decker. "Alive or dead."

"If he was alive, he would surely have made it back here by now." Decker didn't like the idea of abandoning a man out in the jungle, but he was also a realist. Garrett had been missing since the previous afternoon. "Hate to say it, but he's probably dead."

"That might be the case," Ward said. "But Emma and I ended up stuck out there for hours. There was a Cyclops guarding the entrance. Persistent mother. I assume it was hoping you guys would reappear. We only made it in here after it got bored and wandered off. For a while there, I thought it would never give up."

"Thank goodness it did," Decker said. "I'd just about given you guys up for dead, too."

"Tell me about it. Little did we know, it didn't give up. It got spooked. We'd barely broken cover when that multi-headed monstrosity had a go at us. The Cyclops must have sensed it was there and scarpered."

"The Hydra." Decker nodded.

"Exactly. We hoped it wouldn't follow us in here, but it did."

"Unlike the Cyclops, it's not afraid of the pyramid."

"It appears so." Ward turned to look back toward the river. "And that's my point. We don't know that Garrett is dead, and we can't assume as much. He could be stuck out there, unable to reach us."

"I agree we should look for him," Decker said. "But we also have a duty to get those people down below decks to safety. Given how much time has passed, it's unlikely we're going to find any other members of the film crew."

"You want to take them back to base camp?"

"I'm considering it."

222 | ANTHONY M. STRONG

"That's a dangerous trek, given what we now know is lurking in the jungle."

"We don't have a choice," Decker said. "I say we get those people who don't need to be here back to base camp, and then the rest of us return to look for Garrett and explore the pyramid. We left two of your men there guarding the production company people. They might come in useful now."

"I agree," Ward said. "But don't forget, someone is working against us. I don't want to provide that person with an opportunity to take us out."

"We don't know if either of the men back at base camp are working against us."

"We do not," Ward said. "But right now, I don't trust anyone. Besides, if we are going to track out of here, I'd rather do it with Garrett at my side. He's a competent soldier. Experienced. We might need that."

"And if he's dead?" Decker asked.

"Then we find his body." Ward sighed. "I'm not leaving a man behind, and that's all there is to it."

"Fair enough." Decker stepped away from the rail. "I'm going to see if the others are awake yet."

Ward nodded.

"After breakfast, we'll go look for your missing man."

"Sure." Ward looked relieved. "But just the two of us. I don't want to put any more lives in danger."

"Goes without saying," Decker replied. "They can stay here on the ship until we return. It should be safe enough."

"Sounds like a plan."

"You coming?" Decker said, heading back toward the hatch.

"In a minute." Ward was still staring out into the gloom.

Decker nodded and started back below decks. He'd made it halfway down the steps when Ward called out to him, his voice laced with urgency.

"Decker, get back up here."

Decker stopped and reversed direction. He scrambled back up the steps. "What is it?"

"Come and see." Ward beckoned to him.

Decker raced across the deck and joined Ward at the rail again. He followed the commander's gaze and spied a lone figure moving toward them on the dock below.

Kyle Garrett.

He looked the worse for wear, a little dinged up, but he was alive.

He waved and made his way toward them.

Decker stepped back, ready to go down and open the heavy wooden door sealing the ship off from the outside world. But then his eye caught a movement in the water beyond Garrett. The surface was bubbling and frothing, and Decker thought he knew why. A moment later, his worst fear was confirmed.

A serpentine head broke the surface, followed by another, and yet one more. The Hydra had gone nowhere. It was lying in wait, biding its time until they tried to leave, or an easier prey wandered within range.

And that new prey was Kyle Garrett.

## 48

Garrett stopped in his tracks and turned, a look of horror on his face. For a few seconds, he stood transfixed, as if unable to comprehend the reality of his situation.

The massive Hydra towered twenty feet above him, all five wide heads now out of the water. Five sets of eyes observed him with steely malice.

"Don't just stand there, man. Run!" Commander Ward was leaning far out over the deck rail, as if he could somehow reach out and drag his terrified underling away from the looming danger.

Garrett took a stumbling pace backwards.

The Hydra lowered one scaly head toward the dock until it was at eye level with the soldier.

Garrett fumbled in his pocket, never taking his eyes from the swaying head that observed him. When he drew his hand out, he was holding the Makarov pistol that Decker had given him the day before. He held it at arms-length and slowly backed away from the creature.

The creature watched him for a second longer, as if it were summing the man up. Then it fanned all five heads out, rearing further from the water, before lunging forward with a deafening screech.

Garrett pulled the trigger, aiming at the closest head as it swooped toward him.

Decker saw a spurt of blood as the bullet clipped the creature's neck. Not a mortal wound by any means, but enough to fend off the imminent attack. The head recoiled as if it stung. But there were other heads on the way, and Garrett couldn't fire at them all simultaneously.

He didn't bother trying.

Instead, he spun on his heel and took commander Ward's advice, sprinting as fast as his legs would carry him toward the ship.

Decker was already turning back toward the hatch. He shouted down below, hoping the others were already awake. If the dry dock doors gave way, they wouldn't be able to stay on the ship. "Get your gear together. Hurry."

From somewhere within the ship, a voice shouted back. "Already doing it."

Decker recognized it as Rory.

He reached the hatch and came to a skidding halt, ready to tackle the stairs. But before he could do so, there came a mighty crash from his rear.

Decker turned in time to see the Hydra slam against the dry dock gates.

They shuddered but held.

The Hydra tried again, putting the full weight of its immense body into it. All five heads writhed and coiled in anger. It had lost a meal once already. It appeared intent upon not losing another.

This time, the gates bowed and flexed inward.

A spray of water leaked through.

"I don't know how long those gates are going to hold," Ward yelled above the screeching creature.

Decker risked a glance toward the dock below.

Garrett had made it to the gangplank, but he wasn't ascending. At first, Decker wondered why, but then he realized. If the dry dock gates failed, the force of suddenly released water would smash the fragile ship into so much kindling. And probably kill them all if they were still aboard it when that happened. Worse, the Hydra would now be free to pick off anyone who did survive.

"We have to get off this ship," Decker shouted at Ward. "Come on."

He turned and dove forward toward the open hatch, even as the dry dock gates took another shuddering hit. This time, the Hydra was not going to give up.

From below, Decker could hear frantic scrabbling as Rory and the others gathered their gear together.

Decker needed to collect his own backpack. He raced down the steps, had almost reached the bottom, when a final crash came from above. A sickening sound of splintering wood followed. Before he even had time to register what was happening, the ship jolted violently forward.

Decker lost his grip on the handrail and tumbled to the deck, landing hard on his back.

Above him, commander Ward fell through the hatch, swiftly followed by a roaring mass of tumbling water that washed him below. He bounced off the steps and landed on the deck next to Decker with a pained grunt.

"We need off this ship, right now." Ward was already pushing himself up. He reached out a hand and helped Decker to his feet. "The Hydra broke through the gates."

"I kind of figured that out already," Decker said. "Everyone up the steps and onto the deck. Now."

He ushered everyone toward the stairs, then raced back toward the rear of the ship. He scooped up his backpack and grabbed Ward's gear, throwing it to him. Ward caught it with a grateful nod and slipped his pack on his shoulders. Decker grabbed the M4 even though it was useless and tossed it back to him as well, then started back toward the steps.

And not a moment too soon.

The ship lurched and heaved, threatening to throw them all off their feet. Decker gripped the mast post and held on for dear life. Further away, commander Ward was bracing himself against a narrow bulkhead.

Rory stood at the base of the deck stairs, waiting for Emma to ascend. He almost lost his balance but stayed upright, catching Emma's hand as she lost her grip on the steps, catching her before she tumbled off into the gloom. He pulled her back and helped her up and out of the ship.

The others followed, scrambling up the stairs toward the open deck. First Cassie, then Darren Yates.

Decker told Rory to go next.

The archaeologist nodded and made for the hatch, just as another shuddering blow hit the ship.

The bow lifted as the stern pushed lower in the water. Decker thought they would end up completely vertical, but the old vessel wasn't built to withstand such a beating. Instead, it ripped in half.

The Stern section fell away as the bow crashed back into the water. Splintered wood flew in all directions, threatening to impale the three men still left inside.

Rory, halfway up the steps, cried out and almost fell before recovering and heaving himself up and out of the hatch.

Decker risked a glance backwards and saw open space where the back of the ship had been only moments before. And in that jagged hole, weaving toward them with a look of satisfaction, one of the Hydra's monstrous heads.

"Rory. Get out, now." Decker tried to keep his balance and lunged toward the steps.

"We don't have much time," Ward shouted as he pushed

through debris toward the steps, limping on his injured leg. "If that creature doesn't get us, what remains of the ship will sink and drown us."

"I know that already," Decker replied, watching Rory scramble up the steps. "You go up next."

"I'm supposed to be protecting you guys," Ward responded. "Get up there. I'll go last."

"Not a chance." Decker grabbed the commander by his arm and pushed him toward the stairs. "Don't argue with me."

"There's no time for this," Ward grumbled. He gripped the stair treads and started climbing. "You'd better be right behind."

"Where else would I go?" Decker ducked as the Hydra's head darted toward him. The forward end of the ship was filling fast. The water was almost up to his waist. He grabbed a piece of wooden plank that was floating by and swung it as the Hydra darted toward him a second time. The plank caught at a glancing blow on the side of the head and bought him enough time to follow Ward up the steps.

Soaking wet and exhausted, the two men pulled themselves out of the hatch onto the weather deck. Rory reached down and lent Ward a hand, helping him up.

Emma, Cassie, and Darren Yates were already making their way toward the gangplank. Then they stopped.

Emma looked back at Decker. "The plank is gone. There's no way to get off the ship."

"Well, we can't stay here." Decker let Ward lean on him. Rory supported his other shoulder. Together, they hobbled toward the rest of the group, struggling to stay on their feet as what remained of the ship pitched and yawed. The deck slanted down as the interior filled with water.

With dismay, Decker saw the gangplank was indeed missing. He glanced back toward the rear of the ship, or at least the space where it should have been.

The Hydra, one head still stuck inside the ship, glared at them with the other four. It reared back, ready to strike.

Decker felt the sway of the ship beneath his feet. He saw the dock getting closer as they pitched toward it. This was their only chance. "We have to jump."

"Are you crazy?" Emma looked frantic. "We'll kill ourselves."

"And if we stay here, the Hydra will do the job for us."

"It's the only way," Ward agreed. He disentangled himself from Rory and Decker.

"Wait for my command. When the deck pitches close to the dock, we jump," Decker said.

"I don't like this." Rory eyed the dock with trepidation.

"Almost there," Decker said, as the ship took another jarring heave to the left. He waited as the force of water sloshing in the hold crashed back against the hull, tilting the ship's remains sideways. Then, as the dock raced up, it was time. "Now!"

As the hull rotated in the other direction, all six launched themselves off the deck.

The Hydra let out a frustrated shriek. Two heads darted forward, trying to pluck them from the air. Both missed.

Decker landed hard on the dock and rolled, barely avoiding Rory, who landed next to him. He jumped to his feet in time to see the others scrambling up. Garrett quickly joined them.

Decker looked over his shoulder toward the attacking beast. The Hydra had pushed itself out of the river and into the shattered remains of the dry dock. It slammed a head down into the already partially sunken aft end of the ship, crushing it. Wood and other projectiles rained down.

"What now?" Rory screamed, holding his arms up to deflect the falling debris.

"There's an archway at the back of the dry dock. It leads into the pyramid," Cassie said. "It's our only chance."

"Then that's where we go," Decker said.

But before they could move, the Hydra reared up, sending

massive waves lapping over the dock and threatening to sweep them from their feet. And with it came the front quarter of the ship, still stuck on one of the beast's enormous heads. It lifted the shattered hull out of the water, then swung its head sideways to dislodge the broken vessel.

Decker watched in horror as the ship's destroyed bow crashed into one tunnel wall, and then the other. Finally, with an upward flip, the beast freed itself from the fractured piece of hull, and tossed it directly toward them.

## 49

The ship's bow section flew toward them. Or at least, what remained of it. The hull had lost its shape and was now more a tumbling mass of broken planks than a seaworthy vessel. The foremast had collapsed across the bowsprit, snapping off, and now whipped around, attached only by its frayed rigging. Barrels, boxes, and other assorted supplies and cargo now became deadly projectiles that rained down upon the dock.

Cassie and the others were already sprinting toward the archway, ducking, and shielding themselves against the falling debris. Ward hobbled along, lagging until Decker lifted one arm and half dragged, half pushed him toward the archway, and the dark tunnel beyond. They knocked the ancient metal gate aside and tumbled through.

"Lookout," Emma screamed, as a barrel smacked into the door frame with a resounding crack, and ricocheted into the tunnel, bouncing around like some sort of crazy pinball.

As one, they ducked, and the barrel flew over their head and off into the darkness.

More pieces of the destroyed ship followed, most of it too big to fit through the archway. Decker glimpsed the foremast

232 | ANTHONY M. STRONG

tumbling end over end. For a second, he thought it would catch just right to thread the needle of the tunnel and crush them all, but instead, it hit the wall next to the archway and came to a sudden halt with a thundering smack. More debris piled up, blocking the tunnel's entrance like a cork pushed into a bottle. And ahead of it, swept along by the violent force of the ship's demise, a surge of churning water. It gushed into the tunnel, riding up the walls like a tidal wave, and swept them from their feet, carrying the helpless group further into the darkness before receding as quickly as it came.

The silence that followed was eerie.

Decker lay on his back, staring up at the tunnel's vaulted ceiling. Somewhere to his right came a pained groan. He felt a sharp pain in his back. At first, he wondered if he had suffered some dreadful injury, but then realized it was just a sharp object poking through the fabric of his backpack. He pushed himself up on his elbows and looked around.

Rory lay sprawled a few feet away, face down. Nearby, already pushing herself up, was Emma. She looked like a drowned rat, with her hair plastered against her face and wet clothes clinging to her body.

"Need a help up?" Ward asked, standing over Decker awkwardly, with his weight on one leg.

"I'm good," Decker said, climbing to his feet and testing his limbs to make sure they were all in one piece. "You're in worse shape than me."

"Bah. I've suffered worse."

In most cases, Decker would've written this off as bravado, but with Commander Ward, he suspected it wasn't. He gazed around the tunnel, accounting for everyone. "We all good?"

"Took a nasty crack on the head when the water knocked me over," Garrett said. "But other than that, I'm fine."

"Me, too," said Cassie. "Just bangs and bruises."

"I can't believe the Hydra was waiting for us for so long," Emma said. "If we'd tried to leave, we would have been goners."

"Everything in this jungle is too damn obstinate." Rory picked up his backpack, which had become dislodged when the water washed down the tunnel. A broken strap dangled free. He slung it over his shoulder using the other.

"What was that creature?" Garrett asked.

"It was a Hydra." Cassie was ringing the wetness from her hair. "A multi-headed Greek water serpent that was supposed to guard the entrance to the underworld. It was supposed to have up to fifty heads, although that's clearly an exaggeration. If a head was cut off, it would regrow two more to replace it."

"Just as well we didn't lop any of them off then." Ward said. "Although I'm not sure how we would do that, anyway."

"With a gigantic sword," Rory said, deadpan.

"How are we going to get past it to get out of here?" Garrett asked.

"We're not," Decker said, glancing back down the tunnel toward the archway, now blocked by debris from the wrecked ship. "That wreckage will be impossible to move. We'll have to find another way out."

"Suits me," Rory said. "I don't fancy a third round with the Hydra."

"Me either," Emma agreed.

"Guys?" Darren Yates interrupted their conversation. "Has it occurred to anyone else that it should be pitch black in here, but it's not?"

Decker hadn't noticed until now, but Yates was right. With the entrance blocked and no visible light sources, the tunnel should be completely dark. But it wasn't. Even though it had looked dark from the outside, the tunnel was subtly lit by a strange, shimmering glow.

"It's the walls," Emma said, placing her hand against one of the square stone blocks lining the tunnel. "They're giving off luminescence."

"This just gets weirder by the minute," Rory said, turning his attention to the stone walls. "Glowing rock."

"Weird or not, it's true." Cassie looked around in wonder. "This is incredible."

"And fortuitous," Ward said. "Because without it, we'll be stumbling around in the darkness."

"I wonder if the whole place is like this?" Cassie asked.

"Probably. It appears to be a deliberate design feature." Emma was running her hands along the smooth stone surfaces, examining them up close. "I can see what looks like specs of crystalline material in these rocks. That must be what's causing the glow."

"I don't get it. How can rocks be glowing?" Garrett asked.

"It's not unheard of," Rory said. "There are many types of rock that give off luminescence in the dark, including fluorite, autunite, and scapolite."

"Except you normally need ultraviolet light to make a rock glow," Cassie said. "And at least one of those rocks is highly radioactive."

Garrett took a step backwards. "Wait. These rocks are giving off radiation?"

"Hard to tell without a Geiger counter," Cassie said. "I can't even identify the mineral. Like I said, you normally need ultraviolet light to make a rock glow. These are giving off light visible to the naked eye on their own."

"Relax," said Decker. "I'm sure whoever built the pyramid wouldn't have used this rock if it was going to make them sick or die."

"I hope you're right," Garrett said.

"Me, too," Decker told him. "Because we aren't leaving the same way we arrived, so we're going to be stuck inside here for a while."

"You're not making me feel any better."

"I wasn't trying to." Decker adjusted his backpack and looked around the group, then peered past them down the unexplored tunnel. "Who wants to go see what other secrets this pyramid holds?"

## 50

They made their way deeper inside the pyramid, following the strangely luminescent tunnel. It ran on an incline, Decker noted, meaning they were traveling higher into the building. It was also getting colder the further they went.

"I'm freezing," Emma said after they'd been on the move for ten minutes, wrapping her arms around her upper body for warmth.

"The temperature inside the pyramid is always going to be much lower than the jungle," Rory said. "The air in here gets no sunlight and the rocks leech heat, too."

"Plus there's no airflow," Decker said.

"Our wet clothing doesn't help either," Cassie said. "At this rate we'll catch pneumonia before we ever find a way out of this place."

"Cassie's right," Ward said. "We're losing too much body heat. We should change into something dry."

Decker brought the group to a halt. "Our backpacks should have kept most of the wetness out. We'll swap clothes before continuing."

"Right here?" Rory asked. "It's not very private."

"No time to be shy," Emma said. She was already peeling her clothes off. She discarded her sodden shirt and pants, then rummaged in her backpack. "Looks like my stuff survived without getting too wet."

"Mine, too," Cassie said, quickly changing her underwear and pulling on fresh pants and a white shirt almost as dirty as the one she had discarded, only not as wet. "That's better."

Decker waited until everyone finished changing, then picked up his backpack and started along the tunnel once more.

It wasn't long before they came to another archway with a square room beyond. In the middle was a dais made of stone, upon which stood an intricately carved statue. It stood ten feet tall—a bronze figure weathered to a green patina. Upon its head was the Atef crown. In its hands were the crook and flail. Beyond this, on the far wall, a second archway led deeper into the pyramid.

"Oh, my gosh." Emma raced forward. "That's Osiris."

"Another Greek monster?" Ward asked.

"Not Greek. Egyptian," Emma replied. "One of the many gods of the underworld."

Rory said, "Again, with the underworld theme. I'm seeing a pattern here."

"Clearly the Egyptians, and the Greeks that came after, both associated this place with the land of the dead."

"Back at the cliff," Decker said, "when we found that stele, it mentioned the meeting of the two lands."

"Yes." Emma nodded. "Where the beasts from the realm of the gods are free."

"When they wrote realm of the gods, perhaps they meant the underworld." Decker took a step closer, reached out, and touched the statue. He looked at Emma. "Are you okay with all this?"

"I'm an Egyptologist. What do you think?"

"No, I meant-"

"I know what you meant. Osiris was the father of Anubis. At least, depending on which mood the Egyptians were in at the time."

"And we know Anubis is real." Decker ignored the strange looks he received from the rest of the group. "Stands to reason Osiris would be, too."

"If he is, I don't think we have much to worry about," Emma said. "It took a crazy cult to bring Anubis back. I don't see any robe-clad nut jobs around here, do you?"

"Good point." Decker glanced around. "What do you think this room is for?"

Emma studied their surroundings. She stepped away from the statue and approached the walls. "Does anyone have a flashlight? It's hard to see in here, even with the luminescence."

"I do," Cassie said. She rummaged in her pack and produced the flashlight they had used the day before to explore the bottom deck of the ship and the pens. She turned it on and played the beam around the room. What it lit up elicited a gasp of surprise from the small group.

Hieroglyphics.

Lots of them.

They covered all four walls from top to bottom and side to side. It reminded Decker of photographs he'd seen of rooms inside the pyramids on the Giza Plateau in Egypt.

"Wow." Emma's eyes were wide with disbelief. "This is more than I ever expected."

"The Egyptians weren't just here," Decker said. "They were *really* here."

"Can you read it," Rory asked, breathless.

"I think so." Emma took the flashlight and played it across each wall in turn, before stopping in front of one. "This room tells the story of how the Egyptians came to be here. It's a written record of how they discovered the Amazon, and why."

"This is some kind of Egyptian library?" Garrett asked.

"Not so much a library," Emma replied. "But more like one volume inside the library. A big, room-sized history book."

"What does it say?" Rory joined Emma and stared up at the wall as if he could decipher the Egyptian hieroglyphics himself, simply by concentrating on them.

"I'm not sure I have time to read it all, but I can paraphrase," Emma said.

"Make it quick." Decker didn't want to linger any longer than necessary. They still had to find a way out.

Emma spent a few more moments studying the hieroglyphics, her lips moving silently as she took in their meaning. Then, in a hushed voice, she told them what the writing on the wall said.

## 51

"This is a very rough translation," Emma said, her eyes still fixed on the hieroglyphics. "Around fifteen hundred BC, when the Egyptian civilization was beginning their transition from the Second Intermediate Period into the New Kingdom, a strange ship from a far-off land arrived on the Nile River. It was like nothing they had ever seen and crewed by men of complexion even darker than their own who spoke a foreign and unintelligible language. The ship had spent many weeks lost at sea, finally making its way into the Mediterranean. By the time it arrived at the Nile Delta, many of the men on board had succumbed to thirst or were sick.

"There was something else on the ship, too. A towering beast with a single eye on its forehead. At first the Egyptians were terrified, but the animal was not in good shape, and quickly died. Some of the crew though, lived, and over time learned to communicate with their rescuers. They told of a faraway land across a vast ocean, filled with wondrous creatures and untold riches. A place where gold could be dug out of the ground by hand and a mighty river fed a forest of vast proportions."

"Sounds very much like the stories that propelled the

conquistadors thousands of years later," Yates said. "All except the monsters. This is big. Imagine when I announce that we've proved the Egyptians came to the Americas?"

"When you announce?" Rory said. "That's a bit presumptuous, isn't it?"

"Who better than me to tell people about this magnificent discovery?" Darren Yates' chest was puffed out. His eyes glinted. "I'm a world-renowned archeologist. Top of my field."

"Yeah." Rory rolled his eyes. "Sure you are."

"Guys, let her finish," Cassie said.

Emma waited for the conversation to die down, then continued. "Driven on by tales of wealth and curiosity about the one-eyed creature that accompanied the visitors from across the ocean, the Egyptians constructed a ship bigger than any built before. They copied the design of the stranger's vessel, thinking they could sail to this strange and mystical land. But fate was not on their side, at least at first. The expedition was never seen again, probably wrecked in a storm.

"Undeterred, they sent a second vessel, and this one sailed all the way to the Amazon, following a crudely drawn map they had discovered on the stranger's ship. They returned with news of their discovery, and a captured beast with one eye."

"The Cyclops," Rory said. "Can you imagine what they must have thought, arriving here, and seeing what inhabited this land?"

"They thought it was where the Gods lived," Emma said. "After the ship returned, they sent an entire fleet. Six vessels dispatched in secret. Only the Pharaoh and his closest advisers knew this land existed. But it didn't stop them from exploiting it."

"So where does the pyramid come in?" Asked Cassie. "And the Greeks."

"Be patient. I'm getting to it." Emma cleared her throat. "The Egyptians explored the area and found what they describe as an enormous gemstone half buried in the ground near the river. It was said to have mystical properties. When the sun shone upon it, the stone would reveal a second land within the first and bring with it the creatures of the underworld. But the stone lay half buried, and the trees allowed little light to penetrate. The Egyptians wanted to amplify its power, so they built this pyramid to amplify its power.

"They used a modified design borrowed from the smaller step pyramids at the base of the pyramid of Menkaure on the Giza Plateau, mining the blocks from the bedrock around the gemstone."

"I wonder if that's why these rocks glow?" Rory said. "Maybe they have some special quality associated with this enormous gemstone you're talking about."

"It's possible," Emma said. "They dug up the gemstone and used it atop the pyramid. They believed that by building across the river, they would also tap into the natural energy of their surroundings, especially since they believed the river was an underworld representation of the Nile."

"This really is great stuff," Yates said. "God, I wish I had my camera with me."

Decker shot him a look.

"What?" Yates shrugged.

"I want to hear the rest of this," Decker said. He looked at Emma. "Go on."

"Thank you." Emma played the flashlight across more wall. "The Egyptians stabilized the gemstone and the two lands emerged, coming together in one. They established a sect of priests here, whose job it was to converse with these new gods. But the Egyptian civilization was failing, and these new deities did nothing to stop it. The Egyptians could no longer support the sect, and the ships stopped coming. The sect of priests was left stranded."

"What happened after that?" Yates asked.

Emma shrugged. "That's pretty much where the story ends, at least in the hieroglyphics."

"Darn. Just when it was getting interesting."

"It doesn't take much to figure out the rest," Emma said. "My guess is that the priests probably died out since they were all male. We already know from history that the Greeks, who were a rising force in the region since at least the second millennium BC, slowly infiltrated Egyptian culture. They probably learned of the secret Egyptian sect and the land they controlled. They must have mounted their own expeditions to this land. But they weren't interested in worshiping these gods. They wanted to tame and put them to work. Over several centuries, they captured and brought them back to the Mediterranean where they used them for their own nefarious purposes."

"All highly speculative." Yates shook his head.

"I disagree." Rory said, glaring at Yates. "It makes perfect sense. That's how they ended up weaved into the region's mythology. The Cyclops and Hydra, to name a few. All real living creatures removed from this part of the Amazon rainforest."

"But wait," Ward said. "You're saying that the Greeks and the Egyptians merged?"

"It wasn't so much a merger as an invasion," Rory said. "By around six hundred BC, the Greeks and Egyptians were pretty much co-mingling. Egyptian culture was on the decline, and Greek civilization was reaching its pinnacle. By three thirty-two BC, Egypt was under Greek rule, thanks to Alexander the great. Even their gods ended up mingling with each other."

"Which explains why there is both Greek and Egyptian influence here," Decker said.

"Yes." Emma nodded. "The Egyptians found this land, thanks to the timely arrival of a ship from some long-lost Amazonian civilization. It probably got blown out to sea during a storm, or simply lost its way, and ended up traversing the ocean. The

Egyptians apparently kept this place a closely guarded secret through the centuries. But then the Greeks came and decided it was worth plundering."

"There's still one thing I'm not sure about," Ward said. "The giant crystal. What could it have been?"

"Who knows?" Emma said. "But it appears to be why the Cyclops, and all the other strange creatures, are here."

Decker looked at Rory. "The energy source CUSP detected must be coming from the gemstone."

Rory nodded. "Sounds likely."

"What energy source?" Cassie asked.

"The one inside this pyramid," Decker said. "My organization sent a classified satellite over this region. It picked up an unusual energy reading coming from the area."

"You think it's the crystal?" Cassie said.

"Yes."

"And that it's responsible for all the mythological creatures running around in the jungle?"

"That's exactly what I think," Decker said. "And not only that, but I have a theory how."

## 52

"My goodness, this is going to make a great episode," Darren Yates said, his voice tinged with excitement, as Decker led everyone out of the hieroglyphics room and into the dark corridor beyond. "If only I had my camera."

"So you keep saying," Decker said. "And FYI, it wouldn't matter if you did. I'd just take it from you."

"Now look here," Yates said. "I don't know who put you in charge, but this is my expedition. Understand?"

Decker came to a halt and turned on Yates. "This is not your expedition. In case you hadn't noticed, most of the people you walked into this jungle with are dead or missing. I'm in charge now."

"Take it down a notch, Darren," Cassie said. "These people are here to rescue us. You can think about your show later. Right now, I just want to get out of this and survive."

"You need to be careful how you speak to me, Cassie." Yates glowered at his co-presenter. "I'm the one that hired you. I can fire you."

"Don't bother. I quit." Cassie pushed past him and continued along the tunnel.

Decker glanced at Ward, who shrugged, and said, "Guess that's taken care of."

"Yeah. Let's keep going." Decker started after Cassie. He caught up with her and glanced sideways. "You okay?"

"I am now." Cassie was walking at a brisk pace. "Should have quit long ago. Show was stupid, anyway."

"I don't know," Decker said. "I watched a couple of episodes on the way down here on the plane. It wasn't high art, but it was entertaining enough."

"You're trying to cheer me up, aren't you?"

"Little bit."

"Thanks." Cassie managed a smile. "What's the deal with you and the Egyptologist woman?"

"Who, Emma?"

Cassie nodded. "I've been sensing some tension there. Especially when she first showed up. You two have a history?"

"That's one way to put it."

"Want to talk about it?"

"Not really," Decker said. "Besides, there's not much to tell. We dated for a while, and she left. Her career was more important than me."

"I'm sorry to hear that." Cassie shot him a quick look. "You're a nice guy."

"It's all good. I'm with someone else now. We are engaged to be married."

"Well, congratulations," Cassie said. "No wonder it's tense between you and the Egyptologist. Can't be easy having the girl you never resolved things with tagging along on your expedition when you're about to marry someone else."

"We worked things out," Decker said. "At least, I think we have."

"That's good." Cassie cast a furtive glance back toward Rory, who was near the back of the group. "What about him?"

"Rory?" Decker wasn't sure what she was asking.

"Yes. Is he spoken for?" Cassie smiled coyly.

"Oh." Decker nodded. "There is no Mrs. McCormick, if that's what you're asking."

"So, he's on the market?"

"I'm not sure he thinks of himself in those terms," Decker said, grinning. "But as far as I know, he's single. You like him?"

"That would be telling." Now it was Cassie's turn to grin. "But I sensed a little something between us when we were in the ship last night."

"Yeah. He's good at that."

"What does that mean?"

"Never mind." Decker looked at her. "Look, Rory isn't exactly one of the most forward guys on the planet. If you're waiting for him to make a move, it might take a while. Actually, scratch that. It could take forever."

"That's okay. I can be kind of shy, too."

"Well, if there really is a spark there, one of you is going to have to swallow your shyness. And I doubt it will be Rory."

"Good to know." Cassie turned her gaze frontward again. Up ahead was another archway, much like the one they had recently left behind. The room beyond was nothing but a dark void. "What do you think is in there? More hieroglyphics?"

"Maybe, but I doubt it," Decker replied. The corridor they were in had been leading them steadily upward since they left the hieroglyphics room. Decker calculated they were high in the pyramid now, near the apex. "We can't be too far from that gemstone mentioned in the hieroglyphics."

"You think it's up ahead?"

"If it's still here," Decker said. "And if my theory is correct, then it will be."

"When are you going to let the rest of us in on your theory?" Cassie asked.

"When I feel confident that I'm right," Decker said.

"Are you always this mysterious?" Cassie asked.

"Not mysterious. Cautious." Decker approached the archway. The room beyond glowed with the same weird luminescence as the rest of the pyramid, but it was large, and the glow only went so far. The center of the room was swathed in blackness. He stopped at the threshold, overcome by a creeping sense of unease. "I have a bad feeling about this."

"Great. Every time you get a bad feeling, we end up running for our lives." Rory came up behind Decker and peered past him into the gloom.

"Better than walking blindly into danger," Decker replied.

"It's so dark." Cassie took a step closer to the archway. "I can't see anything."

"Me either," Decker said. He turned to her. "Have you got that flashlight?"

"Yes."

"Turn it on. I want to see what's up ahead before we commit ourselves."

"Sure." Cassie turned the light on and swung it past the archway, then jumped back with a squeal. Standing not five feet away, illuminated by the flashlight's beam, stood the motionless figure of a Cyclops.

## 53

The Cyclops observed them with one large, round eye.

Rory let out a strangled gasp and stumbled backwards, almost bumping into Commander Ward.

Decker reached out to pull Cassie back, but then he stopped. "Hang on. Something's not right."

"You're telling me," Rory said. His gaze shifted from the Cyclops to Cassie. "I thought these things didn't come into the pyramid."

"They don't. At least, the few that I've encountered since I got stranded here. I'm not an expert on this stuff." Cassie looked perplexed. "Why isn't it attacking us?"

"Because it's not real." a sense of relief overcame Decker. He stepped forward and studied the Cyclops. "It's a statue. Made of stone."

"Oh, thank goodness for that." Rory laughed nervously. "For a second there, I thought we were all goners."

"It's so lifelike." Cassie approached the statue and peered up at it. She ran a hand across the stone surface and touched the creature's face. "Almost feels like real skin. The detail is incredible."

"The Greeks were master carvers," Rory said, plucking up the courage to enter the room. "I wonder why they put this statue in such an odd place, though? Right in the doorway."

"Maybe this isn't where they meant it to go," Decker said. "They might've been moving it and abandoned the statue here."

"If that's the case, they left a bunch of others, too," Cassie said, sweeping the flashlight around the room. It picked up more statues, all posed in unique positions and facing every which way. "There's no order to any of this. It's like they just plunked them down wherever they felt like it."

"Maybe we're in a storeroom," Ward said.

"Unlikely. This room is high in the pyramid," Decker replied. "It would take a lot of manpower to bring all these here from ground level."

"Maybe they carved them in situ."

"Unlikely. They would still need to bring the blocks here, and that would be impossible in those narrow tunnels."

"And there's no sign this room was used like that," Emma said. "There are no tools or other artifacts relating to carving stone."

"Well, they didn't get here by themselves," said Darren Yates, walking among the statues. Toward the middle of the room, he stopped and turned, calling out to the others. "Hey, this one is different. It's not a Cyclops."

"It's a hoplite," Emma said, rushing across to the statue. "The Greek foot soldier. Look at his shield."

"It's not stone." Yates tapped the shield. "It's metal."

"That's some fancy detail work, giving him a real shield," Rory said, "just to leave him here in this room. Why wouldn't the people who created these move their statues somewhere more prominent?"

"Why bother with the statues at all?" Garrett asked. "It wasn't like there was anyone around to see them. This pyramid is about as far in the middle of nowhere as you could get."

"That's a good question," Decker said.

"There's another soldier over here," Emma said, weaving between two eerily lifelike Cyclops. "Looks like this one is Greek, too."

"The statues don't make sense." Cassie was wandering among the stone figures. Her voice was soft, as if she were talking more to herself than the rest of the people in the room. "Why make so many statues of Cyclops? And why leave them here in such disarray, with no discernible forethought?"

"The Greeks made a lot of statues," Emma said. "Maybe they really were just storing them here until they could ship them back to the Mediterranean."

"I agree with John," Cassie said. "This room is too high in the pyramid to make sense as a studio where they were making these things. I don't believe it's a storage area, either. It would be a tremendous task to get these down to the ship when they could just make them dockside."

"And why sprinkle a few random Greek foot soldiers in?" Rory said. "Those aren't the kind of subjects the ancient Greeks normally bothered with. They made their statues for votive purposes, like to adorn a temple or other such holy place, or as decoration for buildings. If our theory is correct, and the Greeks came here later, long after the Egyptians built this pyramid, then it would have coincided with their classical period, which leaned heavily toward the artistic merit of statuary."

"The material isn't right either," Emma said. "I don't know what the stone is, but it should be bronze or marble."

"It's clearly neither one of those," Decker said.

"Does it matter why these statues are here or what they're made of?" Darren asked. He glanced toward the other end of the room, and a set of stout doors made of wood. "I bet there are better things than a bunch of moldy old figurines around here. I vote we keep going and see what's beyond those doors."

252 | ANTHONY M. STRONG

"A good idea," Decker said. His feeling of unease was returning. A vague sense of disquiet that lingered at the back of his mind. He felt like it had something to do with the statues, but he couldn't quite put his finger on why. "We shouldn't linger in this room."

"You okay?" Rory asked, noticing the strange look on Decker's face.

"Just feeling a little uncomfortable around the statues, that's all," Decker said, keeping his misgivings to himself. Until he could pinpoint what was making him nervous, he didn't want to spook the others.

"They are kind of unnerving," Rory said. "Too realistic. It's like they just walked into this room under their own steam."

"Oh my God," Emma said. "We have to get out of here, right now. I know why the statues are like this."

"Why?" Cassie asked.

"Because they're not statues." Emma looked panicked.

"You're not making any sense," Darren said. "what else could they be?"

Emma was about to answer, but at that moment, a sibilant feminine voice speaking in a strange and archaic tongue echoed through the room.

"It's coming from the corridor," Rory said, glancing back in the direction from which they came. "Something must've followed us in here."

"Rory," Emma said, aghast. "Whatever you do, don't look at what's coming through that doorway."

"We can't fight what we can't see," Ward said, taking a step forward. He hitched a thumb toward the wooden doors at the other end of the room. "The rest of you get out of here. I want to see what we're up against."

"No." Emma ran forward and gripped his arm. "You really don't."

"Why not?" Ward looked confused.

"Because if you do, it will kill you." Emma was dragging the commander forcibly backwards toward the wooden doors. "That's why all these statues are here. They used to be alive, just like us. Until they looked at the Gorgon."

## 54

Decker, Rory, and the rest of the group retreated quickly through the statue chamber to the set of wooden doors at the far end. Decker gripped the ornate bronze handles adorning the doors and pushed with all his might, but the doors would not budge. While to their rear, the strange sibilant voice whispered, enticing them to turn and look at it.

"Is there a latch we have to disengage?" Rory asked in a panic.

"No." Decker felt a prickle of fear run up his spine. They were running out of time.

"Try again." Emma was shaking. "Hurry. The Gorgon is getting closer. I can hear it."

"I am trying." Decker put his back into it. He dug his heels in pushed, grunting with the exertion. "It's no good. The door must be locked from the other side."

"What are we going to do?" Darren Yates asked in a shaky voice.

"Bust it in," Decker said. "In the meantime, whatever happens, don't look at that creature coming up behind us.

Unless you want to spend the rest of eternity in this room as a statue."

"Don't worry about us," Rory said. "You just concentrate on getting that door open."

"That's the plan," Decker said. He stepped away and launched himself at the unyielding doors, slamming his shoulder into them. The doors flexed inward a few inches but did not give.

"Here. Let me help," Ward said, joining Decker on the next attempt.

"Be my guest." Decker lowered his shoulder and barreled toward the door again, with the commander at his side.

The impact of their combined efforts produced a gratifying snap of wood from the other side.

"It's working. Try again," Rory said, keeping his eyes firmly rooted forward to avoid inadvertently glimpsing the deadly creature slinking up behind them. "And hurry. The Gorgon is getting closer."

"Thanks for stating the obvious," Decker said, his voice a low growl, as he and Ward backed away for one more assault on the stubborn doors. He rubbed his sore shoulder. "I sure wish we had something else to do this with. Not sure I enjoy being a human battering ram."

"A few bruises are worth not being turned to stone," Ward said. "You ready to go again?"

"Do I have a choice?" Decker said. He sucked in a deep breath and launched himself at the doors, hoping this would be the last attempt. Which it might well turn out to be regardless of their success. If they didn't get through the door soon, the Gorgon would be upon them. He could sense her drawing closer, but he didn't dare glance over his shoulder. It was an unnerving feeling, fleeing from an enemy they could not look at, even for a moment.

He slammed into the doors, wincing as a sharp jolt of pain

lanced down his arm. Beside him, Ward grunted as he impacted a split second later.

The doors flexed and bowed inward. Then whatever was holding them shut gave way with a sharp crack. The doors banged open. Splintered wood fell around them as Decker and Ward tumbled through, carried into the space beyond by their own momentum.

Decker staggered forward, regaining his balance, before turning back to the others, careful to keep his eyes lowered toward the ground lest he accidentally meet the Gorgon's gaze. "Move. Get through the door. Now!"

But the others didn't need any encouragement. They were already hurrying across the threshold. Rory and Garrett came last. As soon as everyone was safely out of the statue chamber, they took the doors and swung them closed.

Decker looked around, frantic, for something to barricade them with. They were in a square chamber with a smooth flagstone floor and tall walls. A stone staircase wrapped around the perimeter, turning once, then again, and a third time, before ending at another doorway sixty feet above them. Just like the rooms that came before, an eerie, translucent light emanated from the walls.

Apart from the shattered remains of a crossbeam that previously slid into brackets and held the doors closed, there was nothing that would prevent the Gorgon from entering.

In the end, Decker picked up a splintered section of crossbeam, and slid it as best he could into the two brackets closest to the place where the two doors met. It wasn't a perfect solution, and would not hold for very long, but it was all they had.

He turned to the others. "Let's keep moving."

As if to prove his point, the doors rattled.

There was an angry chorus of hissing, as if a nest of snakes were trying to break through, followed by more of the archaic language from the other side.

"Sure wish we could defend ourselves," Ward said, glancing down at the useless M4 which he was still carrying. "I'd love to just riddle that door with bullets, turn whatever is on the other side into a walking pepper pot, and solve our problem."

"Good luck with that. The Gorgon were immortal," Rory said. "All except Medusa, who could be killed."

"And what do you want to bet that this one isn't Medusa," Decker said.

"I'm not a betting man," Ward said, glancing nervously toward the doors. "But I'd say it's a fair bet we wouldn't be lucky enough to run across the one monster we could kill."

The doors shook again, followed by another round of frustrated hissing.

"I think it's time we moseyed along," Ward said. "That bit of broken wood will not hold those doors much longer, and I'd rather not be here when whatever is on the other side makes an entrance."

"Me either," Rory said. He looked at Emma and Cassie, then gestured toward the stairs. "Ladies first?"

"You're a gentleman," Cassie said, touching his arm briefly as she hurried past.

"Me next," Darren said, rushing toward the steps and starting up. "This is one monster I don't want to see, even if I had a camera."

Decker went next, with Garrett and Ward bringing up the rear. They hurried up the steps, taking them two at a time until they reached the first turn. Decker risked a glance back down toward the doors. They were holding. So far, so good.

"What exactly is a Gorgon anyway?" Ward asked as they ascended the second set of steps. "Sounds like some kind of fancy French cheese to me."

"Boy, do I wish it was," Rory said. "And I'm pretty sure I'm lactose intolerant."

"The Gorgon were creatures straight out of Greek mythology," Emma said. "Some scholars believe their origin to be the symbolic sublimation of an invasion by hostile forces early in the Greek civilization. Monsters born from a half-forgotten real event."

"Whatever was on the other side of those doors is anything but symbolic," Ward said.

"Clearly, those scholars were wrong," Emma replied. "Later traditions stated that three sisters were cursed by the Greek goddess Athena and became the Gorgon. Hideous monsters with snakes for hair who turned anyone that gazed upon them to stone. And get this… According to the legends, the Gorgon lived at the entrance to the underworld."

"This underworld theme keeps cropping up," Cassie said.

"Because according to the hieroglyphics in that room back there, the Egyptians apparently considered this part of the Amazon jungle to be a place where the world of the living met the underworld. I bet the Greeks did, too. Hence it ended up woven into their mythology."

"Fascinating as all this is, can we discuss it later and focus on getting out of here," Decker said.

They were almost at the last turn now. The third and final set of steps leading to the upper doorway. Decker resisted the urge to give the barricaded doors at the bottom another glance, and it was just as well. As they started up the third set of steps, there was a sudden crash from below. The Gorgon had broken through.

## 55

With the Gorgon mounting the steps below, Decker and the others reached the upper doors. If these were barricaded like the doors below, they would be in trouble. They were standing on a narrow ledge at the top of the open-sided staircase that ran around the chamber's outer walls, with barely enough room to move. A retreat down the steps was out of the question. The only other option was a sixty-foot drop straight through the middle of the chamber. They were trapped between a creature whose gaze would petrify them where they stood or a plunge onto the hard stone floor below. Except for that door.

"We'd better pray these doors open or we're goners," Decker said, gripping the bronze door handles. He took a deep breath, steeled himself, and pushed.

Nothing happened. These were just like the lower doors. But then, with a groan of protest, the doors swung a few inches inward.

"Give me a hand with these," Decker said, as he struggled to push them open. "They're heavier than the ones below."

Garrett and Ward rushed forward and took one door, while Yates helped Decker with the other. Little by little, they were

260 | ANTHONY M. STRONG

able to push them open enough to slip through. But the doors pushed back against their efforts, as if they were spring-loaded. Decker could feel his muscles giving out under the strain. Another minute or two, and he wouldn't be able to hold on. He could tell the others felt the same way.

"Get inside, quickly," Decker said to Rory, Cassie and Emma. "We can't hold on much longer."

The two women and Rory hurried past, into the room beyond.

Ward looked back over his shoulder, a pained look on his face. "You guys let go of your door and go next. We'll hold this one open enough for you to get through."

"No." Decker shook his head. "There won't be enough room. Besides, the minute you let go of your door, it will swing back, trapping you on the wrong side with the Gorgon."

"A risk we're willing to take." Ward was puffing with the effort of holding the door open.

"There are more handles in here on this side of the door," Emma said from inside the room.

"I don't think that helps us," Decker said. "The two of you are not strong enough to hold the doors open."

"Which is why you have to do as I say," Ward said. "You're just delaying the inevitable."

"Wait," Garrett said. "I have a better idea."

"Then don't keep it to yourself, man," Ward snapped. His feet were already slipping backwards as the door tried to close on them. "Speak up before we're all trapped out here."

Garrett cleared his throat and shouted through the gap. "Emma. Cassie. Rory. Grab ahold of those handles and hold on tight."

"What are you doing?" Decker twisted his head to look at Garrett. "We've already established they can't hold them open on their own."

"But they can buy us a second or two for what I have in

mind," Garrett said. "Darren, on my mark, let go and move to the other side of the door. Help Cassie keep it open. I'll do the same on this side. With five of us holding the doors, Decker and Ward can let go. No need for anyone to get trapped on this side of the doors. You ready?"

"As I'll ever be," Yates said.

"All right then." Garrett counted down. "Three. Two. One. Go."

Yates let go of the door handle and threw himself toward the gap.

Decker felt the sudden release. The door slipped inexorably closer to closing, even with Cassie pulling on the other side with all her might. At the corner of his eye, he saw Garrett perform the same maneuver. Then, just when his muscles were about to fail him, he felt the pressure release as Yates joined Cassie and heaved the door back open a few more inches.

Decker let go of the handle and hurled himself toward the gap between the doors. He barely fit through, his shoulders scraping as he tumbled into the room beyond.

He stumbled forward and almost fell, catching himself and turning just in time to see Ward barreling through the gap a pace behind.

No sooner were the men in the room, then the others released the handles with an audible sigh of relief.

The heavy doors slammed closed with a resounding boom.

"Holy hell," Rory said, breathless. "Those doors must be made of lead. They weighed a ton."

Decker massaged his protesting muscles. He looked at the back of the doors, and how they sparkled with a golden light. "They're not made of lead. They're lined with gold."

"No wonder they were so heavy," Ward said, stepping up to the doors and touching the smooth surface made of precious metal. "Still shouldn't have slammed back on us like that, though."

"They must have some kind of spring mechanism built into the hinges," Decker said. "To make sure no one leaves them open."

"And thank goodness they have," Rory said. "The Gorgon made quick work of those other doors. If these were the same, that creature would be upon us before we could do anything."

"How we got in here before it reached us, I'll never know," Emma said. "But I'm sure glad we did."

"And if the bunch of us struggled to open those doors, I can't imagine the Gorgon will be getting through anytime soon," Cassie said, a hint of satisfaction in her voice.

"Amen to that," Emma said. "I wonder why this room was so special that its builders felt the need to install a set of doors like that. They must have really wanted to keep interlopers out."

"Good question," Decker said. Then he turned and saw what was standing in the middle of the space, and he knew why those doors were there. They had reached the apex of the pyramid. And in the center, towering over them on a pedestal with its tip thrusting through a circular gap in the roof, was the biggest crystal he had ever seen.

56

Decker looked up at the crystal in awe. The stone dominated the room, measuring at least eight feet across by fifteen feet tall. A pear-shaped oval with a rough fern-like textured surface colored a deep olive green, it pulsed with an ethereal radiance. It rested on a raised dais carved with more hieroglyphics. Its top third thrust upward through a circular hole in the ceiling, where it caught the light of the afternoon sun. Nearby was another set of stone steps, leading up and out onto the flat-topped exterior of the pyramid.

"That is incredible," Emma said, transfixed by the crystal. "It looks almost like glass."

"I've never seen a crystal like this," Decker said.

"That's because it isn't a regular crystal," Rory said. He approached the stone and placed his hand against it, feeling the roughness under his palm. "Emma is correct. It's closer to glass. To be precise, it's more like a tektite. And a really big one."

"What the hell is a tektite?" Ward asked, looking perplexed.

"It's a type of projectile rock caused by a meteorite hitting the earth." Rory was circling the stone now, studying it from every angle. "The force of impact fuses and melts the

264 | ANTHONY M. STRONG

surrounding rock into glass debris. But this is much bigger than any tektite I've ever seen. That leads me to believe it isn't ejecta from an impact but might actually be part of the rock that struck the earth."

"Why is it green like that?" Garrett asked. "Aren't meteorites supposed to be black?"

"That depends on what they're made of," Rory said. "Some are composed entirely of stone. Others are made of iron. They can also be a mix of the two. My guess is that this was a crystalline space rock. It almost looks like moldavite. A rare type of mineral that was thought to be formed by a meteorite colliding with Earth millions of years ago. Maybe the impact didn't create the moldavite. Maybe it was part of the original space rock. This could be a bigger example of the same type of impactor."

"Then how did it get here?" Ward asked.

"You remember the cliff that we climbed down?"

"Sure." Ward nodded.

"I don't think that was a true cliff. I think it was the edge of a vast prehistoric impact crater. What we're looking at here is what remains of the rock that caused it."

"So this entire area is a crater?" Cassie said.

"Yes," Rory nodded. "That's my guess. A crater with this space rock sitting at its center."

"That's all very well," Ward said. "But that doesn't explain why there are Greek monsters running around out there, or why we are currently being stalked by a Gorgon."

"Actually, I think it does." Decker had been listening silently to Rory's explanation. Now he stepped forward. He looked at the huge chunk of moldavite that pulsed with an inner fire. "Look at how that rock is glowing with energy. The ancient Egyptians believed it to have magical powers. We know that much from the hieroglyphics chamber. They said it could combine two worlds. I think it really is combining two planes of existence. But not our world and the underworld. It's pulling together two alternate realities. The monsters out there, like the Cyclops and the Hydra, are denizens of that other reality, now mixed with our own."

"And the moldavite is making it possible," Emma said. "Like some sort of bridge between the dimensions."

"Exactly." Decker looked up at the translucent green rock. "I have a theory that this crystal straddles both realities and draws its power from the sun to do so. Anything within range of the crystal's energy becomes an amalgam of both realities."

"So why don't the monsters disappear at night," Ward asked. "After all, if the crystal is keeping the two realities merged, and it's powered by the sun, then it shouldn't work after dark."

"It stores energy deep inside, so that even when there is no sunlight, the crystal is still full of power," Rory said excitedly. "Not only that, but I think John is right. It's a crazy notion, but maybe the impact of this meteorite was so great that it shattered the membrane between realities, at least in this spot. Quantum mechanics hypothesizes we live in a multi-verse and that there are many billions of realities layered atop each other like an enormous pile of copy paper, with each sheet separated by a thin barrier yet existing simultaneously in what's called superposition. Within those paper-thin realities, every possible outcome can occur."

"That's ridiculous." Yates snorted and shook his head.

"Is it?" Emma turned to the others. "We've seen what's out there. It shouldn't exist, at least not in our world."

"It explains a lot," Cassie said, agreeing with Emma. "You, of all people, should keep an open mind, Darren. You are hosting a show on the supernatural, after all."

"A lot of good it does me without my camera. All this stuff and I can't record any of it."

"Boo-hoo." Cassie shook her head. "You should be glad just to be alive."

"That's enough bickering. There are more important issues. Like getting out of here alive," Emma said. She turned to Decker. "You got any thoughts on that?"

"We keep going up," Decker said, glancing toward the set of stone steps leading up and out of the pyramid.

"I agree," Ward said. "I got a good look at the pyramid when we were out in the jungle. It looks very much like a standard Mayan design with stepped blocks up to the apex, and an exterior staircase on each side leading back to ground level from the flat-topped roof. Once we get up there, it should be no trouble to access those steps and make our way all the way back down to the jungle floor."

"Not Mayan," Rory said. "A modified Egyptian step pyramid that the Mayans later copied at places like Chichen Itza."

"What about this crystal?" Emma asked. "Is there some way to turn it off and get rid of the monsters?"

"I don't think so," Decker said. "The only way would be to destroy it, and we don't have any means of doing that. There's no choice but to make our way back to base camp while avoiding the monsters out in the jungle."

"That's a shame," said Rory, glancing toward the set of heavy golden doors through which they'd come. "Because I can hear the Gorgon, and she does not sound happy."

Decker could hear the Gorgon too, hissing and talking in that strange archaic tongue. Every now and again, the doors shuddered as she tried to bust through, but so far, their incredible weight had proved too much for the creature. He wasn't sure how long that would be the case. "We have to leave, right now."

From somewhere high above, outside of the pyramid, came the steady thrum of a helicopter's rotor blades, getting louder.

Emma looked up, surprised, then to Decker. "Did you arrange an airlift?"

"No." Decker moved toward the steps. "But I'd sure welcome one. Maybe Hunt decided to come get us."

"Don't bother. It's not Adam Hunt. This ride is for me." Garrett stepped away from the group, raising his M4 semi-automatic assault rifle. He waved it at Decker. "Get back over there with the others."

Decker hesitated, weighing his odds of taking Garrett out. But he couldn't be one hundred percent sure the M4 was truly disabled even though Garrett hadn't been able to fire it back in the jungle. He could have been faking, or he might have replaced the firing pin at some point after. In the end, Decker held up his hands and rejoined the group. "Whatever you say."

"Garrett, what in the blazes are you doing?" Ward asked, glaring at his underling. "Put that gun down, right now. That's an order."

"Sorry, commander. No can do." Garrett retreated further toward the steps.

"How?" Decker asked, watching Garrett with narrowed eyes.

"How what?" Garrett shook his head.

"How did you get a helicopter all the way out here with such perfect timing?"

"GPS locator." Garrett removed a small device from his pocket and showed Decker before putting it back. "I activated this a couple of hours ago. Figured I'd need a way out of this godforsaken jungle."

"It was you who put the snake in my tent," Decker said.

"A little surprise." Garrett tutted. "Shame it didn't work."

"So now you're going to shoot us?" Decker decided to test whether Garrett's gun really was out of action. "That gun doesn't work, remember? And I'm pretty sure you used all the bullets I gave you for the Makarov."

"Yeah." Garrett glanced down at the gun. "I had to disable this bad boy when I took the firing pins from the other guns.

Couldn't have the only working weapon. That would give the game away."

"Then what's to stop me from coming over there and knocking you into next week?" Decker asked, taking a step toward the soldier.

"These guys." Garrett jerked a thumb toward four men in battle fatigues and helmets who appeared at the top of the steps. Each carried an M16, which they leveled at the huddled group. "Mister Decker, say hello to your executioners."

## 57

The four soldiers descended the steps, guns at the ready. They wore additional arms at their side. Glock pistols. Each of them also carried a pair of M67 spherical frag grenades on their belts.

The men joined Garrett and looked to him for instructions.

"Not yet," Garrett told them.

"Why?" Ward glared at Garrett. There was a look of hurt in his eyes. "After all the years we've served together, this is how you repay me?"

"This is nothing to do with you, commander. Collateral damage, that's all."

"That doesn't answer my question."

"Why do you think I did it?"

"Money." Decker said. "I remember what you said back in the jungle about CUSP paying better than the military. I guess someone else pays even more than CUSP."

"My employers paid me well enough, I'll admit," Garrett said with the barest hint of a smile. "But it's not just that. Look at the anomalies we investigate. The creatures we collect and put in the zoo. The gadgets we hunt down—like that orb you recovered from the German submarine. CUSP wastes them all.

They're shortsighted. Blind to the possibilities. Think what we could do to make the world a better place with all that technology and all those creatures."

"Or a worse place," Decker said.

"I disagree." A thin smile touched Garrett's lips. "Take that Gorgon out there, the one trying to bust through those doors. If we could capture it, control it, think what it would mean on the battlefield. Our military could go where they want, unopposed. No one would be able to stop us. We would be invincible. Think of the lives we could save."

"Think of all the lives you would take." Decker was horrified. "It's unconscionable."

"It's the only way to guarantee world order."

"Listen to yourself, man," Ward said. "You sound like the very people we used to fight against."

"I'm nothing like them. I'm a realist."

"You're a mercenary," Decker said. "Selling out to the highest bidder. And what about all that technology that you want to get your hands on? Does that go to the highest bidder, too?"

"What if it does?" Garrett folded his arms. "It's out there, anyway. One way or another it's going to end up in the wrong hands. Why not make a profit along the way?"

"So all that talk about protecting our military was a load of bull."

"Nothing of the sort. If they want to pay for it, they can have it. If not, someone else will pony up and gain the advantage. And when the smoke settles, the world will be at peace regardless of who the victor is."

"You want to live in a world like that?"

"Better than the one we have now."

"And you're going to kill us all in cold blood just to get your hands on what's in that jungle out there?" Emma asked. "How can you be so heartless?"

"You misunderstand." Garrett shook his head. "It's not about what's in the jungle. Sure, we'll come back and harvest the Cyclops, and the Hydra, and all the other nasty beasties. Waste not, want not. But this isn't about that."

"Then what is it about?" Decker asked.

"Revenge." A thin smile touched Garrett's lips.

"I don't understand," Decker said.

"Really? It's not that hard to figure out. You've got on the wrong side of some very powerful people, Mister Decker. People who wanted technology that you deprived them of."

"Habitat One." Realization dawned upon Decker. "I stopped Thomas Barringer from stealing the alien technology on that sunken U-boat."

"Very good. Go to the top of the class."

"The attack in Manaus, those gunmen who came after us. They weren't trying to get their hands on the coordinates for this place, after all. It was a hit job, pure and simple."

"We saw an opportunity, and we took it. Unfortunately, the local gangsters that we hired to take care of the situation didn't prove as effective as we hoped. Amateurs."

"And the snake?"

"My way of taking care of the situation without revealing myself. I could hardly come right out and shoot you. That would have blown my cover with CUSP, and I spent years working on that."

"Looks like it's blown now," Emma said. She glared at Garrett.

"Not really," Garrett said. He nodded toward the soldiers. "My men here shoot you all, and I leave with them. Then all I have to do is show up back at base camp and say unknown forces attacked us. They killed everyone except me. My cover stays intact."

"And all for petty revenge against me," Decker said. "Hardly seems worth it."

"Oh, it's not just about you. Don't be foolish. We're sending a message."

"To whom?" Decker said, although he thought he already knew.

"Why, Adam Hunt, of course."

"What did he ever do to you?"

"Not me. My employer. He and Hunt go way back. This storm has been brewing for a long time."

From their left, the heavy gold-clad doors rattled and bowed inward. Decker resisted looking toward them, for fear he would glimpse the Gorgon.

"Looks like those doors won't hold much longer," Garrett said. "It's going to be bad when that Gorgon gets in here. Not that any of you will care. You'll be dead already." Garrett turned and started up the steps. "Now, I think that's my cue to leave."

The four soldiers aimed their guns.

The doors into the room shuddered with another impact as the angry Gorgon tried to break through.

Garrett was almost at the top of the stairs. Another few steps and he would be on the roof of the pyramid. He stopped and looked down at his men. "Whenever you're ready. Make sure they're all dead before you leave."

"Aye, sir," one of the four responded.

Decker guessed he was their leader. He stared down the barrel of the man's gun and tensed for the bloodbath that was about to come.

Garrett disappeared through the opening in the ceiling and out onto the exterior of the pyramid. At the same moment, the Gorgon hit the doors with a chorus of angry hissing. This time, they didn't hold. The doors slammed inward and smacked back on their hinges. Then all hell broke loose.

## 58

All four soldiers' gaze swung to the right when the doors crashed inward. Directly into the stare of the Gorgon. For the closest three, the effect was immediate. Their skin lost its color, their faces contorted in agony. One of the three let out a strangled scream. He took a step forward, then froze, caught mid-stride. His skin lost the elasticity of flesh and took on the hue of stone. Then, with only one foot on the ground and his center of gravity off, the man pitched forward. He slammed face first into the floor and broke into four pieces. His petrified head rolled a few feet and came to rest at the base of the steps, sightless eyes, now nothing but pebbles, looking upward toward the ceiling. One hand still gripped his M-16, a stony finger curled around the trigger. The other two men fared no better, but at least stayed on their feet.

Emma screamed.

Cassie averted her eyes with a choked sob.

The last remaining soldier, his view of the Gorgon blocked by his comrades, made a fatal mistake. He stepped out to see what turned his friends to stone, readying his gun at the same time.

And in that instant, Decker saw an opportunity.

He broke ranks and lunged forward, reaching out for one of the grenades hanging from the soldier's belt, just as the man's eyes widened with pain and his skin took on the mottled hue of stone.

Decker's hand closed over the grenade, and he slipped it free.

If the soldier even registered Decker's sudden movement, the man didn't have time to react. Instead, he froze in place. "Everyone, keep your eyes away from the door," Ward shouted. "Unless you want to end up like those men."

"Everyone, up the stairs," Decker said, aware that the Gorgon was in the room with them even though he didn't dare glance in her direction. "Before she walks into our field of vision. Hurry."

Emma pulled herself together and dashed for the steps. Cassie followed right behind, and together they started up. Decker waited for Yates and Rory, then made Ward go next before following up the rear.

They raced upward, even as the creature below let out a frustrated howl.

Decker couldn't be sure, but he sensed the Gorgon start up the stairs up behind them, intent upon claiming more victims.

Emma and Cassie reached the top of the steps and hurried onto the pyramid's flat outer top.

Decker could hear the helicopter hovering above. He expected to hear the chatter of gunfire, for them to be picked off one by one as they exited the pyramid. But none came and soon he emerged into the late afternoon sunlight.

Now he realized why they weren't being fired upon. The helicopter-a Sikorsky UH–60 Black Hawk-hovered directly above, the angle too oblique for any gunman to get a bead on them. The side door was open, with ropes dangling onto the pyramid, left behind when the four soldiers rappelled down.

One of those ropes was now being used by Garrett, who was

climbing back up toward the helicopter's waiting hatch. He was almost at the top. After that, the helicopter could circle around and fire upon them.

There wasn't much time.

Decker glanced around. The top third of the crystal emerged from the pyramid and soaked up the sun. Around it was a gap of a couple of feet. A vertical drop straight back down inside. But there was another way out of the line of fire. Just as Ward had said, a set of exterior steps sloped downward into the jungle on each of each of the pyramid's four faces.

"Get to the other side of the crystal," Decker said, realizing they could use it for cover. "Then start down the steps toward the jungle floor."

"What about you?" Emma asked.

"I'm going to take care of the Gorgon," Decker said. He was still gripping the hand grenade. He hoped it would be enough.

"I'm not leaving you up here on your own," Ward said.

"There's no time to argue. Do as I say. I know what I'm doing."

"I hope you're right," Ward said, taking off behind the others.

"Me, too," Decker said under his breath. He risked a glance back up toward the helicopter, equally aware that the Gorgon could not be far from the top of the steps.

Garrett was clambering aboard now. He scurried into the darkness within and disappeared from view. Decker wished he'd grabbed one of the M-16s, but there was no time, and he wasn't sure he could even get them out of the petrified soldier's hands.

Decker took a step backwards, intending to dive for cover should the need arise, but no gunfire came. Instead, the side door slid closed. But before it shut all the way, a figure appeared in the helicopter's hatchway.

Decker saw the man for only a second. Just a brief glimpse

before the door slid home. But he recognized the face all the same.

Thomas Barringer.

# 59

---

Decker's breath caught in his throat. He stared up at the helicopter, unable to believe his eyes. Thomas Barringer was looking right back at him, large as life. The man met Decker's gaze, his lips curling upwards in a smug, superior, half-smile. Then the helicopter's side door slammed shut, severing their silent exchange.

The helicopter banked, circled once, and flew off over the treetops.

Decker glanced around, careful not to look toward the stairs, where he could hear the Gorgon's snakes hissing as she climbed toward him. He was relieved to see that the rest of the group had taken his advice and were already starting down the steep staircase leading to the pyramid's base.

But now there was another problem. Above the group scrambling down the outside of the pyramid was a winged creature that flew in lazy arcs, silhouetted against the low hanging sun. It observed them with deadly intent, getting closer with each pass. This was, he guessed, the same beast that had carried Cassie's producer off days before.

He shouted out, hoping someone would hear him over the

noise of the retreating helicopter's engines. But they didn't need any warning. They had seen the beast too and quickened their descent.

But it wasn't enough.

The creature made one more pass over their heads and then swooped toward them.

Decker heard startled cries, saw the group frantically beating the winged beast away, to no avail. It screeched and slashed at them with deadly talons before settling on Emma and taking hold. She screamed and struggled against the beast as it tried to lift her up and away.

And now, Decker remembered the other danger. The Gorgon, which must by now surely be at the top of the steps. If his gaze even swept across her countenance, one accidental glimpse, he would be a goner.

His only chance to save Emma, and everyone else, was the grenade still clutched in his hand.

Without another moment's hesitation, he pulled the pin and raced forward toward the gap where the crystal emerged from the pyramid. Praying that his hunch was right, he dropped the grenade down through the gap and into the room below.

It had a five second delay.

Just enough time to get clear.

But he would still be atop the pyramid. He'd never used a grenade before and didn't know how much damage the blast would do. He hoped it would destroy the crystal, but it might also take the entire top of the building. If that happened, he would be toast.

But none of that mattered.

The Gorgon was moving toward him across the pyramid's flattop. He could sense her. Hear her sibilant voice calling for him to glance her way. He had no intention of doing that. Decker raced to the edge of the pyramid and started down the steps after his companions.

The winged beast had lifted Emma off her feet and was now engaged in a tug-of-war with Ward and Rory, who held on to her legs to prevent it from carrying her off.

She twisted and turned, struggling against the beast. Her terrified screams sent a shiver down Decker's spine.

If the grenade didn't destroy the crystal, or he was wrong about its role in keeping the creatures here, Decker knew it would cost Emma her life. It would probably cost all of them their lives.

He was about to find out.

From inside the pyramid, there came a rumbling bang.

A shudder ran through the steps under Decker's feet. The grenade's concussion wave. But the stonework didn't cave in around him. The building had contained the blast.

But had it destroyed the moldavite crystal?

Decker stopped and turned, squinting back up toward the top of the pyramid despite the danger of inadvertently looking into the Gorgon's face.

His heart fell.

The crystal was still there. He could see its tip protruding from the apex, catching the sunlight and soaking it in.

Below him, Emma was still screaming.

Then, just when Decker thought he had failed, there was a sharp cracking sound. A spider web of lines weaved their way up through the crystal, becoming deep fissures. It stayed that way for a moment, held together by nothing but the oppressive air around it. And then the crystal caved in upon itself and dropped from view through the center of the pyramid.

Decker turned back toward the others, further down the steps. The winged creature was still there, battling to carry Emma off. But not for long. It let out a frustrated squawk, beat its mighty wings, and released her, even as it faded. A moment later, it vanished as if it had never even been there.

Decker raced down the steps and joined his companions.

When he looked back up toward the top of the pyramid, only a cloud of dust billowed where the crystal had formerly been.

Of the Gorgon, there was no sign.

He let out a long sigh of relief. And then Decker noticed something. The air was full of birdsong. Further away, in the treetops, he could hear monkeys chattering and calling out to one another. The jungle, which only seconds before had been the playground of monsters, was back with its rightful inhabitants, maybe for the first time since a prehistoric meteorite slammed into the ground and shattered the barrier between worlds.

He looked at Emma, and she looked back at him. And in that moment, an understanding passed between them. She had her career, and he had Nancy. They were both where they wanted to be, and that was the end of it. The only thing left to do was hike out of the jungle and leave this godforsaken place behind for someone else to clean up.

Decker looked around the tired and bedraggled group, noting how Cassie had taken Rory's hand and was gripping it tightly. He smiled, and started off back down the steps toward the pyramid's base, calling over his shoulder. "Come on, last one back to base camp is on dish washing duty."

## 60

They arrived back at base camp three hours later. By then, it was already getting dark. The four men waiting there were relieved to see them. The soldiers greeted Ward with open arms, while Hugh Henriksen, the producer, rushed forward and embraced Cassie and Darren Yates. Tristan Cook even grudgingly admitted he was pleased to see them, even though Decker suspected he was secretly a little disappointed that he would not get to host a TV special, lamenting the loss of his rival in the jungle.

They stayed at base camp that night, building a fire and huddling around it, talking of their adventures, and passing around a bottle of bourbon that Henriksen had retrieved from his backpack. It was, he reminded them, New Year's Eve. They should celebrate fresh beginnings and tip a glass to those who hadn't made it back.

Later, as Decker stood at the cliff's edge, gazing over the dark forest below, Emma approached and joined him.

"We should probably clear the air," she said. "I know you've never forgiven me for what I did, and I understand that, but I'd like us to part as friends."

"Me, too," Decker admitted. "I've moved on, and I'm happy now."

"I'm pleased to hear that." Emma turned to look at him. "It was really hard when I left you. I've always been so career driven, and CUSP made me an offer I couldn't refuse. Unlimited funding and resources. The ability to dig anywhere I wanted. It was the chance of a lifetime."

"I get that," Decker said. "I just wish you'd told me."

"I wanted to. You have to believe that. But their terms of employment were very clear. I couldn't tell anyone what I was doing or where I was going. And they wanted me to leave right away." She reached out and touched Decker's arm. "I almost said no."

"Almost."

"Yes. You would never be happy with me, anyway. I'm just not the domestic type."

"It wasn't your place to decide if I was going to be happy or not. I knew what your job demanded when we got together. I knew you'd have to go on digs, and I was fine with it."

"I know. But you would always have been second to the job. I'm not saying that to hurt you. I'm saying it because it's the truth, even though it makes me look heartless and unfeeling."

"You're anything but heartless and unfeeling," Decker said, turning to meet Emma's gaze. "It's okay. Like I said, I'm happy now. It all worked out for the best in the long run."

"Yes. I suppose it did." Emma looked thoughtful. "You know, I really didn't have a clue you worked for CUSP now. If I did, I might have reached out earlier."

"It hasn't been that long," Decker said. "Still, you didn't look very surprised to see me."

"That's because I already knew you were coming. You weren't the only one to have a briefing."

"Right. Of course."

"I was terrified of what you'd say when you arrived at base

camp." Emma ran a hand through her hair. "I've never been good with confrontation. You know that much. I decided attack was the best form of defense. I know I came on too strong. It's just that I didn't want you to see my vulnerability."

"You came on a little strong." Decker said. "And if I wasn't with Nancy, you might have tempted me."

"I'm pleased that you're with Nancy," Emma said. "And not because I would have broken your heart again, which I probably would have, but because you're happy."

"That's good to hear." Decker glanced back toward the fire, and the group huddled around it. "Want to go see if there's any more of that bourbon left?"

"I think there's plenty," Emma said with a grin. "Henriksen just found a second bottle. I don't think he brought anything but booze in that backpack of his."

"In that case, I feel it's our duty to help him dispose of it," Decker said. "Don't you?"

"Absolutely." Emma took Decker's hand and led him back toward the fire pit. "I think it's time we toast your upcoming nuptials."

"You do know I'm not inviting you, right?" Decker said as they rejoined the others.

"Well, that's just mean," Emma laughed. "But I guess it's fair payback, even though I'd make a great bridesmaid."

## 61

ONE WEEK LATER.

Decker sat in Hunt's office at CUSP headquarters on the tiny
island off the coast of Maine. He'd already been debriefed, as
had Rory and Emma, but what he wanted to talk about with
Adam Hunt now was of a more private nature.

"Thomas Barringer," Decker said, watching his boss's face as
he spoke the words. "He was supposed to be in prison."

"Not prison." Hunt corrected him. "A secure facility run by
us. A place that was supposed to be escape proof and secret."

"Except it clearly wasn't," Decker said. "Or we wouldn't be
having this conversation."

"Correct."

"And you didn't think it was worth mentioning that
Barringer was out there, running free?"

"No." Hunt sat straight in his seat, meeting Decker's gaze
with cool detachment. "I absolutely did not. As with many
things around here, it was need to know."

"And apparently I needed to know," Decker said. "He sent
hitmen after Rory and me in Manaus. He almost succeeded in

killing us. It also affected the mission because I didn't know why we were being pursued. I made a false assumption based on faulty knowledge."

"And I take responsibility for that." Hunt didn't sound apologetic. "But I had no way of knowing Barringer would come after you. Our assessments of the mission risks did not include that parameter."

"Because it was nothing to do with the mission." Decker could feel his anger rising, but he swallowed it. "Kyle Garrett said that my death was not just meant to be revenge for thwarting Barringer's plans on Habitat One, it was also meant as a message to you. What did he mean by that?"

"Your guess is as good as mine," Hunt said, shrugging. "The man is clearly deranged. I wouldn't worry about it."

"There's something you're not telling me."

"If there is, it's for a reason."

"Not good enough."

"It will have to be."

Hunt wasn't budging. Decker could see that. "Then answer me this. How badly compromised is CUSP? Considering how secretive you were at the beginning of this mission, you already suspected there were people within our organization working against us."

"I did." Hunt nodded. "And I still do."

"Kyle Garrett was a member of the Ghost Team. A low-level operative. That means we can't trust anyone."

"I'm aware of that," Hunt said. "But nevertheless, there are some people I trust within CUSP. People who are working to find and remove those who have other allegiances."

"Garrett told me that a storm was coming. This thing with Barringer isn't over."

"I'm aware of that, as well."

"When the time comes, I expect you to brief me in full,"

Decker said. "He tried to kill me. I'm a part of this, whether or not you like it."

Hunt nodded. "When the time is right, I'll tell you everything. You have my word."

"And in the meantime?"

"You go about your business and do your job," Hunt said. "On another note, I have some good news."

"What's that?"

"Your taxi driver in Manaus, Paulo. We've taken care of his son's medical situation. The boy will get all the care he needs."

"That's very nice of you," Decker said.

"The least I could do, considering he saved your life. Rory's too. Probably more than once." Hunt smiled. "We've also brought him on board as a resource in Brazil. It's low-level stuff, nothing too dangerous. Going forward, he will serve as a liaison for operatives in the area."

"I see."

"It's always good to have local help, and it means that he and his family won't have to worry about money again."

"Does that include his sister?"

"Naturally. We made sure she was taken care of, too," Hunt said. "We also retrieved Rory's watch from that helicopter pilot. He seemed attached to it. The settlement made for her services was well received. It was more than generous and will ensure her help in the future, should it be needed."

"Good." Decker stood. "I think that just about covers everything. At least for now."

"Not quite. There is one more piece of business."

"Another assignment?"

"Nothing of the sort." Hunt's smile turned to a grin. "This is about your wedding. I hear you're planning to hold it in the spring."

"We are," Decker said, suspicious.

"Have you picked a venue yet?"

"Nothing is set in stone," Decker said, instantly regretting his choice of words as memories of the Gorgon filled his head. "We were thinking something small. We might even have it at the house."

"You will do no such thing." Hunt got to his feet. "CUSP owns a small island in the Bahamas. It has everything you will need, including a private beach resort. We'll also make the jet available to get everyone down there. How does that sound for a venue?"

"What's the catch?" Decker asked.

"No catch. My wedding present to the pair of you. It's the least I can do."

"In that case, I think Nancy would love a Bahamas wedding," Decker said.

"Perfect. Let me know the dates, and I'll make it happen."

"Absolutely. And thank you." Decker nodded and turned to leave.

"Wait," Hunt said. "There is one caveat."

"I knew it," Decker said, turning back to his boss. "All right, let's hear it."

"I have to be there. As do Rory and Colum. It's non-negotiable." There was a gleam in Hunt's eye.

Decker looked back at Hunt for a long moment, resisting the urge to smile. Then he turned toward the door and said over his shoulder, "We'll see."

The end.